Chatfield Hollow

A New En

Sharon Snow Sirois

LIGHTHOUSE PUBLISHING

North Haven, Connecticut

LIGHTHOUSE PUBLISHING
P.O. Box 396
North Haven, CT 06473

Illustration by Beverly Rich
Computer Graphics by Jane Lyman

All Scripture quotations are from the Holy Bible,
New International Version ©1978 by
N.Y. International Bible Society, used by permission of
Zondervan Publishing House

Library of Congress Control Number 2003090107

International Standard Book Number 0-9679052-5-7

Printed in the United States of America

I would like to thank God for the privilege of serving Him through my writing. As God gives me each story, I learn and grow so much closer to Him throughout the process of writing each book. My heart is filled with joy as God shows me new things about the Bible and life that I have never seen before. Looking at life through God's eyes changes my perspective entirely. He simply overwhelms me with His love. Draw close to God and He will draw close to you. He will give you a glimpse of heaven, fill your heart with joy like you've never known before, and have you standing humbly in awe at what a truly awesome God He is.

"Let us draw near to God with a sincere heart."
HEBREWS 10:22

To the Readers

Dear Friends,

Thank you so much for all your letters and your prayers. Your letters are very encouraging to receive and something that I treasure. Your prayers humble me. I value them more than I can say. Thank you!

Chatfield Hollow is the exciting conclusion to *Stony Brook Farm*. When I started writing this story, I never anticipated that it would turn into two books. As the story grew, and I had a manuscript before me the size of a dictionary, plans began to change. My publisher looked at the manuscript and plainly stated, "That's two books!" I immediately explained that it was one very long story. He looked carefully at the manuscript again and then back at me. He slowly repeated his earlier statement. "That's two books!" As a smile spread across his face, he leaned toward me a bit and whispered, "The second one is called a sequel, ya know".

Amidst the snickering around the room, I narrowed my eyes at him. "I know what a sequel is!" I quickly admitted. I really do. It's just that I never thought I was writing one. I had to laugh. Apparently I was! There's a lot of joking and teasing that goes on at Lighthouse, from both sides, and from pretty much every angle. It keeps the atmosphere light and makes it a fun place to work.

As the romantic comedy continues in *Chatfield Hollow*, Annie and Ryan's friendship continues to grow. Through prayer, time, love, hope, tears and laughter, Annie is finally ready to accept the second chance at love and happiness that God is offering her. As she and Ryan Jones prepare to take their relationship in the direction of forever, Annie soon finds out that everyone is not happy about the news.

Through the battles, Annie and Ryan grow closer to the Lord and closer to each other. Annie learns to stand up and face her accusers instead of running away. She comes to realize that Ryan Jones is not only a man worth fighting for, he is a man that she is head-over-heels in love with and doesn't want to live without.

One thing that I hope you take with you from this story is to follow God no matter what others say. He is a faithful God, and He will stay faithful to what He has called you to do and give you the strength and power to accomplish it. He can see the whole picture of life. The path that God is leading you down is a path that He knows, and with His help, you can walk it. He has confidence in what He has called you to do. Walk with Him, and He will lead you to places that you never thought were humanly possible to go.

I want to thank you again for your letters and prayers. They touch my heart deeply. I am incredibly humbled and honored that you've taken time out of your busy schedules to read *Chatfield Hollow*. I hope you enjoy our time together.

God Bless,
Sharon Snow Sirois

I love to hear from my readers!
You can write me through Lighthouse Publishing, P.O. Box 396, North Haven, CT 06473 or email me at sharonsnowsirois@hotmail.com

Acknowledgments

Lighthouse Publishing. I'd like to thank the team of people at Lighthouse Publishing. You are all such an incredibly talented group of people and it is my honor and privilege to work with you. You help me take the ideas that my imagination spins off and turn them into a story. Thank you for your dedication to God and your high commitment to excellence. Thank you for your prayers, support, guidance and encouragement.

Editorial Staff. William Burrill and Patricia Stearns. What a joy it has been working with you! Your long hours, insightful directions and comments help makes this book the best it can be. Thank you for your prayers, support, time, encouragement, and advice. Thank you for using your expertise to patiently guide me through this process. You are two of the most gifted people I've ever worked with.

Beverly Rich. I'm worse than a kid at Christmastime waiting to see your latest illustration. You capture the story in your painting in your own special way with little surprises tucked in here and there. Thank you so much for your wonderful illustration. You really amaze me with your talent.

Jane Lyman. Thank you for the excellent job you did with the computer graphics. Thank you for your time and patience. All those endless, little details that you take care of help make this book the best it can be. Thank you!

The Snow & Sirois Families. Thank you for all your prayers, support and encouragement. It means more to me than words can ever say. You all are such an incredibly special group of people, and I am so overwhelmingly blessed to have you in my life. I treasure you with all my heart. I love you!

Peter. I can never seem to find the right words to explain exactly what you mean to me. My feelings for you run deeper than any words could possibly describe. You have touched my life in more ways than I could ever count. You are such a wonderful husband, father and best friend. I am so proud of you! Your prayers, love, encouragement and support are something that I treasure and cherish. I love you with all my heart!

Jennifer, John, Robert, Michael. Being your mom is such a wonderful blessing! You guys are so special to me. No words could ever describe it. Your love for the Lord and concern for others shines brightly in so many of the little everyday things that you do. I am so proud of you. I love you with all my heart!

This one is for my mom and dad,
Kenneth and Sheila Snow

It is a great privilege and honor to dedicate this book to two people that I love and admire so much. You taught me so many things by example: to love God, our family and our friends, and to be proud of this great country that we live in. You showed me how to love others and what the joy of giving is all about.

You were always so proud of us kids growing up. You were excited about our accomplishments and comforted us in our defeats.

The three of us kids often felt that you were doing the parenting techniques of James Dobson before there was a Dobson. You made our home a place where we were loved and accepted. Thank you for expecting our best and accepting our best even when our best might fall short of the goal. Unconditional love and acceptance is a wonderful gift to give a child.

I cherish my childhood memories and often times find myself drawing on those experiences as I write. I loved our camping and hiking adventures throughout New England. I loved sailing the ocean coastline and exploring all the little islands along the way.

We had the most wonderful backyard to grow up in. I'm not surprised that most of the neighborhood kids ended up there. The bobsled, twenty-two passenger war canoe, tee pee, round and round, and the awesome tree fort, complete with its own emergency escape zip line were things that you couldn't possibly find in stores. The hours you spent building them gave us years of fun and a lifetime of great memories.

Now that I am a parent, I often look back and wonder how you had the energy and wisdom to do everything you did for us. I don't know how you kept up with us; I can hardly keep up with the memories.

You made our home special and fun and a place where we wanted to be. Who else could say that they had climbing ropes three stories high built right into the center of their house or ladders fastened to the ceiling of their central hall to climb on and ambush friends as they unexpectedly came down the hall? Remember trying to explain all the footprints on the hallway ceiling long after the ladders had come down? Those were such fun times.

Thank you for the lessons you instilled in me as a child. They are lessons that I try to pass on to my own kids. Thank you for placing the value on each person and not material possessions. Thank you for giving so much of yourselves to your kids. I am so proud to be your daughter. I love you with all my heart.

Put your hope in God,

for I will yet praise Him,

my Savior and my God.

PSALM 42:5

One

*C*hristmastime, with all its splendor had finally arrived, and Annie and her family excitedly boarded an airplane bound for Chatfield Hollow, Tennessee. Annie's brother Bob, her sister-in-law Jude, and her five-year-old niece Heidi drove down from Maine to Annie's Stony Brook Farm in Boston so they could all fly out together. Little Heidi was so excited about her first plane ride that she had already talked nonstop across four states. Annie kindly volunteered to put Heidi next to her for a while so that her parents could have a break from the energized chatterbox.

After ten minutes of listening to Heidi yak, Annie knew she was going to have to come up with an alternative plan to quiet the motor mouth down for a while. "Heidi," Annie said firmly, "I'll make a deal with you." The five-year- old loved making deals and her ears immediately perked up. "How would you like to have this yummy lollipop?"

The little girl nodded her head so vigorously that Annie was afraid she'd get whiplash. "Oh, yes, Auntie! I want the lollipop!"

"OK," Annie unwrapped the grape pop, "but there's one condition." Heidi looked at Annie anxiously. The little girl loved candy and her face clearly displayed the message that she would do anything for the pop. "If you take my pop," Annie waved it in front of her, "you've got to promise to keep it in your mouth."

"I can do that!" Heidi squealed. As she eagerly accepted the candy from her aunt, muffled laughs went up from behind Annie's seat. Annie leaned around her seat slightly and spoke to her children in a voice that was full of warning. "Knock it off, you two."

Tyler and Amy looked like they were going to explode in laughter. "Mom," Ty leaned forward and whispered, "I can't believe that Heidi's falling for that old trick!"

"Shhhh," Annie commanded. "Don't ruin it or I'll put the chatterbox next to you." The amusement drained from Tyler's face immediately, and he suddenly became very serious. "Besides," Annie grinned mischievously, "you guys always fell for it, why wouldn't Heidi?"

Annie turned her attention back to Heidi. She was enjoying her lollipop but had a puzzled expression on her face. "What's wrong, Honey?" Annie asked her curiously. Heidi garbled a response to her aunt but Annie couldn't understand because the pop was still in her mouth.

"Sweetie, take the pop out of your mouth for a second so Auntie can understand what you're saying."

The little girl shook her head emphatically no. She didn't want to take any chances of Annie taking her pop away. Her determined blue eyes stared up at Annie again, and in a louder voice, she slurred out the word, "Sorree."

Annie studied her for a moment feeling more confused than ever. "Sorry? Sweetie, what are you sorry for?"

The little girl shook her curly blonde head again, and in an even louder voice, with more determination, she screamed out, "SORREE!"

This was not going according to plan at all for Annie. Instead of Heidi talking non-stop, she was now shouting out slurred sounds. They had no connection to any words Annie recognized; yet the assumption was clear, that if she yelled them louder at her slightly dense aunt, she might get the message. Annie soon realized that Heidi was playing the same game but with new rules.

"Mom," Amy sounded amused, "I think Heidi wants you to tell her a story." Heidi confirmed this by jumping excitedly in her seat with loud giggles escaping her slurpy mouth.

"Oh," Annie responded less than enthusiastically, "do you want Auntie to tell you a story?"

Heidi nodded excitedly. She tucked the pop firmly in the right side of her cheek and clearly said, "Bout the rancha."

"You want to know about the place we're going to?" Once again, a firm nod from Heidi confirmed this was true. Annie groaned inwardly. She had figured out a way to keep Heidi quiet for a while, but Annie knew there would be no peace and quiet if Heidi succeeded turning her into the story time fairy.

Annie looked at her niece. "Heidi, I'll tell you a short story and then we're both going to be quiet." Heidi nodded her head a little reluctantly and then Annie, even more reluctantly started talking about the ranch.

Annie went on to describe the horses, the wagons, the sleighs, the barns, the fields, and the mountains. She described what each of Ryan's children looked like and a little about their personalities. When she finished, Heidi gazed up at her anxiously.

"What?" Annie asked in a low grumble. Heidi looked anxiously at the pop stick in her mouth, and Annie gently pulled it out of her mouth. "What is it, Honey?"

"What does Mr. Jones look like?"

"He's tall," Annie handed the pop back to Heidi, "and he has brown hair."

"What color are his eyes?" Heidi studied her aunt intently before putting her pop back into her mouth.

"His eyes are blue."

Heidi pulled her pop back out. "Do they twinkle like mine? Mommy says that my blue eyes twinkle."

Annie laughed. "I guess they do." She felt a bit embarrassed discussing Ryan's twinkling eyes with a five-year-old. It was time to end the conversation, before her inquiring mind went into its investigative reporting mode. "OK, Heidi, I want you to rest some now. We're going to be there soon." Heidi stuck the pop in her mouth and to Annie's amazement, she was quiet the rest of the trip.

Ryan, Beth, Nicole, and David excitedly met the passengers when their plane landed in Nashville, Tennessee. Ryan immediately scooped Annie into his welcoming arms and hugged her tightly. Annie hugged him back just as tightly.

"I've missed you so much!" Ryan looked at her so tenderly that she got the feeling she would melt in a puddle at his feet.

"I've missed you, too! We're all so glad to be here."

Ryan winked at her and then went to greet the rest of the family. Amy and Tyler gave Ryan big bear hugs, and Bob and Jude shook his hand firmly. Bob held Ryan's hand a moment longer than necessary. Ryan knew, in that brief time, a fifteen second inspection was being done by Annie's very protective older brother Bob.

"I look forward to getting to know you." Bob's voice was firm and his manner extremely serious. He definitely wasn't friendly; then again, he wasn't all-out frightening either. It was a place somewhere in the middle that wasn't intended to be comfortable for Ryan. It was at that point that Ryan knew without a doubt that he was going to be interrogated by Bob. He could see it in his eyes. He didn't care that Ryan was a celebrity, rich or had fans circling the globe. What his eyes plainly told Ryan was that all he cared about was his interest in his little sister.

Ryan smiled as the big man released his hand. Bob's attitude toward him actually made Ryan like and respect him more. He knew if he ever had a sister he'd react the same way. Bob was Annie's self-appointed bodyguard. He was caring and kind, but noticeably protective, defensive, and clearly warning those around her that he wouldn't hesitate to permanently maim or destroy if necessary. It was all in a day's work and all part of doing the brother job.

As Ryan glanced around, he spotted Heidi. He went over to her and squatted down to see her. "Welcome to Tennessee, Little Lady. Ryan offered her his hand, and she shook it seriously. Heidi stared at Ryan so intensely that he finally asked her if something was wrong.

"You have blue eyes," she stated in a matter of fact way.

Ryan's eyes lit and a huge grin spread across his face. "Yes," his voice was amused, "I do have blue eyes, and" he tweaked the tip of her nose playfully, "so do you!"

Heidi nodded seriously. "Auntie says that you have twinkling blue eyes."

Ryan picked up the five-year-old in his arms and stood up. His laugh could be heard throughout the terminal. He glanced at Annie impishly and then turned back to Heidi. "Oh, yeah, Short Stuff, what else does your auntie say about me?"

Heidi instantly knew she was part of a game. She let a loud stream of giggles flood the air. Before she could answer any more of Ryan's probing questions, Annie gently scooped Heidi out of Ryan's arms. She didn't want Heidi giving him the five-year-old version on anything else that pertained to her. Kids definitely had a way of bringing an entirely new level of humility to adults.

"Come with Auntie, Dear. Let me show you where you get your suitcases." Heidi took off with Annie to the baggage area and the group curiously followed the fleeting pair.

As Ryan caught up with Annie and wrapped a loose arm around her shoulders, Jude discreetly took Heidi's hand and pulled her back with the rest of the group. "Why don't you want me talking with Heidi? She seems very informative." The grin on

Ryan's face told Annie that she was going to get teased.

"She's too informative for a five year old."

"Information's good." Ryan grinned wickedly.

Annie cleared her throat. "Yes, well, at times it can be, but I'd like to make two points here. Information is good as long as it's not about me, and if it's coming from your five-year-old source, it's likely to be watered down a bit."

Ryan laughed loudly. "Yeah, well, I may have to take whatever info I can get on you because I remember you telling me that you didn't like to talk about yourself. You're a very private person."

Annie smiled. "You can ask me whatever you want. If you go to Heidi for info on me first, I'll clobber you."

Ryan stopped walking for a second and stared at Annie. "I thought you didn't want to answer my questions. I distinctly remember you saying that your life was none of my business."

Annie laughed. "Did I say that?"

"You know you did."

"Listen, you can ask me anything. I've become a very open person."

Ryan's eyes narrowed. "Oh really? Then the first question that I'm going to ask you is why the sudden change of heart?"

Annie laughed. "Because…Heidi is staying at your house for the next two weeks, and she's a non-stop talker."

Ryan howled with laughter. "Gee, if I knew that would have worked, I would have invited Heidi down to the ranch months ago!"

"Very funny!"

"I'm serious."

Annie stopped walking and turned to face Ryan directly. "You'd better not be."

"Are you threatening me?" Ryan laughed. "Remember, I have a talkative five-year-old staying in my house who seems to freely volunteer all sorts of interesting information. Besides," Ryan wiggled his eyebrows up and down, "I'm very good at opening kids up." He shrugged his shoulders. "Kids like me."

"That's because you're a big kid yourself."

"Thank you."

Annie sighed. "Promise me you'll come to me first?"

Ryan grinned. "This is a very interesting situation."

"No, it's not."

"You're getting nervous about what Heidi might say."

"If you were smart, you'd get a little nervous about what Heidi might say, too. Just remember, she doesn't limit her conversation to just me; she talks about everyone and soon that will include you, too."

Annie sighed. "If only you knew all the stuff she's blabbed about Bob and Jude. I mean, the kid answers questions far too openly and is entirely too informative. She has absolutely no discretion at all. I can't tell you how embarrassing it is at times. There are things that I now know about Bob and Jude, because of Heidi's big mouth, that I definitely didn't want to know. She's really awful. You should watch what you say around her."

Ryan laughed. "You see, I wasn't planning on saying a whole lot around her. I was just planning on doing a lot of listening. You know, there's so much you can learn about people if you just sit back and listen."

"I think coming here was a very bad idea."

"I think coming here was a very good idea."

"You're a pest."

"That's nothing new to you. Actually," Ryan grinned, "I believe you called me a pest shortly after we met."

"That's because you are."

"I'm so glad that you're all here." Ryan slipped his hand in Annie's and squeezed it tenderly.

Annie had to laugh. "I just bet you are-especially Heidi!"

Ryan smiled down at her. "Yeah, I bet I'm going to learn all kinds of things about you."

"About everyone else, too. She never stops talking."

"I'm mainly interested in what she's going to say about you."

"I'm sure you are."

Ryan grew serious. "Annie, I'm sure everything's going to be fine. Don't worry."

"That's easy for you to say. You don't know Heidi."

"She's a kid."

"That's just her disguise. She's lethal."

"I'm sure we'll have a great time."

"I think I'd have a better time if Heidi got laryngitis for the next two weeks."

"I don't think anything can stop her."

"You're probably right."

"Hey, now, we've been down this road before." Ryan pointed to himself, "I am always right. You know that."

Annie laughed, but her mind was still on Heidi. It was amazing how much damage the little rug rat could do with her loose lips. It wasn't as if Annie had anything awful to hide, it was just that Heidi had a way of revealing life's most embarrassing moments to the entire world. There was a limit on how much someone could be humiliated before permanent damage took place. Annie knew that she needed to leave this in God's hands. As she prayed, she tossed the idea of laryngitis up to her Heavenly Father. It really did seem to her that it would help the situation all the way around.

Two

After they had retrieved their luggage, the merry group made their way to the parking lot, dragging their suitcases behind them. Ryan had brought his large, nine-passenger black Suburban, along with a slightly jacked up black Dodge pick-up truck.

"I thought we'd toss all our luggage in the bed of the pickup," Ryan unlocked the truck. "That way, we'll have more room in the Suburban."

Ryan, David and Tyler quickly loaded the luggage into the bed of the pickup and then secured a tarp across the top. David drove the pickup, while Tyler rode shotgun with him and everyone else squeezed into the Suburban.

Ryan quickly took Annie and Heidi's hands. "You two ladies are riding up front with me. I think Heidi has some interesting stories to tell." Annie rolled her eyes at him while Heidi giggled loudly.

As they drove the hour ride home, Ryan talked excitedly to Heidi. "Do you like horses?"

"Oh, yes!" Heidi squealed. "I want a horse just like Black Beauty but I don't want her black I want her brown and I want her to be able to talk like Mr. Ed. Do you know who Mr. Ed is?"

Ryan laughed and nodded his head. "Isn't he that horse on TV that talks?"

"Yes," Heidi bubbled excitedly, "and he really talks." She looked at Ryan seriously for a minute and decided that more conformation on this subject was needed. "My daddy said so."

Ryan muffled another laugh. "Well, daddy's are never wrong."

"Just like you," Annie whispered, "never wrong."

"You see, that's because I'm a daddy."

Annie laughed. "I don't think I want to go there with you."

"You know that you do." Ryan grinned.

"Nope. I've thought about it, and I don't. It would only lead to a huge argument, because I don't think that daddys are always right, and I don't think you are always right."

Heidi gasped. "He's not always right?" she whispered to Annie.

Ryan choked on the laughter that he was trying to keep inside. Annie just smiled at him. "Heidi," she reassured the little girl, " no one is always right but Auntie."

"Uh, I'm having major problems with this conversation here." Bob leaned over the front seat some so he could look directly at Annie. "I know for a fact that you are not always right."

"You don't know anything," Annie said between fits of laughter.

"Oh, yeah?" Bob leaned a little closer to her.

Annie covered Heidi's ears for a moment and leaned up to whisper in her brother's ear. "What do you know? Weren't you the daddy that told her that Mr. Ed really talks?"

Bob grinned. "And your point here would be?"

Annie laughed. "She's going to be going up to all the horses on Ryan's ranch thinking that they're going to talk with her." Annie laughed again. "I think it's going to be disappointingly quiet in the pasture, if you know what I mean, big brother." Annie took her hands off Heidi's ears and the little girl stared at them quizzically.

"Hey Sweetie," Bob said gently to his daughter, "you know that only Mr. Ed talks right? Other horses can't."

"Why not?" Heidi asked him innocently. "Maybe no one's ever taken the time to listen to them."

Once again, Annie and Ryan were choking on their laughter. "That could be true, Bob." Annie looked at her brother and wiggled her eyebrows at him. "Have you ever taken the time to listen to a horse?"

Bob cleared his throat loudly. "Not lately, Ann." Annie turned her head so Heidi wouldn't see her laughing. "I do know this. Mr. Ed is the only talking horse. He is the only one with the gift." Everyone in the Suburban broke out laughing.

"Ryan," Bob asked as he looked at his watch, "how far are we from the ranch?"

"Trying to run away, big brother?" Annie laughed.

"No," Bob laughed, "I'm just feeling the need for a little more space."

"I'll bet." Annie laughed again.

"Bob, we're thirty minutes from Chatfield Hollow." Ryan had a huge grin on his face. "I imagine that's going to be a little longer then you wanted, but it should go by pretty quickly."

"Yes, and that gives us plenty of time to explore the subject about talking horses." Annie couldn't keep from laughing. She loved teasing Bob. It wasn't often she could get him into a corner on anything.

"Change the subject, Ann." Bob's voice held a clear warning that Annie quickly chose to ignore.

"Now, Bob, I'm really interested in this. It isn't every day the subject of talking horses comes up."

"It isn't every day I think of killing you either, Annie." Bob exhaled loudly. "Change the subject."

Annie laughed. "OK." She turned to Heidi. "Hey, Sweetie, what do you want to talk about?"

"Horses!" The little girl squealed.

Everyone laughed. "Bob," Annie asked innocently, "is it OK with you if we talk about horses? I don't want the subject to be offensive to you."

"I'm glad I'm not the only one that you pick on," Ryan mumbled with a playful smirk on his face.

"I wish you were," Bob moaned from behind them. "Listen, you can talk about horses all you want, just don't talk about talking horses."

"I really think those are more fascinating." Annie turned in her seat to smile at Bob.

He put a hand on the top of her head and messed her hair up. "You are such a pest. Ya know that?"

Ryan gasped. "You're a pest, too?" He grinned charmingly at her. "I guess we're both a couple of pests."

"You're worse," Annie pointed a finger at him.

"I bet your brother would disagree with that."

"I would and I do," Bob boomed from behind them. "No one can out pester Annie. She's the queen of pests."

"Now stop. You're just mad because of the talking horse thing. I wasn't the one that started that."

"Yes, you were, you little antagonistic bug."

"I was not," Annie shook her head firmly. "I never told Heidi that horses talk. You did."

"How did we ever get back to talking horses?" Bob sighed. "I said we could only talk about the horses that don't talk. Do you have non-talking horses on your ranch, Ryan?"

Ryan laughed. "Well, to be honest with you, I'm not totally sure a few of them don't talk. Like Annie said before, I've never taken the time to listen to them."

"They could have something very interesting to say," Annie admitted quickly. "You just never know."

Heidi tugged on Ryan's sleeve. "How many horses do you have on your ranch?"

"We have ten horses."

"Ten horses!" Heidi exploded. "Can I see them?"

"You bet," Ryan winked at her. "If your parents say that it's OK, I'll even teach you how to ride."

"Really?" Heidi squealed loudly. Ryan nodded his head. "Can he teach me to ride?"

"Only on the non-talking horses, Dear," Jude answered. Everyone laughed but Heidi.

"Why mommy? I'd like to ride one like Mr. Ed." Heidi asked determinedly.

"No, Dear. It just won't do. If you get on a talking horse, then it will distract you from the lesson that Mr. Ryan is trying to give you."

"Good one, Hon," Bob whispered to his wife.

"Besides," Annie turned to look at Heidi, "some of those talking horses never shut up. I think that could get really annoying after awhile. Yak, yak, yak…"

"OK, that's it," Bob sighed loudly, "no more horse talk for the rest of the trip. Talk about anything else but horses. Please." Everyone laughed.

"Bob," Annie leaned back to whisper to her brother, "you know this talking horse thing just isn't going to go away for Heidi. She's going to bring it up again. You know her."

"In the meantime, I'll think of some brilliant answer."

"I'd love to hear it," Annie admitted.

"I think we'd all love to hear it." Jude nudged her husband with her elbow.

"Heidi," Ryan asked quickly, "do you like dogs?"

"I like horses better, but I also like dogs."

"Well, you'll see plenty of horses, but right now I want to tell you about my dog."

"What's his name?" Heidi turned her head so she could look at Ryan.

"Banjo." Ryan smiled at his new little friend.

"Banjo?" Heidi repeated with a confused expression. "I thought a banjo was an instrument."

Ryan and Annie laughed. "It is an instrument, but in this case, it's a dog, too."

"You named your dog after an instrument?"

Ryan nodded. "Yes. My grandpa played the banjo very well. I've always loved the sound of a banjo, so I named my dog Banjo."

"Do you have any other animals on the ranch named after instruments?"

Ryan laughed. He was enjoying his conversation with Heidi. "You mean," he asked wiggling his eyebrows at her, "like do I have a cow named piano or a horse named guitar?"

Everyone in the Suburban broke out laughing but Heidi. She stared at Ryan seriously and nodded her head.

Ryan laughed. "Banjo is the only animal named after an instrument. You're going to like him. He's a big Golden Lab and as friendly as dogs come."

The ride back to the ranch passed quickly. Ryan cheerfully played tour guide to the group. He talked about the mountains, area attractions and different Christian celebrities that lived in the area.

After about fifty minutes, Ryan pulled off the main road and onto a dirt road. "Ten minutes this way," he smiled at Annie, "and then we're home."

"What's the name of this road?" Annie asked him curiously.

Ryan laughed. "It's not a road Annie, it's my driveway."

"Your driveway?" Ryan nodded. "Your driveway is ten minutes long?"

Ryan smiled. "Longer if you're walking or riding a horse."

Annie smiled at him and then focused her attention on the beautiful mountains and woods around them. "Ryan, I'm so glad that you invited us here. It's simply beautiful."

Ryan smiled at her lovingly. "I'm glad you think so. God's creation is awesome."

When the ranch came into sight, both Annie and Heidi let out a loud gasp. Ryan smiled at them and slowed the Suburban for them to look around. The ranch was in the middle of a large meadow. Surrounding the meadow were gently rolling mountains. The picturesque view looked like it belonged on a calendar page or a postcard.

The ranch itself consisted of five, large, white barns graciously spaced apart. Four of the barns had classic, white-board corral fencing. There was a big group of horses grazing in the largest corral. The fifth barn was red with white trim. It reminded Annie more of a quaint carriage house than a barn. She smiled. It certainly was one high class looking barn.

"Horses!" Heidi screamed.

Annie turned around to look at her brother. She had a huge smirk on her face. "Think any of them talk?"

"Don't start with me, Ann. I mean it."

"You're going to have to face this issue sooner or later."

"Later is fine with me."

"Yeah, that would work for me, too. Just make sure I'm around OK? I don't want to miss this."

"Turn around," Bob ordered, wiggling a finger at his sister.

"Do the horses all have names?" Heidi asked Ryan eagerly.

Ryan smiled. "Yes, they do. I'll introduce you to each one later."

A little further down the road, still in the same meadow as the barns, a huge, rambling, two-story ranch house came into view. The house was painted white with black shutters decorating the windows. A wide country porch ran around the entire house. Annie noticed the white rocking chairs that were on the front porch. There were at least six of them, and they looked very inviting.

"I love your rockers. What a great place to sit!"

"Yeah," Ryan smiled at her, "they're a great place to sit and visit. We've had some wonderful times on that porch. I've written some of my best songs there," Ryan added reflectively. "It's such a peaceful spot."

They unloaded their baggage, and Ryan headed the troops up the stairs to the second floor to show them their rooms. "This place is huge!" Amy turned to Ryan. "I think I'm going to need to map."

Annie laughed. "Maybe you could get one in the gift shop." She glanced at Ryan. "Do you sell little souvenirs and tee shirts?"

Ryan looked embarrassed. "We have friends and family all over the country and the world. I wanted to have a place big enough to accommodate them all as often as possible. I've always loved to entertain and have family and friends around as much as possible."

"Tyler," Ryan pushed open a door, "you'll be bunking with David. He's got two full beds in there so you should be pretty comfortable." They went down the hall a few feet to the next door. "This is Beth's room," Ryan swung the door open. "She and Nikki are going to bunk together."

As Ryan went down the wood paneled hallway a little further, he turned to Heidi and winked. "This is where you and your mom and dad will sleep. There's a bed for your parents and we put a comfy cot in the corner for you." Heidi immediately went over and sat down on her bed. "Heidi," Ryan pointed to the large window that faced the meadow, "you can see the horses from your room." Heidi squealed, flew off her bed and ran over to the window.

Annie made a face at Bob. "Don't say a word, Ann. I mean it."

Annie laughed. "It's not me that I think Heidi is dying to listen to. It's going to be a very interesting time. Don't you think?"

"Why didn't God give me a little brother instead?"

Annie went to jab him in the ribs, but Bob jumped away. "You would miss me so much."

"Yeah, like a migraine or a bad toothache," Bob grumbled.

"Now listen you two," Jude stated firmly, "if you don't knock it off, I'm going to take away your dessert tonight."

"What's for dessert tonight?" Annie quickly asked Ryan.

"I'm not sure. Why?"

"I'm just trying to figure out if I should keep picking on Bob and lose my dessert." Annie laughed. "Sometimes, if the dessert isn't that great, it's better to keep picking on Bob."

Ryan laughed. "I think I'm going to take away your TV for tonight. You're being bad."

Annie smiled. "Well, you see, that still might not make me behave. It all depends what's on TV tonight. If nothing good is on, I should keep picking on him. This talking horse thing has endless possibilities."

Bob folded his arms across his broad chest and narrowed his eyes at his little sister. "I would think twice before I bring that subject up again."

Annie shook her head. "Nope. Don't have to. It's a golden opportunity that I don't think I should let pass."

Ryan pointed a finger at Amy with one hand and with the other hand he grabbed Annie. "You two better come with me." They walked down the hall a little ways and Ryan swung the door open. "This is our presidential suite!" He waved his arms around the large room. There was a comfortable sitting area and a large canopy bed. Off the far end of the room Annie could see part of a bathroom.

"Ryan, you're going to spoil us!" Annie looked around the room in shock. It was a beautiful little suite.

"I doubt that," he smiled at her. "This is where the grandparents usually stay. We wanted to make the place special for them."

Annie nodded. "Mission accomplished. This place is great."

As Annie and Ryan began to head back down the long hall again, Amy stayed in the room to unpack. A thought suddenly struck Annie, and she turned and looked at Ryan a bit nervously. "Where's your room?"

Ryan stopped walking and laughed loudly. "Annie, you have nothing to worry about," his voice was full of amusement. "My room is actually on the other side of your room."

Annie's eyes widened. "I'd say that's something to worry about."

"When we have female guests staying on this floor," Ryan gently touched the tip of Annie's nose, "I always sleep in the small bedroom just off the kitchen. I try to avoid situations where people may get the wrong idea. You know," he added seriously, "that whole avoid the appearance of evil thing. I take it pretty seriously. I think that avoiding certain situations can keep you from falling into a lot of trouble and temptation."

Annie felt immediately embarrassed by her concern. She could feel the red rising in her face. Pretty soon she'd be glowing like Rudolph's nose. It wasn't a good look for her. "I just needed to ask. Protecting both our reputations is very important to me."

"Me too," Ryan added quickly.

"I'm sorry we've kicked you out of your room."

Ryan laughed. "Annie," he gently took her hand, "I don't mind sleeping in the spare room. I'm so excited that you're here that I'd sleep in the barn with the horses." He squeezed her hand again and then let it drop. "Let me show you around the place."

Ryan led Annie down the stairs and into his great room. It was a large family room area, probably about half the size of her farmhouse back in Boston. There were two huge fireplaces at either end of the room with couches and coffee tables attractively sectioning off the middle of the room. French doors and large windows decorated the back of the room, giving a breathtaking view of the mountains. In the back corner of the room was a large, black, baby grand piano. Ryan walked over to it and gently played a few notes.

"I'd love to play for you later."

"A private concert by the world renowned Ryan Jones." Annie bowed slightly as a grin tugged at the corners of her mouth. "I would be honored, Sir…"

Ryan shook his head slowly. "I still can't believe that you are actually here." A shy expression quickly slipped across his face. "I wasn't sure if you'd really come."

"It's not every day that I receive an invitation from one of my favorite singers. How could I have said no?" He looked at her tenderly and she smiled warmly. "Besides, I was really looking forward to coming. You've been such a good friend to me."

Ryan walked over and hugged Annie. "Thanks. You've become a good friend too. He lifted his head back slightly and gazed deeply into her brown eyes. It was only seconds but Annie felt the moment lasted for hours. His gaze dropped down to her lips, and he lowered his head slightly. Suddenly, he jerked away. He released Annie from the embrace, and took a full step backwards as he ran a hand nervously through his thick brown hair.

"Annie," Ryan sighed loudly, "I promised to be good and in order to do that, I think we'd better keep moving. You know," he laughed, "stay in big groups, with lots of people as chaperones. You're too tempting for me when we're alone, Sweetheart. Besides," he laughed again, "if Heidi got wind of this, she'd make it front page news. I've got to keep her in mind. Little kids are great spies. They're often secretly watching you when you think no one is around."

Annie smiled at him lovingly. She admired his honesty and his discipline. "That's a good idea," Annie agreed as they exited the great room, "because you know, after all, we are just friends."

Ryan laughed loudly as he followed her. "Annie, this relationship is going to kill me!"

As they walked into the kitchen, a large Golden Lab approached them with his tail wagging so enthusiastically that his entire back end was wiggling. "You must be Banjo," Annie stoked the dog's head lovingly.

"Hey there, Boy," Ryan knelt down to hug his dog, "I've been wondering where you've been hiding. You had better not be going through the garage cans again looking for leftovers." Banjo looked mildly guilty and then planted a few sloppy, wet licks on Ryan's face.

As Ryan stood up, the back door opened and two people that Annie had never seen before confidently entered the kitchen. The woman and the man looked to be around sixty-five or so. As soon as they noticed her, they extended their hands welcomingly.

"Well, hello there," the man's voice was warm and kind, "you must be Annie. I'm Tag," he grabbed Annie's hand and shook it enthusiastically, "and this here is Sadie." Tag put a loving arm around the plump woman standing next to him. "She's my bride of forty-seven years." Sadie quickly shook Annie's hand but her greeting was noticeably reserved.

"Tag and Sadie came to live with us about ten years ago." Ryan smiled lovingly at the pair. "They are such a blessing to have around. Tag takes care of the horses and Sadie helps out in the kitchen. They're a great team."

Tag smiled gently at Annie. "Ryan really lifted us out of a hard spot. Our place in town burned to the ground and he offered us his guest house." Tag laughed loudly. "I guess we aren't very good guests because ten years later we're still here!"

Everyone laughed. "Don't believe a word he says." A loving smile spread across Ryan's face. "They are one in a billion and we're lucky to have them here."

As Ryan and Annie went to join the others that were now seated around the table, she couldn't help but get the feeling that Sadie didn't like her. The older woman had been pleasant but definitely kept her distance. There was a wall there and Annie didn't know why. As she tried to push these thoughts out of her head while she ate dinner, several times she caught Sadie staring at her in a cold, analytical way. Her expression was hard and penetrating until Annie's eyes would lock with hers. Then Sadie would plaster a quick, fake smile across her face. The smile bothered Annie as much as the firm expression, because the smile was void of the slightest bit of warm or sincerity. Annie tired to shrug it off, but she'd never been good at such games. She was the type of person that liked to resolve issues and problems between people, not let them linger and smolder until they destroy.

After dinner, everyone went into the great room. The kids hung out at one end of the room playing board games, and the adults sat in the couches by the fireplaces and talked. As Sadie began talking about what a wonderful person Ryan's wife Kay was, Annie cuddled a little closer to Heidi, who had fallen asleep in her lap. Somehow, Heidi's blonde, curly head resting upon her cheek comforted her.

After listening to Sadie go on and on about how incredible Kay was, Annie was quite sure that no one could complete with the superwoman. Jude and Bob began casting Annie curious glances. They were openly surprised at the older woman's thoughtlessness. Sadie was being overbearing, arrogant and rude. It was clear that she wanted Annie to know that she could never live up to Kay or even come close to replacing her.

Ryan and Tag tried unsuccessfully to change the subject many times but Sadie was a determined, strong willed woman. She didn't seem like she would stop until Annie packed her bags and left the ranch.

Slowly, Annie got up and passed Heidi to Bob. "I'll be right back," she looked at Ryan for a moment. If Sadie thought she could dump on her, she was greatly mistaken. Annie was never one to sit idly on the sidelines. She didn't start whatever was happening between them but she would defend herself.

She went up to her bedroom and retrieved her pocketbook. She got two pictures of her late husband out of her wallet and headed back to the great room with them.

As Annie entered the room she was praying that God would help her control her temper. She was so mad that a red haze danced before her eyes. She knew she was at the boiling point. Annie went to stand directly in front of Sadie. "Are you done yet?"

The older woman seemed shocked but then slowly nodded her head. "Yes, I believe that I am. I'm going to leave now."

"Not so fast. You've had your say, now I'm going to have mine."

"I'm not interested," Sadie answered boldly.

Annie's eyes narrowed. "That's too bad because you're going to listen anyway." Annie slapped the pictures of her late husband down on Sadie's lap. The unsuspecting woman stared up at Annie in pure shock.

"Those are pictures of my Ryan," Annie's voice was full of emotion. "He was a wonderful, godly man who was ripped out of our hearts and lives forever." By this time the kids had crossed the large room and had ringside seats to the show. "He was sensitive, kind, and loving," Annie pushed on as the tears stung her eyes, "and I miss him every second of every day. If you think I came here to replace him," Annie seethed, "then you're wrong!" Annie snapped the pictures up and ran off to her room. Amy, Tyler and Bob immediately followed. Jude picked up Heidi and followed the group up the stairs.

Ryan stood up and glared at Sadie angrily. "You know, she is my guest here. It took me four months to convince her to come here for Christmas, Sadie. Annie has never, in any way thrown herself at me. I," Ryan pointed to himself, "have been the one actively pursuing her from day one." He paused and looked at the confused lady before him "Sadie, you owe her a big apology."

Ryan left the great room quickly, taking the stairs two at a time toward Annie's room. He could hear the muffled sobs as he approached her door and he felt like each one was a knife through his heart. He softly knocked on Annie's door, and as it opened he was greeted by a very serious Bob.

He opened the door just enough for him to see Tyler and Amy sitting on the bed next to their mom. Tyler shot Ryan an angry, spiteful look. There was no doubt in Ryan's mind that Tyler and Bob would be fighting over who was going to get to kill him.

"Bob, I'd like to speak with your sister."

Bob stepped into the hall and shut the door behind him. "She's not available."

"All I want is five minutes of her time before she starts packing," Ryan asked desperately.

Bob grinned wickedly. "She's already started packing. Tyler and Amy stopped her."

Ryan's blue eyes opened wide in surprise. "Listen, I know you don't like me…"

Bob interrupted him. "The jury's still out on whether I like you or not." Bob answered frankly. "What matters is I know my sister does and because of that, I'll go ask her if she wants to speak to you. If she says no," Bob's voice held clear warning, "then the answer's no. You've got to respect her wishes. If you don't, you'll answer to me. Got it?"

Ryan nodded. Only a complete idiot wouldn't have gotten it. Bob was more than ready to pound him. This would give him the perfect excuse.

A few minutes later, a shaken Annie opened the door. She saw Ryan leaning against the wood-paneled wall, with his arms folded across his chest. When he turned his eyes toward her, she could see that his eyes were puddled in tears.

"I need to go back to Boston," Annie quickly blurted out. "I don't belong here."

Ryan didn't move. "I was afraid that you'd say that." Annie noticed the hopeless defeat in his tone.

As Annie turned to go back into her room, Ryan literally jumped off the wall. He grabbed one of Annie's hands. He had to stop her before Bob came out to defend her. "We need to talk."

Annie studied him for a moment and then said reluctantly, "OK. Come in for a minute."

Ryan shook his head firmly. "I can't go in there, Annie."

Annie looked startled at first, but then the truth of the situation dawned on her. "You're right. I'm sorry." That's all she needed for people to find out that Ryan had been in her room, and they'd assume the worst.

"Come with me for a short drive. I'll bring you back as soon as you ask. In the Suburban, we'll have all the privacy we need to talk." Ryan sighed and shook his head. "As long as Bob's not in the back seat we'll have all the privacy we need to talk."

Annie smiled as she studied him carefully. His plan did make sense, and she knew that she owed it to him to talk before she left. "I'll meet you outside in five minutes."

Annie grabbed her jacket and met Ryan on the porch. They walked in an awkward silence to the Suburban. After they both had gotten in, they slowly made their way down the dirt road. About four minutes into the ride, Ryan shifted the vehicle into four-wheel drive and made a left turn up another dirt road.

Annie glanced at Ryan. "We're going up the mountain in the dark?"

Ryan smiled slightly and nodded. "It's all right, Annie. This is just a rural country road. There's a meadow on the top of this mountain. It's a great place to sit and see the stars." Ryan paused thoughtfully and then whispered in a choked up voice, "You've got to see the Tennessee stars before you head back to Boston."

After another five minutes of driving up, Ryan pulled the Suburban into a meadow and shut off the engine. "We're here. Even though it's wintertime and it's cold, you've got to get out and see the stars. They're unbelievable this time of year."

They both got out of the Suburban and Annie immediately zipped up her leather bomber jacket. As she walked a few feet from the truck, Annie glanced up at the sky and loudly gasped. Never before had she seen a sky so loaded with stars. It looked as though there wasn't room for one more in the sky.

"It's beautiful!"

"Yes," Ryan agreed quietly, "it always reminds me of how wonderful God is."

Annie stared at the sky for at least fifteen minutes. She couldn't seem to pull her eyes away from the captivating show. She felt eyes on her and quickly glanced over at Ryan. He was watching her through tearful eyes. In a choked-up voice he quietly said that they needed to talk.

They got back in the truck so they wouldn't freeze, and Ryan began speaking immediately. "Annie, please hear me out for a minute." Annie slowly nodded and Ryan continued. "Sadie has been with me for ten years. Never," he sighed deeply, "in all that time has she ever done anything like she did tonight. She was rude and just plain awful." He paused and looked at Annie intently. "I'm not making excuses for her...what she did was very wrong. I spoke to her right after you left and set her straight. I'm sure tomorrow things will go better."

"Ryan," Annie began in a choked up voice, "tonight was a real eye opener for me. Sadie is just the beginning of it. Every time you introduce me to your friends, they're going to assume that I'm out to snag myself a rich and handsome husband." Annie paused and took a deep breath. "I would never make it through that type of daily criticism. My heart is just beginning to mend. If people criticize our friendship and treat me as though I were a gold digger, I'd crack. I can't go through any more issues of the heart right now. I'm not that strong."

Ryan nodded. "I understand what you're saying," his tone was compassionate as he unbuttoned his deerskin coat, "but things will be different next time. I was totally unprepared for Sadie's comments. I was shocked and quite honestly completely taken off guard. Next time," Ryan sounded firm; "I will be on guard and set the record straight immediately. There will be no doubt in anyone's mind that I'm madly in love with you."

Annie laughed nervously. "Oh yeah, Slick, and just how do you think that you're going to pull that off?"

Ryan grinned mischievously. "I was thinking," he began slowly as he flashed her a big charming smile, "that I'd grab you and kiss you passionately."

Annie stiffened. "You wouldn't. Would you?"

Ryan laughed loudly. "OK then," he winked at her, "I guess we could always go to plan B."

"Plan B?" Annie asked questioningly.

"Yep," he nodded thoughtfully. "Anyone who really matters to me and knows me at all can clearly see that I am a man in love." Ryan paused and smiled. "Tag spotted it right away as soon as I got back from Boston."

"What about Sadie?"

"She knew, too, Annie. That's why I was so surprised when she laid into you. If," Ryan looked at Annie seriously, "it ever starts to happen again, I will put a stop to it immediately and then take you away from the stone throwers."

"Stone throwers?" Annie smiled at him.

"Words can hurt worst than rocks." Ryan closed his eyes for a moment. "I'd rather be stoned than tossed into a room full of people that were angry at me and criticizing me unfairly." Ryan glanced at her. "How about you?"

Annie laughed loudly this time, and Ryan was glad. "Yeah, I'll take stone throwers over cutting remarks. It would be a less painful way to die." They both laughed again.

As Ryan tenderly took Annie's hand, he became very serious again. "Will you stay Annie? Please. We can still make a special time of it."

Annie slowly nodded. Ryan scooted across the bench seat and hugged her tightly. After a moment, he let go of her but continued to sit right next to her.

"Annie," Ryan's face was full of smiles, "I want you to close your eyes for a minute." Annie looked at him curiously, but then closed her eyes. She could hear him rustling under the seat for something and was tempted to open her eyes, but she didn't.

"OK," Ryan said excitedly, "open your eyes."

When she did, Ryan was holding a dozen long-stemmed roses out to her. Annie accepted them, a little mechanically, and stared wide-eyed at her admirer. "Annie," Ryan whispered tenderly, "I love you and would haul you off to the church right this moment and marry you." Annie's eyes widened even more, and Ryan laughed softly and tapped the tip of her nose with his finger. "I know you're not ready for that …yet," he smiled understandingly. "So don't worry, I'm not asking you to marry me…tonight anyway." He winked at her, and then continued. "What I'm going to ask you is something that I believe you're ready for, Annie." Ryan gently took hold of her hand. "I want you to be my girlfriend."

Annie looked at him and no words came out of her mouth. Ryan smiled at her lovingly. "I know I've shocked you. You can take your time and think about this, Sweetheart. You don't need to answer me tonight."

Annie visibly relaxed. "Ryan, I need to know what your expectations are."

"You make it sound like I should be giving you a job description for being my girlfriend," Ryan answered in an amused tone.

Annie just continued to stare at him seriously. "OK," Ryan winked at her, "you want a job description, I'll give you a job description!" Annie nodded. "Annie, not much is going to change from our friendship. But," he squeezed her hand, "I want to be able to tell people that you're my girlfriend. It may sound juvenile to say that I'm going steady with you or going out with you at my age, but I don't care; I want to be able to say that." Ryan turned and looked at Annie. "Do they still say going out or going steady? I think I may not be up on the latest jargon."

"It works for me," Annie shrugged and smiled. "That's all that matters."

"Tell me more about the job description."

Ryan smiled. "OK. I want to be able to hold your hand for the rest of my life."

Annie's eyes widened. "Ryan…"

Ryan laughed. "Just concentrate on the hold-your-hand part. We'll work on for the rest of your life part a little later. One thing at a time."

"OK." Annie eyed him closely. "What else?"

Ryan dropped his gaze to her lips. "I want to feel welcome to kiss you. Now mind you," Ryan held his hands up towards Annie, "nothing too physically, just a lip touch every now and then. Nothing too wild and crazy."

Annie turned away from him to hide her smile but Ryan caught it anyway. "I saw that. For the record, I want you to know that I saw that."

Annie smiled at him and for a moment he was lost in her love. He shook his head to clear his mind from the fog. "Do you want to go back out and look at the stars before I bring you back?" Getting out of the small space they were in seemed like a wise idea. He suddenly felt all too close to her.

Annie nodded and they got out of the truck. As she began to walk toward the center of the meadow Ryan was beside her in a flash. "Oh, there's something that I forgot to tell you about the job."

Annie looked up at him curiously. "There's more?"

"Yes." Ryan nodded his head. "I want to be able to put my arm around you."

Annie giggled. "Then why don't you?"

Ryan didn't need any more of an invitation than that. He immediately put his arm around Annie and pulled her near. She smiled up at him and his heart soared.

"If I was interested in this job," Annie asked teasingly, "how would I go about applying for it?"

Ryan grinned broadly at her. "Oh, you'd have to apply in person."

"OK, then, I'd like to apply for the job of being your girlfriend."

"You sure?" He studied her carefully.

"Yes. I'm sure. It's something I've been thinking about and praying about for a long time."

"Well, the job is all yours." Ryan picked her up and spun her around. As he set her back on the ground, he hugged her tightly. "I love you so much, Annie!"

Annie hugged him hard, unable yet to say the words that were in her heart. Some day she would be able to say those words but not quite yet.

When Ryan let go of her, he took her cold hand and held it tenderly. "Get used to this, girl, cause I love holding hands."

"Me too!" Annie laughed.

Ryan looked at Annie impishly, and she curiously asked him what was so funny. "It's going to be fun giving you your job evaluations!" He roared with laughter. "There's always room for improvement, ya know?"

Annie smacked his arm playfully. "You are something else. You know that?"

"Why, thank you," he beamed proudly at her. "I'm sort of one of a kind."

"Definitely." Annie laughed. "I don't think I've ever met anyone quite like you."

"Thank you again." Ryan turned and looked at her. "Was that a compliment? I just want to make sure. You're not ranking on me or anything. Are you?"

Annie laughed. "I'm not sure. I may be. It's true, I've never met anyone like you before."

"And that's a good thing?"

Annie laughed again. "Yeah, that's a good thing."

"So," Ryan grinned proudly, "it was a compliment after all. I knew it all the time!"

Annie smiled at him. "Hey, do you know what time it is?"

"No, and I don't care. I'm having too much fun."

Annie laughed. "Don't you have a watch?"

"I," Ryan gestured a hand toward himself, "never wear a watch. I hate the things."

Annie mouth dropped opened. "How on earth do you ever get through life? I loaned Heidi my watch and I've been going nuts without it."

"How do I get through life?" Ryan repeated her question.

Annie nodded. "Yeah, how?"

"By asking people like you who always wear a watch what time it is."

Annie's mouth dropped open a bit. "That would make me crazy."

"Hey, the system works quite fine for me, thank you very much."

"So you really don't know what time it is?"

"Not a clue."

"It's probably time to be heading back."

"Yeah, but you don't know that for sure."

Annie laughed. "If I had a watch I would know it for sure."

"See, watches are a pain. They interfere with life's fun. They always cut you off just when you're starting to have a good time."

"Ryan, whether or not you wear a watch, time just cuts into life whether you want it to or not. Time marches on. We can't stop it."

Ryan let out a low grumble. "You're probably right. We'd better head back before they send out a search party for us."

Annie laughed. "I have the feeling that Bob would be leading it up with a double barrel shotgun."

Ryan laughed. "I have the feeling that Bob could flatten me if he wanted to."

"He wouldn't do that. He likes you."

Ryan shook his head. "No, I wouldn't go all the way to like. He clearly told me that the jury was still out on me. That's a warning if I ever heard one." Annie laughed. "Yeah, you go ahead and laugh but I'm not turning my back on that guy anytime too soon."

"I really don't think that you have anything to worry about."

"I'm not really worried, just kind of cautiously concerned." Ryan sighed. "Has he always been so protective of you?"

Annie smiled lovingly. "Yeah, we were always close as kids; and as we grew up we continued to stay very close. He's a good guy Ryan. He'll like you once he gets to know you. I'm sure of it."

"Yeah, well let's just say that you have a lot more confidence about this whole thing than I do. I'm still not turning my back on the big guy. If he's going to flatten me, at least I want to be able to see it coming."

As Ryan opened the door to the Suburban, he suddenly stopped. "Annie," he whispered lovingly, "is it all right with you if I kiss you?" Annie nodded and Ryan leaned down and held his lips with hers for a moment. At that minute, Annie and Ryan saw more fireworks go off than they'd ever seen at any Fourth of July celebration.

Annie felt like someone had turned a song on inside her heart. She felt like dancing for joy. As she took both of Ryan's hands in hers, she didn't notice the cold, or the stars, or the beauty surrounding them. All she noticed was him. Just him. It was a magical moment that melted away any doubts she had and replaced them with love. It was at that moment that she knew for sure in her heart that she would one day marry Ryan Jones. It was at that moment that she knew, beyond a shadow of a doubt, that God had made them for each other. It was a match made in heaven.

As she gazed into Ryan's eyes, she knew that he had read her heart. He squeezed her hands tightly and kissed her on the top of the head.

"Just say the word, Annie," Ryan's blue eyes smoked with an intensity that matched her own. "Say the word and we'll get married tomorrow if you want. All you need to do is let me know that you're ready."

As Annie shook her head, her eyes welled up with tears of frustration. "I'm not sure why I feel this way, Ryan," Annie voiced was pained. "I just know that I'm not completely ready yet. I wish I were…"

"So do I Honey," Ryan whispered softly as he wiped her tears away. "God will help us. He will be the one to heal you so you are ready. I'm sure of it."

"Thanks," Annie squeaked out in a choked up voice.

"You're welcome." Ryan encompassed her in a huge hug. "I love you Annie."

It was no surprise to Annie or Ryan to find Bob waiting on the front porch when they pulled up to the house. "It looks like he's waiting for us," Ryan said wearily.

Annie laughed. "That's because he is."

"I am about to get pounded?" Ryan studied Bob for any clues that big man might give.

"No," Annie squeezed Ryan's hand, "not tonight anyway."

Ryan laughed nervously. "Does that mean that I'm going to get pounded in the near future?"

Annie smiled at him. "Bob hasn't personally pounded any of my boyfriends for years."

"Annie," Ryan stated anxiously, "you haven't had a boyfriend in years."

Annie nodded. "Good point. You should probably be careful then."

"Great time to mention this," Ryan slowly got out of the Suburban.

"I thought you'd appreciate it."

"You are so not funny."

Bob was at Annie's side instantly when she got out of the truck. "Is everything OK?" He studied her carefully.

"Fine," Annie tried to reassure her bodyguard. "We talked everything out."

"OK," Bob nodded his head thoughtfully. He stared intently at Ryan. "We should talk soon." It was not a request by any means. It was a demand. It was an appointment that Ryan knew he shouldn't be late for. The consequences could hurt.

"How about tomorrow?" Ryan felt like he was scheduling his own execution.

"Fine," Bob replied quickly. "We'll talk tomorrow." He stared at Ryan for a second longer and then marched into the house.

Ryan looked at Annie skeptically. "Should I be picking out the flowers that I want at my funeral?"

Annie laughed. "No, just talk to Bob."

"It might not be a bad idea if you find him in the morning first and talk to him a little. You know," Ryan waved his arms, "kind of soften him up a bit."

"You don't need to be afraid of him."

"Annie, the man has arms the size of tree trunks. I think being afraid of him is very smart."

"You'll be fine."

Ryan laughed. "Famous last words…"

Three

The next morning before breakfast, Heidi came running up to Ryan. "My daddy's looking for you."

"Is he?" Ryan tried to ignore the knot in his stomach.

"Yes. He wants to talk to you."

"Oh, won't that be nice." Ryan's enthusiasm came out sounding fake and artificial.

A moment later, a very serious-looking Bob appeared in the doorway. "Ready to talk?"

Ryan felt like a prisoner that had been holding out from the police. He laughed nervously. "Sure."

"Let's go outside." Bob turned and headed for the door.

Ryan laughed again. Yeah, Bob wouldn't want to kill him in front of little Heidi. It would be too much violence for a tyke to see.

They both put on their coats and grabbed a cup of coffee before heading out. There was no time for an awkward silence to develop, Bob jumped right in. "Annie made me promise that I wouldn't hit you or anything."

"Really? She's no fun, is she?" Ryan tried to break the tension with a joke. To his relief, Bob almost smiled.

"I haven't hit many of her boyfriends," Bob looked across the meadow. "I'm concerned that your relationship has progressed very quickly. I know that my sister really cares for you."

"Permission to speak openly."

Bob smiled this time. "Permission granted."

"I love her," Ryan said honestly. "I have loved her since the first time we met."

"I know," Bob gripped his coffee cup tightly. "I can see it in your eyes but what happened last night was very upsetting. I don't like to see my sister ambushed."

"That completely caught me off guard. I have known Sadie for a long time and she's never behaved that way. I can guarantee you that Sadie will never do that again. If I need to make a choice between Annie and Sadie, Annie will win hands down. I really love your sister with all my heart and I intend to cherish her for the rest of my life."

Bob studied Ryan's eyes for a minute and saw the determination they held. "Good," he said in a satisfied tone. "I think I could like you."

"Not sure yet?" Ryan asked amused.

"Too soon to tell." Bob actually smiled again. It was a good sign. "The jury's still out, but things are looking promising."

"Sounds good," Ryan nodded his head. "I'm sure Annie's told you a lot about me, but if you ever have any questions, feel free to come and ask. I'm an open and upfront type of guy."

"Good. I'm sure I'll take you up on that." A smile began to cross Bob's face that soon turned into a loud laugh. "Annie has told me a lot about you. I probably know more about you than you know about yourself."

At that moment, Annie came out unto the porch. "You two haven't traveled far."

"Just hanging out on the porch." Ryan smiled lovingly at her.

"Looks like you're getting along with each other." Annie felt more relieved than she showed.

"Yeah," Bob replied sarcastically, "we're playing nicely."

Annie smiled at Bob. "Glad you learned something from me!"

Bob narrowed his eyes at his little sister. "I guess now is a good time to tell you that my little sister is the most competitive woman on the face of the earth." Bob laughed loudly.

"That is so not true!" Annie threw her hands on her hips.

"In all fairness, I should clarify that." Bob smiled at Annie. "She is very competitive in sports. If she loses, she demands a rematch. If she wins, she takes out a full page ad in the Boston Globe declaring her victory to the world." Bob laughed again. "She's not only a sore loser, she's a sore winner!"

Annie came at Bob like a speeding train and Bob quickly handed his coffee off to Ryan. He wanted two hands to fight off his attacker.

"You are such a big, fat liar!" She glanced at Ryan and saw he had a grin spread from ear to ear. "You had better not be laughing!"

"No, ma'am," Ryan quickly tried to wipe the smile off his face, but he found he couldn't. The show in front of him was just too funny.

Annie turned her attention back to Bob. "You're just jealous because I can play ball better than you!"

"See what I mean about the competitive thing?" Bob quickly glanced at Ryan.

"I am staying out of this." Ryan held his hands up. "There's no way I'm coming between you two."

"Smart man," Bob mumbled as he watched his sister carefully. "You know," Bob pinned Annie with a hard look, "you're lucky that you're a girl and being the gentleman that I am, I have made it a policy to never hit girls. Even ones with sassy mouths."

"Oh, yeah," Annie threw a finger in Bob's chest, "you're lucky that I don't hit girls either!"

Ryan choked on the coffee that he was drinking. It came flying out of his mouth in the direction of the squabbling siblings. They saw it coming and took a step back and continued their argument.

"You always were in a hurry to catch up with your ambitions." Bob smiled down at his little sister. "Unfortunately for me, most of your ambitions involved beating me in some way. You always wanted to do everything that I did." Bob sidestepped a quick right that Annie threw at him. "You always thought you could do everything better than me."

"That's because I could!" Annie stated proudly. "Sometimes the truth hurts."

"She never gives up and she never shuts up!" Bob howled. He loved picking on his little sister. It would be great if every day could start this way. "She always has to have the last word. I'm going to be the mature one here and walk away."

"You are so juvenile," Annie mumbled under her breath.

"See," Bob looked at Ryan, "always has to have the last word."

"Go away!" Annie demanded. "You're being such a pain."

"There it is again," Bob said in a matter-of-fact way, "the last word."

As Bob disappeared into the house, Annie turned and saw a very amused Ryan Jones. She had to smile. She knew that the sparing that she and Bob did was quite a sight.

"Well, at least I know that he likes you." Annie smiled again. "He never would have picked on me in front of you if he didn't like you."

As they walked back into the house, Ryan knew it would be a while before he could get the smile off his face. The show he had just witnessed had been one of the funniest things he had seen in a long time. Comedy at someone else's expense was usually funnier than it was if it was at your expense.

As everyone gathered around the breakfast table, Ryan proudly announced that he and Annie were boyfriend and girlfriend. A loud cheer went up from the kids and they were instantly surrounded by hugs.

"It's about time!" David declared loudly.

"Yeah," Amy teased, "you guys were driving us nuts!"

"It was obvious that you two belonged together." Beth gave Annie a big hug.

After another round of hugs, Ryan told the group that they were going on a trail ride up the mountains. "Anyone interested in going should be at the barn in an hour."

"Heidi's never been on a horse before." Jude was clearly anxiously.

"She can ride with me," Ryan answered the worried mom confidently. He smiled at the little blue eyed, blonde haired girl. "I even have a small riding helmet that should fit you."

After the crowd left the kitchen, Annie and Ryan started making sandwiches to take on the trail ride. Annie seemed unusually quiet and Ryan asked her if everything was OK.

"I didn't see Sadie this morning…" Annie studied the sandwiches she was making intently. "I was hoping to see her and get things straightened out. I hate having something between us."

Ryan nodded understandingly and put an arm around Annie's shoulders. "I talked to Tag this morning. He said Sadie was up all night pacing the floors and crying. The Lord really convicted her Annie. Sadie's real sorry for what she did. I'm sure she'll be around later in the day and then you two can work this all out."

Annie nodded seriously and after they finished putting together their picnic lunch for ten, they headed to the barn to saddle up the horses. Annie enjoyed working with Ryan. They made a good team and worked efficiently together like they had been doing it all their lives.

When everyone showed up at the barn, the Jones family helped everyone get situated on a horse. After Ryan climbed up on his huge, muscular horse, General, David handed an excited Heidi up into his father's arms. Ryan tucked Heidi in front of him and wrapped an arm protectively around her waist.

"Now Heidi," Ryan's voice was stern, "you can't bop around up here on General. He doesn't like it and it will make the poor boy nervous. You need to sit calmly as if you were in church."

Heidi nodded firmly and asked seriously, "Is it alright if I talk? I'm not allowed to talk in church when the preacher's talking."

Everyone laughed and Ryan gave Heidi a quick squeeze. "Darling, you can talk all you want. General loves a good story and so do I."

The group made a single file line and headed slowly across the large meadow. Annie's horse, Lilly, was right behind Ryan's horse and they were able to talk back and forth.

"I love your cowboy hat and your cowboy boots!" Annie smiled at her handsome cowboy.

"Thanks there, Little Lady." Ryan turned around in his saddle. He tipped the front of his hat, in a gentlemanly fashion and winked at Annie. Annie rewarded him with a loving smile. It was so good to be at this stage in their relationship. It felt so comfortable and just plain natural to be together.

Ryan kept a slow, steady pace and played tour guide for the group as they passed ponds, mountains and a small lake. He was the perfect, gracious host and Annie could tell that he enjoyed the part.

As they started up one of the mountains, Heidi darted her head back and forth. She kept repeating the action until Ryan asked her what she was doing. Heidi turned slowly in the large saddle until she could look up at Ryan's face. "I'm looking for Robin Hood. He lives in a forest like this. I know," Heidi spoke confidently, "because I have seen it on TV."

Ryan turned around and grinned broadly at Annie. His eyes were full of twinkles and Annie could tell that he was working hard at suppressing his laughter. After a few seconds, he spoke to Heidi warmly. "Little Lady, I've never seen Robin Hood in this particular forest, or even Little John for that matter. I think they pretty much hang out in Sherwood Forest." Heidi looked up at Ryan disappointedly. "But," he tapped the tip of her nose, "this forest is loaded with deer. Maybe you can help me spot some."

Heidi's disappointed look immediately faded and her blue eyes opened wider. "You mean like Bambi?" she asked in awe. "I love Bambi!"

"Well, I think there's a good chance you'll see him today." Ryan smiled tenderly at the little girl in his lap. She was precious.

After about an hour of slowly climbing the wooded mountain trail, Ryan led the crew into a clearing. It was simply breathtaking. As Annie sat on her horse, she could look out for miles. The different mountain ranges that she could see seemed to go on forever.

Ryan pulled his horse up next to Annie's and touched her arm lightly. "Look down there," he pointed excitedly, "you can see the ranch."

Annie immediately looked in the direction he was pointing. You could see the entire layout of the ranch. It was beautiful and looked to Annie as if it should be on a postcard. "I feel as though I'm in an airplane! This is an unbelievable view. Thanks for bringing us up here."

Ryan smiled at her lovingly and then whispered softly, "Follow me." He led Annie and the others to the far side of the meadow. "Look over there."

As Annie turned her eyes toward the right, she could see a large winding river. The river snaked its way around the different valleys, disappearing for one moment, only to reappear on the other side of the mountain. It was an awesome sight.

After they tied the horses up to some trees at the far end of the meadow, Ryan and David spread plaid blankets from their saddlebags on the ground. Annie slowly walked toward them. She felt sore and stiff and moved like her legs were made on concrete.

Ryan laughed at her as he noticed her rubbing her backside. "Are you a little saddle-sore, Annie?"

Annie turned and looked back at him. She laughed loudly and then mumbled, "My buns are killing me! They're so numb I can hardly feel them."

He laughed again. "Keep walking around. It will help some."

After their lunch of turkey sandwiches, chips, apples and double chocolate chip cookies, Ryan and David retrieved a series of games from their saddlebags. Soon, a football and a few Frisbees were flying through the air. Annie and Ryan stood off a bit, watching the group with amusement.

"It's so great that the kids get along so well." Annie watched Tyler pass the football to David.

Ryan took her hand and slipped his fingers through hers. "God is so good Annie. We've all been through so much. I know that my kids are healing better since they've gotten to know your kids. I think they bonded so quickly because they have all been through similar experiences."

Annie nodded thoughtfully. "That's true."

Ryan smiled tenderly into Annie's eyes. After a moment, he let his eyes drop down to her lips. He kept his eyes there for a second, and suddenly turned away laughing. "You are lucky, Sweetheart that we are surrounded by so many people. I find it takes all the discipline I have and then some to be a good boy around you."

Annie giggled. "Whoever said that you were a good boy?" Just then, Annie dropped his hand and caught a football that was flying in their direction. She tucked the ball into her arms and began running. At first, Tyler made moves to cover her but then he abruptly stopped. The wide grin that spread across her son's face could only mean one thing. Ryan was in hot pursuit after her. As she took a quick glance behind her, to her surprise he was almost right on top of her. In a last minute, good-hearted effort, Annie kicked it into high gear. She gave it everything she had but she was still no match for the quick cowboy grinning behind her. Ryan made it beside her and carefully dropped her to the ground. She fell with a thud on the ground and the ball rolled free. Annie turned toward Ryan and looked at him with surprise spread across her face. "You're quick!"

"So are you!" Ryan was still trying to catch his breath. "For a minute there, I wasn't sure if I was going to be able to catch you. These cowboy boots are awful to run in."

"Oh," Annie teased, "you're blaming it on the boots!"

Ryan scooted over and leaned over Annie as she lay on the grass. "The boots did make me slow," his voice was very determined. "And, to answer your earlier question about me being a good boy," Ryan beamed with amusement, "I am being a very good boy. There's been plenty of opportunity to liplock with you My Dear, but," he winked at her, "I'm trying to limit myself."

Annie laughed and then quickly rolled away from him. She got up and as she was brushing herself off, she glanced back at Ryan. "You're good because you're a gentleman."

Ryan laughed loudly. "A gentleman! Let me tell you, it's not always fun being a gentleman. You're pushing me to the limit here, Annie." They laughed and headed back to the group walking hand in hand.

On the ride down the mountain, much to Heidi's delight, they spotted a group of deer not far away. As Heidi squealed with excitement, the deer raced off. She didn't care. She was thrilled that she had gotten to see Bambi.

The next morning at breakfast, Ryan announced that they would be going off in search of the perfect Christmas tree. Everyone excitedly met at the barn and waited patiently as Ryan and David hooked up the team of horses to the two large wooden wagons. David drove one team and Ryan drove the other. The younger people hopped in David's wagon, while Bob, Jude, Heidi and Banjo got into Ryan's wagon.

"Come sit up here with me." Ryan took Annie's hand. He settled her beside himself on the passenger bench seat. He whistled sharply and then snapped the reins in the air. The two large horses eagerly took off.

"I feel like I've gone back in time to an old country-western movie. You're spoiling me Ryan. This is so much fun." Annie squeezed his hand tightly as she took in the sights.

"That's the idea, Annie," Ryan whispered in a low voice, "to make you love it here so much that you'll never want to leave." Annie looked at him in surprise, and Ryan winked at her.

This time, Ryan led the group up a different mountain. In a clearing, he halted the horses and jumped off the wagon. "Time to start looking!"

After he secured the horses to a large tree, Ryan led the crew down a wide, heavily wooded path. They had not gone more than a few hundred feet when Annie stopped and stared at the sight in front of her. "Ryan, there have to be thousands of Christmas trees up on this mountain. I've never seen so many in one place in all my life."

Ryan laughed at Annie. "Yep," he smiled proudly, "probably thirty thousand or so, though we've never actually counted them all."

Annie turned and looked at him. "Never counted them all, huh?"

"It's on my 'To Do' list."

Then Ryan instructed the group. "OK folks," he sounded remarkably like a Boy Scout troop leader, "team up in pairs and let's find our tree. Don't go far from this general area."

Instead of going out in pairs, everyone, including Banjo, excitedly took off down the path together leaving Annie and Ryan alone. Ryan dropped an arm around Annie's shoulders and chuckled softly.

"What?" Annie asked him curiously.

It seems to me that we've been given quite an opportunity here."

Annie laughed. "Just what opportunity are you referring to, Mr. Jones?"

Ryan didn't answer but his grin widen. He studied Annie's face for a moment and saw the welcoming look in her eyes. Slowly, he leaned down and brushed a kiss across her soft pink lips. She smiled up at him lovingly and that was all the encouragement he needed. He took Annie in his arms, cradling her in a loving embrace, and leaned down and kissed her tenderly. This time, it was not the type of kiss that someone gave quickly in greeting. It was the type of kiss that two people in love give each other that heats up hotter than a blazing fire and stirs the very heart and soul. It took every ounce of self-control Ryan had to force himself to push away from Annie. Everything inside him was screaming for her. Yet he knew, until she wore his wedding band, she didn't entirely belong to him. He knew it, she knew it, and more importantly, God knew it. As Ryan pulled away from her, he couldn't help but smile at the dreamy expression that covered Annie's face. He took her hand and led her toward the Christmas trees.

"Annie, I think we'd better find a tree quickly before we get into too much trouble."

Annie smiled up at him and he stopped for a second to look at her. "What is all that smiling about, Young Lady?" He took a step away from her but was still holding her hand.

Annie giggled. "You're a good kisser, Mr. Jones."

Ryan grinned. "Thank you."

Ryan took a step closer to her and held both of her hands lovingly. His expression became serious. In a quiet but firm voice he spoke from his heart. "Annie, I'm not going to be able to kiss you often. I think I should stick to once a day." Annie looked at him with a confused expression and Ryan continued on. "Honey, I want to honor God in this relationship and respect you completely." A loud sigh escaped from Ryan's lips as he ran a hand nervously through his hair. "That's a hard thing to do Annie. You're kisses are like a sweet candy bar to me. Once I've taken a little bit of the candy bar, I want the whole thing." Annie smiled and nodded understandingly.

"You know," Ryan dug at the dirt with the tip of his cowboy boot, "when Kay and I fell in love, we were determined to honor God in every aspect of our relationship." Ryan sighed heavily. "That included the physical side too. God says to wait until marriage before you become sexually involved, and," Ryan spread his arms wide, "we did. It was one of the hardest things I've ever had to do but with God's help, and not allowing ourselves to be in certain situations that could be tempting, we made it." Ryan paused for a moment. "Well, this time around it's going to be a whole lot harder. The physical relationship that Kay and I had was great. You know, it's easier to wait for something that you've never tasted the pleasure of it. Well," Ryan laughed loudly, "not only have I tasted the pleasure of it, I loved it. You see Annie, this time around I know exactly what I'm missing. That makes it all the harder. I need to set up very strict boundaries here or I know I'm not going to make it." Ryan sighed again. "Do you know what I' saying?"

"All too well." Annie smiled tenderly. "I think it's wise that we set up tight boundaries. If we don't, you're right, we won't make it through this visit."

"I agree." Ryan said quickly. "We need to be very careful."

"Now," Ryan intently looked at Annie, "if you're ready to take that walk down the church aisle, I'll drive to the preacher's house right now."

Annie slowly shook her head. "Not yet," she answered barely audibly.

"That's what I thought." He put a loving arm around her. "I'm OK with that. I'm not one to rush God's perfect timing. But," he tapped the tip of her nose, "I am a man who knows my own limits."

Annie completely understood. "One kiss a day?"

Ryan nodded. "Yes," he smiled charmingly at her, "that's about all I think I can handle. I'm calling it my one-a-day plan. It's kind of like a vitamin. Just one a day, and I'll tell you, I'll look forward to it with all my heart." He paused and looked at her tenderly. "Right now, I think we need to be in a group. It's the second best thing to a cold shower!" He hugged her quickly and then they went in search of the others.

As they walked through Christmas tree land, looking at the large trees reaching up to the sky, Annie quietly thanked the Lord for Ryan's judgment and discipline. She knew the decision she had made was awfully hard on him but she also knew that his desire to do the right thing in God's eyes was even stronger. Annie knew that she and Ryan were both very passionate people. The temptation to cross the line physically would be great at times. By setting their boundaries up early, she knew they were safeguarding themselves against trouble and that was smart.

"Thank you, God," Annie prayed earnestly, "thank you for bringing Ryan into my life. Heal me, Father, so that one day I can truly make him my Ryan."

Four

The next morning they began to decorate their twenty-foot Christmas tree. "Do you have enough decorations for this huge monster?" Amy asked Ryan.

He laughed as he looked up at the giant tree. "If we put a lot of lights on the tree and space the decorations out a lot, we should be fine."

Ryan climbed a long extension ladder as David and Amy handed him strings of colored lights. As Annie watched the process in amusement, a hand lightly tapped her on her shoulder. Annie turned to see a serious looking Sadie facing her.

"Annie, can we talk for a minute?" Annie nodded and then followed Sadie into the kitchen. Sadie pointed to the chairs around the kitchen table and Annie quickly slid into one. Annie watched Sadie carefully and soon the older woman's eyes began to fill with tears.

"I knew Kay for a long, long time. I helped take care of her children and took care of her when she was sick. When she passed on, it was an awful blow to Kay and Ryan's family, and to Tag and me. We'd felt as though we'd lost one of our own." Annie nodded compassionately at the older woman.

"Right away, when Ryan came back from Boston, I knew he was in love. He was beaming brighter than the sunshine." She paused and shook her head smiling at the thought of it. "Anyway, a funny thing happened to me. Even though Tag and I had been praying for Ryan's heart to mend and that God would bring him another lady to love, I wasn't prepared for the time that it actually started to happen." Sadie paused again and took out a handkerchief to dab her eyes. "At first I felt shocked that he was in love again, and then when I got used to the idea a bit, I felt angry. I was really very angry. I shouldn't have been because two years had already passed. It was more than enough time." Annie watched Sadie through sympathetic eyes. "Somehow, I began to feel that Ryan loving you was being disloyal to Kay. I know it's not true, but that's how I felt at the time. I'm sorry."

Annie nodded again and touched the tearful woman's hand. "Sadie, that's the exact reason I wouldn't date Ryan for months. I felt like I would be cheating on my late husband if I did. I had a lot to work through to get to this point and," Annie ran a hand through her brown hair, "I still have a lot to work through."

Sadie smiled. "Ryan Jones is one patient man Annie. I'm sure he understands. Take your time."

Annie laughed. "Yeah, he's patient, but man, is he persistent!" Both women laughed. They both knew it was all too true.

"Annie," Sadie had grown serious again, "I need to ask you for forgiveness. I am so sorry that I acted the way I did. I was wrong. I know God has forgiven me but," Sadie looked directly into Annie's eyes, "I need to know that you have forgiven me, too."

Annie took both of Sadie's hands and squeezed them tightly. "I have forgiven you, Sadie. I hope we can be friends."

"I'd like that very much." When the women got up, Annie went around the table and hugged Sadie. As they returned to the great room, both women had a lighter step and a lighter heart.

When Ryan saw Sadie coming back in the room, he climbed down the ladder and immediately went over to her. "Where did you disappear to?"

"Sadie and I had a little talk," Annie answered quickly. Ryan's faced clouded in protective alarm, and he took on the look of a German shepherd guard dog. Annie loved him for it. She loved the feeling of being protected by the man she loved.

"It's OK," Annie took his hand in hers. "We talked everything through and things between us are fine now." She gave his hand a reassuring squeeze.

"You sure?" His voice still radiated concern.

Annie nodded and smiled confidently up at Ryan. "Good," he visibly relaxed. "I was praying a lot about this."

"Thanks. It means a lot to me."

"Well, Honey, you mean a lot to me." Ryan hugged her tightly. "Besides, there is never any reason to thank me for praying for you. I love to pray." Ryan kissed her on the cheek and then they headed back to the tree.

Annie let out a giggle and called after him. "Excuse me, but I believe that's two!"

Ryan stared at her with a confused expression on his face and slowly walked back to her. "Huh?" he muttered.

"That's two." Annie was trying hard to control her laughter.

"Two what?" Ryan asked coming to stand directly in front of her.

"Two kisses, Romeo. You said," Annie wiggled her eyebrows at him, "I believe the exact quote was…that you were only going to kiss me once a day. Remember- your one-a-day plan?"

Ryan's face exploded in amusement. "Sweetheart," he took her hand gently, "I was talking about kissing you on the lips. I'm only allowing myself one kiss on the lips." Ryan's grin broadened. "It's a good one a day plan- for now." They laughed and the others around the room looked at them curiously. Ryan ignored them and continued to speak to Annie.

"Now," he brushed a quick kiss across her rosy cheek, "the cheek is another matter all together. There are no limits on cheek kissing. How about you?"

Annie laughed. "I would recommend that you keep it under four."

"Four?" Annie noticed the disappointment in his voice. "Are you kidding?"

Annie smiled. "Yeah, keep it under four thousand. Any more than that and we might make a spectacle of ourselves!"

Ryan let out another loud laugh and took Annie in his arms. He dipped her low and planted a big, wet, mushy kiss on her cheek. "Girl, you're going to keep me on my toes!"

"I hope so!" Annie whispered into his ear. "I'm planning on it."

Annie and Ryan laughed as Banjo strolled by. Someone had decorated the dog with gold garland and a Santa's hat. He proudly showed off his new duds, going from person to person in the room.

As the Jones and Smith families continued to decorate the tree, Christmas music was being pumped throughout the house by a large stereo system. As Annie was helping wrap the gold garland around the tree, she suddenly stopped and made a puzzled face at Ryan.

"What?" he asked curiously.

Annie laughed. "I think that this is the seventh straight time that Silent Night has been played. You guys must really love that song."

Ryan laughed, suddenly realizing it was true. "Oh boy, where's Beth?" he asked glancing around the room quickly.

Annie looked around the room too. "I don't see her."

"That's it then." Ryan snapped his fingers together and ran out of the room.

Annie watched him run off, feeling completely in the dark about the situation. When she turned her questioning face toward David, he broke out laughing.

"Beth loves Silent Night," David began quickly, "it's her favorite Christmas carol." Annie nodded, thinking she understood the situation but David waved a hand at her. "It's not what you think. Beth made a repeating tape of Silent Night and the tape can go on forever!" David laughed as Annie's mouth dropped opened.

"One Christmas, Beth put the tape in the stereo system, which is located in dad's office and locked the door. Beth refused to unlock the door, even for Dad." David paused and shook his head. "Dad started getting mad because the song had already played through the entire house at least fifteen times!"

"You're kidding!" Annie laughed. "That would drive me crazy!"

David laughed loudly. "Yeah, it was making us all nuts! Anyway, Dad stormed out to the barn and got his tools and threatened that if Beth didn't unlock the door, he was going to pop it off its hinges."

"Oh boy…" Annie could picture the scene clearly. "What happened?"

"Well, I think she thought Dad was faking it. She didn't open the door and Dad popped off the hinges."

Annie laughed. "What happened to Beth?"

"Oh, that was pretty funny. Once the hinges were getting popped off the door, Beth realized she had pushed Dad too far. She escaped out his office window."

"The window?" Annie repeated in shock. "Isn't your dad's office on the second floor?"

"Yeah, why?" David shrugged.

"David, how did your sister get to the ground?"

"Oh that. It's no big deal. She slid down the drain pipe."

"No way!"

"Yeah, we've all done it at one time or another. It's a great escape route from the second floor. You know," David added thoughtfully, "the one outside your window works great too."

Annie laughed. "No thanks. At my age I'll stick with the stairs. At your age, I might have tried the escape route."

"You aren't very adventurous, are you?"

"Not anymore. I used to be. I'm going to live to be an old lady because I'm not pulling stunts like sliding down drainpipes."

"Yeah, well she used to be very adventurous." Bob had joined the conversation. "Boy could I tell you stories."

"But you're not going to." Annie said firmly.

"Why not?" Bob challenged.

"Because…I've got plenty of stories to tell about you too." Annie laughed.

"You're blackmailing me?" Bob threw his hands on his hips.

"Absolutely and do I have great stuff on you!"

"Well, her stories aren't that good anyway," Bob admitted quickly.

"I know when I'm missing something good," David stared at Bob.

"OK, I'll admit the dirt on Annie is good, but it's also privileged." Bob smiled at his sister.

"You see," David picked up a ornament that was rolling by his feet, "I'm old enough to know that what Aunt Annie has on you is better than what you have on her. I know how this works. I have two sisters. Blackmail is part of any normal sibling relationship. You spill the dirt on her and she's going to blab on you. Believe me, I know how this works!"

"Then you understand why I'm taking the Fifth." Bob smiled.

"Yeah, unfortunately I do."

"Now that that's out of the way, finish your story." Annie smiled obnoxiously at Bob, "What happened to Beth after she slid down the drainpipe?"

"Oh," David was fiddling with gold garland, "she went and hid in the barn." David turned and looked directly at Annie. "The barn has a lot of good hiding spots."

Annie folded her arms across her chest. "Why are you looking at me when you say that."

"Thought you might want to know," David replied casually.

"Do you honestly think I'm going to be hiding from someone?"

"Well, I was just thinking about the Super Soaker fight we had back in Boston." David laughed. "You might need a good hiding spot."

"Thanks," Annie said sarcastically.

"Any time." David smiled at her.

"I want to know what your dad did to your sister," Bob asked curiously. "I especially enjoy these stories when I'm not personally involved in them."

David smiled at Bob. "I'll bet!" He paused for a moment. "Oh, this is funny. Dad can be pretty creative with his punishments. Since we had been tortured by two hours of Silent Night, Dad sat Beth on the bench in the kitchen and made her listen to a repeating tape he had made of Jingle Bells for two hours."

"Didn't that punish everyone in the house?" Annie asked scrunching up her nose. "Listening to the same song straight for two hours would drive anyone batty."

"No," David waved a hand at her, "Dad made her wear her Walkman. He sat at the kitchen table for two hours, doing paperwork and watching to make sure she kept her Walkman earphones on. I don't think he did much paperwork." David laughed loudly. "He was too busy laughing at the agonizing faces that Beth was making." Annie and Bob laughed as they pictured it. "You know, to this day, Beth still hates Jingle Bells. She just about goes crazy every time she hears it!"

They laughed again as Ryan came into the room waving a cassette tape. "Did David tell you the Silent Night nightmare?"

Annie and Bob laughed. "It's the stuff that great memories are made of!" Bob laughed loudly. "We have a few of our own," Bob paused, "unfortunately I'm not free to share any of them because Annie has reduced herself to blackmailing me."

Ryan smirked. "She must have good stuff on you to keep you quiet."

Bob's eyes narrowed. "I don't want to talk about it."

Annie laughed. "I'll bet! I really could enlighten Jude and Heidi on a few issues."

Bob took a step closer to her. "I know you're not going to do that."

"Feeling confident, are you?" Annie smiled at him.

"Extremely." Bob smiled. "Remember, it's a two way street, sister. You enlighten my people and I'll enlighten yours!"

Annie's smile disappeared. "OK, moving on…"

"Not so quick," Ryan dropped an arm around Annie. "Let's rewind here for a second."

"Let's not," Annie whispered quickly.

"See, you're making me very curious here." Ryan squeezed her shoulders.

"Curiosity killed the cat."

"I'm not a cat." Ryan looked at her closely. "What stories are you hiding?"

Bob laughed. "Stupid childhood prank stories and I can pretty much guarantee that Ann and I will take most of them to our grave."

"That's the truth," Annie mumbled under her breath. "What you don't know won't hurt you."

"Now that's not true," Ryan folded his arms across his chest. " Several times in my life, thus far, what

I didn't know has come back to bite me in the behind. Ignorance is not a blessing; it's like a bad rash. You can try to ignore it but it just spreads. I know this for a fact."

"Rashes do spread," Annie agreed.

"I'm not talking about rashes," Ryan was adamant.

"You just were."

"I was simply using that as a picture to put in your mind."

"Yeah, kind of an itchy picture," Annie laughed.

"You are such a pest," Ryan ran a hand through her hair to mess it up.

"I believe we've been down this road before," Annie smiled at him.

"Dad," David smiled at his father, "I want to know what you're going to do to Beth? Is she going to get the Jingle Bells treatment again?"

Ryan laughed. "No other person on earth enjoys hearing the punishment of another, like a sibling does when it involves another sibling. They like to be judge, jury and executioner." Everyone laughed.

"Dad," David became very serious, "I'm not like that."

Ryan's eyes narrowed. "Oh yeah?"

David nodded his head from side to side. "OK, well, like, sometimes, once in a great while-maybe. But, in my own defense, living with two sisters, both of them being older than me, is by no means an easy thing for a guy. I mean, really...the bathroom situation alone is an unbelievable trial for me."

Everyone laughed. "David," Annie said objectively, "girls have more things to do in the bathroom than guys."

"With all due respect," David's voice held a measure of disgust, "I don't think you want to go there with me. I mean, Beth and Nikki go in the bathroom, right before I need to go, and stay in there for hours, doing who knows what. When they finally come out, they look exactly the way they did before." David shrugged his shoulders. "I honestly don't get it."

"Uh, a word of advice here," Bob smiled at David, "if you learn early on that you shouldn't try to figure out women, it will save you from a life time of misery. Just go by their rules, be advised as to when they change them or update the standing rules, and life will go much better for you." Everyone laughed but Annie. She smacked Bob in the arm.

"You are such a pig sometimes. Don't pollute this young boy's mind."

"Hey," Bob became defensive, "I know what it's like to have to go to the bathroom and not be able to get into it because a sister has camped out in there with her chem. lab of makeup and other girl junk. It's tough on a guy."

"Oh you poor baby," Annie hummed, "you have my deepest sympathies."

Bob laughed. "I don't think I've ever had your sympathies."

David turned to his father. "It never ends. Does it?"

Ryan smiled. "No, it doesn't, David. You'll probably be fighting with Beth and Nikki the rest of your life." Ryan laughed.

"That's true," Bob laughed, "long after you have a bathroom of your very own, you'll still be fighting with them." Bob smiled at Annie. "When you become an adult, you'll call it discussing something and not fighting with them."

David groaned. "Do they still always think they're going to win?"

Bob smirked. "Some things never change."

"Speaking of change," Annie looked at Ryan, "I believe we've lost our focus here."

"What was our focus?" Ryan asked scratching his head. "Did we ever have one?"

Annie laughed. "Yes, we did. Remember, Beth and the Silent Night nightmare?"

"Vaguely," Ryan laughed.

"Aw, come on Dad, is she going to get grounded? I bet I could help you think of some punishments." David appeared more than willing to help.

"You shouldn't be so eager to watch your sister do hard time." Ryan looked at his son seriously.

"Dad, I tend to start thinking of punishments when they lock me out of the bathroom." Everyone laughed. "After years of this, I have a long list."

"I don't need help in this area," Ryan tried not to smile at his son.

"Well, if you ever do, come see me."

"I'll keep that in mind."

"So, what are you going to do to her?" David asked eagerly.

Ryan laughed. "Beth was in the office with Amy and Nikki. When I knocked on the door, she opened it right away and handed over the tape."

"Does this mean she's not going to get punished?"

Ryan shook his head. "Sorry to disappoint you, son, but not this time."

"Gee," David's voice sounded disappointed, "if I had known she wasn't going to get grounded I'd have done something."

"Son," Ryan put a firm hand on David's shoulder, "you don't want to try anything. Trust me on this. Premeditated crimes have a harder punishment than those off the cuff stupid things you do without really thinking about things."

"OK…" the light was going on for David. "You know, I was only kidding."

"Really?"

"I think so but to be perfectly honest, I'm not really sure."

"Kids!" Ryan shook his head.

Annie smiled at the girls as they returned to the room. "Hey guys!" Ryan sounded tired, "gather around. It's getting late, and we need to finish decorating this tree." The group set to work like busy bees attacking the tree from every angle. After an hour, the last ornament was finally hung.

"Tomorrow evening," Ryan addressed the group, "we will have our traditional tree lighting ceremony. We do a devotion about Christ's birth, sing Christmas carols and eat too many Christmas cookies. Go off to bed now and we'll make a plan for the day at breakfast."

As everyone was going off to bed, Ryan grabbed Annie's hand and pulled her into his arms. "I need a hug, Sweetheart." He wearily dropped his head on Annie's shoulder.

Annie gave him a big hug. "Now you need some rest buster! Off to bed!" Ryan obeyed without a word and Annie quickly headed off to her own room. She was exhausted and fell asleep before Amy even finished changing.

Five

$\mathcal{T}$he next morning at breakfast, Ryan announced that he was going to head into Nashville, to go to the mall, and finish up some Christmas shopping. Anyone that wanted to go should meet him at the Suburban in an hour.

"You're going Christmas shopping the day before Christmas?" Annie looked at him in shock. "You must be crazy. The crowds will be awful."

Ryan laughed loudly. "Annie, the crowds only make it more fun!"

"I have never heard anyone refer to Christmas crowds as fun. Usually people are trying their best to figure out how to out maneuver the crowds and get to stores before the lines get really bad." Annie paused and stared at Ryan for a second. "Have you ever been to the mall the day before Christmas? Do you really know what you're getting yourself into?"

"I go every year the day before Christmas. It's fun."

"I'm not sure we have the same definition of fun."

"Come with me. I'll make it fun for you."

Annie's eyes narrowed. "See, there you go with that fun thing again. I really don't see how going to the mall right before Christmas is fun."

"Please," Ryan begged.

"I'll tell you what. I'll go with you, but just because I don't have any shopping to do. There's no pressure. I'll think of it as a cultural experience. Fighting for that parking spot, trying to find the impossible gift for the impossible person, and then standing in long, never-ending lines." Annie laughed. "Gee, you're right, that does sound like a lot of fun. Let's go!"

"I think Bob and Heidi and I will stay here," Jude added quickly. "The mall this time of year sounds like too much fun for an excited five-year-old. Sadie said we could help her with the Christmas cookies. That sounds like an activity that is more up our alley."

Ryan nodded. "What about you, Bob? Are you into making Christmas cookies?"

Bob laughed. "My cooking abilities pretty much max out at peanut butter and jelly."

Annie smiled at her brother. "Anytime someone's making cookies, Bob kindly volunteers to do his part."

"And what part would that be?" Ryan asked curiously.

"Oh," Bob answered offhandedly, "I'm the official taster." Ryan smiled at him. "Hey, someone's got to do it, and since I have a strong stomach, I figure I'm the man for the job."

"You are too kind." Annie threw a potholder at her brother.

"I know. Jude says I'm a real gem." Bob chuckled. "You know, after years of her saying this, I'm finally starting to believe it. I'm a gem." Everyone laughed.

As Ryan and Annie and the five kids made the hour ride into the city, they talked excitedly about Christmas Eve and Christmas Day. Annie enjoyed Ryan's family as if they were truly her own. Suddenly she realized how close she was growing to them all. They were very special people. They loved each other, teased each other and opened up very honestly with each other. They were there for each other on a very deep level and she knew that she wanted to be part of his family.

At the mall, the kids headed off in one direction and Annie and Ryan in the other. Ryan had told the kids to meet him at the indoor ice skating rink in two hours. He felt that would be enough time to pick up the gift he needed to get. Besides, two hours at the mall at Christmastime would probably be the limit for Annie. He wanted their time together to be fun not stressful.

As Annie and Ryan walked hand in hand through the mall, Annie cast Ryan a curious glance. "So, what do you have to get at the mall?"

Ryan smiled mischievously at her. "Christmas presents are supposed to be a surprise, Annie." He grinned broadly at her. "You know I can't tell you that!"

Annie laughed and squeezed his hand tightly. "Well," she smiled up at him, "in case you haven't noticed, I am kind of following you around here. I'm bound to see a thing or two!"

Ryan laughed. An amused expression covered his face. "For the record, I did notice that you were kind of following me."

Annie smiled. "Still trying to figure out how to lose me, huh?"

Ryan laughed. "I would never try to lose you! How could you say such a thing?"

"Well, that brings me back to my earlier point. Since I'm standing right next to you, I am probably going to see what you're buying. I mean," Annie shrugged her shoulders, "I am more than likely to see a thing or two."

"Maybe not," Ryan answered casually.

"Hey, buster, I'm telling you right now that I'm not, under any circumstances, going to wear a blindfold. That is just not going to happen."

Ryan laughed loudly. "I hadn't even thought of that." Ryan winked at her. "Thanks for the suggestion."

"It wasn't a suggestion." Annie laughed. "I'll tell you, quite honestly, it's not even a remote possibility."

"Didn't you ever play pin-the-tail-on-the-donkey when you were a kid?"

"You see, the funny thing about that game is that we always played in someone's house or back yard. I never once remember playing at the mall. That could be the reason for my hesitation."

"You're never too old to try something new."

"Well, that goes both ways. Did you know that Bob once taught me an interesting thing?"

"And that would be…" Ryan waved a hand in the air.

"That a blindfold works really well as a gag, too. If you don't mind your prisoners seeing where they're going, you can use the blindfold as a gag if they're making too much noise. It's a convenient little tool."

Ryan stopped walking and stared at Annie hard. "Young Lady, I think we'd better have a serious talk about your childhood. I'm starting to think that what I don't know really may hurt me."

Annie laughed. "Who said this happened in my childhood? You should never just assume stuff like that, ya know?"

"We are going to have a really deep heart to heart talk."

"And you know," Annie threw a hand across her chest dramatically, "I'm really looking forward to it."

Ryan's eyebrows shot up. "Uh huh. I'm sure."

"No, really. I am. I know there's a lot of stuff you've done that I haven't heard about yet. I can't wait. When do you want to talk? Is tonight good for you?"

Ryan laughed. "Annie, I was thinking that you were going to talk to me about your stuff."

"Hey, if you want to hear about my stuff, then I want it in writing that you're going to tell me about your stuff. It's only fair."

Ryan smiled at her. "We're going to have a great life together."

Annie smiled. "Yes we are, especially when you've told me your stuff." Ryan laughed. "So, are you going to tell me what you're looking to buy? Maybe I can help out. I am actually very good at shopping."

Ryan dropped an arm around Annie's shoulders. "I wanted to pick up something for Heidi. I would have done it earlier, but I wanted to meet her and get a feel for her personality."

Annie laughed. "Well, I think you've got a feeling for the little chatterbox's likes and dislikes."

"Yeah, I've got her number. She's quite a ticket!"

Ryan directed Annie toward a huge toy store. He poked his head down different aisles expectantly until he spotted what he was looking for. "Here it is, Annie." He picked up a child's tape recorder with a handheld microphone.

"She's going to love that!" Annie picked up the friendly red, white, and blue child's tape recorder. She couldn't help but smile at it because the tape recorder, with a big yellow smile on its face looked like it was actually smiling at her. It was very cute.

"Yeah," Ryan smiled, "she likes to talk so much that I figured she'd get a kick out of recording herself."

After they waited in line thirty minutes to pay for their purchase, Ryan, who was holding Annie's hand, dragged her into a music store that was right next door. "I want to pick up a pack of blank tapes for her along with some Christian kid's sing a longs."

As they squeezed their way down the jammed packed aisle, Annie suddenly stopped. Ryan, who was just ahead of her, turned and looked at her curiously. "What's up?"

Annie didn't speak but continued to stare at something slightly off to her right. Ryan followed her gaze until he spotted what had her glued. An embarrassed expression flooded his face. "Annie," he whispered, "it's just a promotional thing. It's no big deal."

When Annie didn't respond, Ryan made a joke to try to lighten the moment. "That guy over there is a real stiff."

Annie turned and looked at Ryan and smiled. She dropped his hand and headed over to the display. There, in front of her, was an eight-foot cardboard picture of Ryan Jones. Around the cut out cardboard figure were tables holding Ryan's latest CD. Annie picked up the CD and studied it carefully. The picture on the front was a photo of Ryan at his piano, live in concert.

"This is a great picture of you." Annie looked up at him sincerely.

"Thanks, Hon, but we'd better get out of here before someone recognizes me." Ryan put on his sunglasses and threw on a baseball cap he had tucked away in his back pocket. "Things can get pretty zooy at times, so I always carry a disguise with me." They found the blank tapes and the kid's sing-a-longs and waited in line for twenty minutes before they reached the cash register.

After they exited the music store, Ryan took Annie's hand tightly and made a beeline for an empty bench. "Annie," he took off his sunglasses and tucked them away his jacket, "we need to talk for a minute." Annie nodded curiously and they both dropped down on the bench. "Sweetheart, I saw that panicked look on your face when you saw that display of me in there and I felt just awful."

Annie turned her eyes away from him but Ryan gently took her face and turned her eyes back to meet his. "I know you so well, Honey. I'm sure you felt shocked and overwhelmed by the display."

Annie nodded. "Ryan, sometimes I just forget that you're this world famous singer. It's a little intimidating at times."

"Kay felt the same way you did at times but I'll tell you what I told her. Don't blow things out of proportion. I consider myself a musical missionary. Through my music I'm able to reach so many hearts for God. That's what it's all about Annie. I want to reach people for the Lord. God showed me a long time ago that I need to be bold and stand up for Him. If I get lax in my stance or shy about it, or afraid I might be offending someone with my faith, someone else will come along and take a stand in my place. What happens if the person taking my place doesn't love God at all or realize how they can reach so many hearts for the Lord? There are always people willing to stand up for things but how many are willing to stand up for God? We can save the whales, save the bay, save the rain forest but how many people know the One that can save their souls? It's so easy for us to fill the emptiness in our hearts with temporary things when God is all we need. Nothing can take His place or fill our souls like He can. I want people to come to know God personally and find the hope and peace that they can only find in Him. If it takes stores putting up cardboard figures of me to do that, then I need to choke down my shyness about it and let it be used for the glory of God."

Ryan sighed loudly. "It's important to keep your focus on God. If you ever let the flashy side of this business become your focus you'll drown for sure." Ryan paused and squeezed Annie's hand. "I am just a simply country boy being used by God. It's all about Him and not about me."

Annie leaned over and hugged Ryan. "Thanks. I needed to hear that from you."

Ryan smiled. "Annie, I don't ever want anything to come between us. God, family, ministry…that's what's important in life."

Annie nodded but her expression remained serious. "What is it?" Ryan put an arm around her shoulders and squeezed them reassuringly.

"Well, are you ever afraid that you'll get recognized in public and trampled?"

Ryan laughed. "Trampled, huh?" Annie nodded seriously and Ryan answered her question directly. "No, not really, Sweetheart. Most people don't seem to recognize me out of the concert scene. People walk by me and sometimes give me a curious glance. I have heard them saying to the friends they're with, 'Gee that guy looks a little bit like Ryan Jones.' " Ryan laughed and shook his head. "It's actually kind of funny, especially when you hear someone say, 'he doesn't look at all like Ryan Jones'. Sometimes, I even get people coming up to me and saying, 'Hey, you look like Ryan Jones!' "

"What do you say?"

Ryan laughed. "It all depends."

"On what?"

"If I'm with my kids, I usually say something like, yeah people tell me that all the time. I have to carefully guard my public outings with my kids. I don't want them to turn into fan club gathering. If I told people who I was, my kids would never get a minute of my time."

"That's true," Annie admitted thoughtfully.

"I've never desired fame or fortune. I'm just a simple man and that part of this business that I have to work really hard to adjust to. People want to put you up on a pedestal and turn you into some kind of a superhero or someone larger than life." Ryan paused. "I won't let that happen. It's not fair to them and it's not fair to me. I can't be anyone's Superman, ya know? I'm a friend to help them along the way but they need to turn to God. I'm just a light hopefully pointing them toward God."

"I understand what you're saying. If someone sets you up as their personal Superhero, you're going to crash and burn. It's so much better if you can just be their friend."

"That's right. That's what I try to do. I mean, if someone comes up to me and I'm by myself and they recognize me, I'll hang out with them for a while. I take it as an opportunity to be their friend and also tell them more about God. I want the attention on Him and not me."

They sat quietly for the next few minutes, watching the crowds of people go by. "When I'm in a crowded place like this," Annie said softly, " I often wonder how many people here have a personal relationship with God. I start getting this overwhelming urge to go up to people and witness to them."

Ryan nodded understandingly. "That's why I sing, to reach them. And," he tweaked her nose, "that's why you write, to reach them."

Annie nodded and Ryan softly kissed her on the cheek and then pulled her to her feet. "We'd better head off to the rink to meet the kids. If we're late, we'll never hear the end of it!"

Ryan took Annie's hand firmly and began weaving in and out of the mall rush hour traffic toward the ice rink. When they got there, the kids were sitting on benches around the rink watching the skaters as they wobbled by. The song Jingle Bells, sung by a group of very talented barking dogs, was blaring out so loudly, that Ryan and Annie were able to sneak up behind the kids. When Ryan touched Beth on her shoulder, she screamed loudly.

"Dad!" Beth scolded her father, "You scared me half to death. Don't ever do that again."

Ryan smiled. "I was just trying to let you know that I was here Beth."

"Yeah, well next time, tap Nikki. When she screams, then I'll know that you're here!"

Ryan nodded. "OK, I'll keep that in mind. By the way, did you notice that they're playing your favorite song?" Everyone laughed.

Beth narrowed her eyes at her father. "Don't remind me. I will be tortured for life with this song. It makes me crazy."

Ryan laughed. He loved being a dad and he loved teasing his kids. Now that they were older, they teased him back a lot and he loved that too.

Ryan put an arm around Annie. "Do you skate?"

Annie let out a loud laugh. "Yes, but never in crowded malls."

"So," Ryan smirked at her, "I can't convince you to get on the ice?"

"Not here," Annie replied firmly. "Why, do you skate?"

"Yep," Ryan nodded his head. "I play hockey at the pond at the ranch with the kids. We have a lot of fun."

Annie smiled at him. "So, are you planning on skating at the mall rink today?"

"No way!" Ryan scrunched his face up at her. "Everyone hangs out at the mall rink and you become their entertainment as you wobble by." Ryan shook his head and laughed. "I know less crowded ways to embarrass myself, thank you very much."

Everyone around them laughed because they knew it was true.

"Yeah, and if you wiped out," David had become very serious, "people will remember it the rest of their lives and remind you of it every time they see you. It's awful."

Annie looked at him for a moment. "How old were you when you wiped out?"

"How did you know?" The shocked expression that spread across David's face made Annie laugh.

"Just a gut feeling."

"I was eight years old and my "friends" at school still talk about it." David paused a moment. "It really eats away at my sensitive male ego." Everyone laughed. Annie knew exactly where David got his sense of humor. Like father, like son. They were one funny pair.

"Hey! I know!" Ryan snapped his fingers together. "We could recruit the whole gang and play hockey on our pond!"

"Are you sure that your pond at Sleepy Hollow is frozen over?" Annie asked thoughtfully.

The kids laughed but Ryan just stared at her hard.

"What?" Annie mumbled.

"What did you say?"

Annie couldn't read Ryan's face. It had gone blank without the slightest hint of expression.

"You called Chatfield Hollow, Sleepy Hollow." Ryan's tone was completely flat.

Annie laughed. "I did not."

"Yes you did." Ryan folded his arms across his chest. "You said it and I've got witnesses to prove it."

Annie glanced at the kids and they nodded and then laughed. "Do you really think you can get any of them to testify against me? I almost always have some sort of candy on me. You can bribe all kinds of people with candy."

Ryan laughed. "Just don't do it again. I don't want Heidi thinking that Chatfield Hollow is Sleepy Hollow. All we need is for her to start looking for headless horsemen riding through the ranch."

"How do you know you don't have headless horsemen riding through the ranch?"

Ryan cleared his throat loudly before answering. "This is just the type of logic you used to drive your brother crazy about the talking horse thing. I'm not falling for it."

Annie sighed loudly. "That's because I'm right. People don't like to argue with you when you're right." Ryan put a hand out to try to tickle Annie but she jumped away. He continued his advance as she slowly retreated backwards from him. "You see, you don't know for sure. Just maybe, on some of those moonlit nights, a headless horseman has ridden through Sleepy Hollow, oops, I mean Chatfield

Hollow, and you missed the entire event because you weren't looking out the window at the time. What a shame." Annie paused and looked him straight in the eye. "It could have happened you know."

"You read too many kid's books."

"I happen to like kid's books a lot."

"Yeah, but you think they're real. Somebody should have told you long ago that they're just fairy tales." Ryan paused and looked at her with a pompous face. "That means they're made up, ya know, not real."

Annie just looked at him for a second through narrowed eyes. "Yeah? Says who?"

Everyone around them started laughing. "Did you ever see Superman fly?"

Annie smiled. "Maybe I have, but I'll tell you right now mister, with that lousy attitude you have I'm not going to tell you anything." Annie leaned toward Ryan. "You know, there are believers among us and nonbelievers. I think I know what category you fall into."

"I think you're the only adult I know that believes in fairy tales."

"You don't know a lot of adults, do you?"

"Do you believe in Santa Claus?"

"I'm not talking to you."

Ryan continued. "OK. How about the Easter Bunny or the Tooth Fairy, do you believe in them?"

"You know, if I were you, this year, I would not bother to hang my stocking by the chimney with care."

Ryan laughed. "Oh yeah, why not?"

Annie laughed. "Because, I don't think that Saint Nicholas will soon be there." Annie laughed and Ryan grinned at her. "Here's a well known tip, Big Boy. Santa only fills good boys and girls stockings with toys and stuff."

"So?" Ryan looked amused by the conversation.

"Have you ever heard of coal?"

"Yes…"

"That's what you'll get if you hang your stocking up."

"And why's that?"

"Because your bad," Annie answered in a matter of fact tone. "That's what bad children get."

Ryan laughed. "Annie, I haven't gotten a stocking in years. Besides, you're not that good yourself."

"Better than you," Annie replied quickly.

"And I suppose you have proof of that."

"As a matter of fact I do." Ryan raised questioning eyebrows at her. "I'm still getting a stocking from Santa. I have every year. You see," Annie smiled confidently, "I'm good."

Ryan smiled and shook his head. "I'm not convinced."

"So, are we going to play ice hockey at home?" David asked expectantly. "I would love to see you on the ice, Aunt Annie."

"I just bet you would!" Annie laughed. "I don't mind trying as long as no one runs me over or slams me into the wall."

"I'll play on the opposite team Annie and guard you myself!" Ryan had that distinct twinkle in his eye that Annie loved. It was just another way that he showed her he loved her.

"That sounds interesting and all, it really does," Annie smiled at Ryan, "but unfortunately for us, no one from New England brought any skates with them. We'll just have to do it another time."

Ryan grinned at her like he knew a secret and she soon found out that he did. "The barn is full of old skates- all different sizes. I'm sure we can find skates to fit you all, unless," Ryan laughed, "you were just being polite and trying to get out of playing hockey."

"For your information, I am always polite." Everyone laughed and Annie scowled at them. "I would love to play some hockey on your pond. Do you think you have skates to fit Ty? His foot is pretty big."

Ryan glanced skeptically at Ty's feet. "What size shoe do you wear?"

"A thirteen," Tyler smiled at his uncle.

"Really?"

Ty laughed. "Yeah, you should have seen the Coast Guard trying to outfit me. I got to wear my sneakers for the first two months there because they couldn't find shoes big enough to fit me."

"I can imagine," Ryan smiled at him. "Did they special order your shoes?"

"Yep. That's the only way I get anything to fit. I have to special order almost everything."

"Well, we'll figure something out for you."

On the ride back to Chatfield Hollow, they sang a variety of Christmas carols, including both Silent Night and Jingle Bells. Ryan turned to Annie. "You've got a great voice, Sweetheart. I hope I get to hear it more often."

"Ryan," Annie's voice was firm, "I do not have a great voice. Actually," Annie laughed, "I think my voice is pretty awful."

"Awful? Are you kidding? I just heard you now. You have a wonderful voice."

"Ryan, we were singing Jingle Bells. Everyone sounds good singing Jingle Bells."

Ryan laughed. "Annie, you're too hard on yourself. Tell me why you don't like your voice?"

Annie laughed loudly. "Well, I just never seem to be able to reach the key that something should be sung in. I feel more comfortable in my own key and unfortunately; it's usually the wrong key! It doesn't make for a pretty sound. Trust me!" Annie laughed again.

Ryan grinned and shook his head. "Sorry, I don't believe that."

Annie smiled at him. "What do you know? You don't believe in Santa, either. Nonbeliever…" Annie whispered. Ryan smiled at her and laughed softly.

"Listen, Ryan," Annie grew serious and thoughtful, "God has given us all gifts, and I know that music is not mine. I love to listen to it, but I know I don't sing that great. I mean, it's not like every time I sing all the dogs in the neighborhood star howling…" everyone laughed. "But I do know that I don't sing good."

"You don't sing well, you mean." Ryan teased her.

"Listen Buddy, I know that I don't sing well or good." Annie laughed. "My voice is more of a joyful noisemaker type of voice." Annie paused. "I'm fine with it." Annie smiled.

"What?" Ryan asked curiously.

"Well, I'm fine with my joyful noisemaking voice except when I'm at church and someone turns around and stares at me because I made a less than joyful sound. That is actually quite embarrassing."

"You're exaggerating."

"Actually, I'm not. When my voice goes off on it's own little unmerry tune and I'm packed into church and people turn around to see who just made the foghorn type sound, I want to die. There I am, packed into the church pew with nowhere to run and hide. It's very humbling."

Ryan smiled and winked at her. It was obvious he didn't believe her. "We'll see."

When they got home, they were given a royal greeting by Banjo, whose muzzle had red and green Christmas sprinkles on it. As Ryan bent down to pat his dog, he turned and glanced at Sadie for a minute. "How many Christmas cookies did Banjo weasel out of you this year?"

Sadie made a loud huff sound. "Banjo has every right to enjoy the holidays too."

"Not what I asked…"Ryan narrowed his eyes at the kitchen queen. "How many? He's not going to get sick on my bed again, is he?"

"Now listen here, you," Sadie approached Ryan waving a wooden spoon in the air like a sword, "no one ever, and I mean no one ever has gotten sick on my cookies." Sadie pointed the spoon at Ryan like a dagger. "And, that includes your dog." Sadie paused. "I still believe that it was something that he got into outside."

Ryan laughed. "I can't ever win this argument with you."

The older woman smiled at him confidently. "I agree. I honestly don't know why you even try. It's pathetic."

Ryan shook his head and laughed. "I don't know why I ever argue with any woman. I never win."

After they had eaten a quick lunch and some of the sugar cookies that Sadie and Heidi had made, they set out to finish decorating the house for Christmas. "We waited to put up most of the decorations so you could help us."

"That was nice of you." Annie smiled. "I love decorating for the holidays."

"Oh, I almost forgot…" Ryan took Annie's hand and led her back to the great room where the others were making a great mess with the decorations. Ryan eyes the group seriously.

"Dad, I know it looks like a big mess right now," David was speaking quickly, but not quick enough.

"I agree with you son, it does look like a big mess and the reason for that is, because it is a big mess."

"We're going to get all this straightened up soon."

"I'm counting on it." Ryan paused, looked at Annie and shook his head. "I always forget that it has to look worse before it looks better."

"That's the way it goes with holiday decorating. You start with a clean house and drag all these boxes out of your attic and put them in the center of your clean house so it looks like it got hit by a tornado."

"Sounds about right."

"After everything is decorated and cleaned up, it looks terrific!"

"That sounds about right too." Ryan leaned down and kissed Annie on the cheek. He winked at her, straightened back up and put his thumb and fore-finger in his mouth and let out a loud whistle. Everyone stopped what they were doing and looked at him. "I forgot to mention earlier that we always go to the Christmas Eve candlelight service in town. It starts at five so we'll be leaving around four thirty."

After the announcement, all the girls took off upstairs to change and get ready for church. Annie looked at Ryan curiously. "How do the people in your church dress? Are they fancy or casual?"

"Well," he dropped an arm around her, "usually pretty informal. On holidays a little more formal. I'll probably throw on my black suit and tie and the girls will probably wear dresses or skirts."

Annie smiled. "So, my old jeans with the big holes in the knees are probably out, huh?"

Ryan smiled. "Probably. Got anything else?"

Annie smiled again. She loved teasing him. "Hum, I really was counting on that grunge look. I even have an old flannel shirt to go with the jeans. The outfit's complete. You sure I can't wear it?"

Ryan laughed. "You can wear whatever you want but I can almost guarantee that on Christmas Eve most everyone is going to be dressed up." Ryan smiled down at her. "You would be original."

"You see, I like that. I don't want to look just like everyone else." Ryan went to tickle her and Annie jumped away. "OK, I guess I should put on the skirt thing that I brought."

"Yep," Ryan wrapped his arm back around her, "that would be good. Oh, another thing I forgot to mention. I made reservations for us at our favorite restaurant in town. It should be fun."

Annie stared up at him. "Do you do that a lot?"

"What?"

"Forget to tell people things."

Ryan smiled. "Only around you. I find you very distracting."

"I don't think it's that," Annie pondered thoughtfully.

"Oh yeah? What is it?"

"You're old," she stated matter-of-fact.

As soon as the words left her mouth Annie saw him coming. As she began to escape, Ryan quickly went after her in a very determined pursuit. She managed to get the couch between them and felt glad for the boundary.

"You know, even though you're old you're very fast." Annie smiled at him. "I'm going to have to remember that."

Ryan laughed. "Think you'll be able to?"

"Definitely." Annie smirked. "I'm not as old as you!"

Ryan threw a couch pillow at her and she immediately threw it back. The war had begun and Annie was having second thoughts about the battle.

"Hold on there, cowboy…" Annie tried to thwart off her attacker. "We don't want to do this."

Ryan let out a loud laugh and leaned over the couch toward Annie. "We, Annie?" He laughed again. "You may not want me chasing you around the house to tickle you, but I," Ryan pointing to himself, "definitely think it's a great plan!"

Annie couldn't help but laugh too. He really could be so funny. Annie spotted David coming into the room. She quickly slid out from behind the couch and went over to him. "You look great!" She gave him a big hug. He had changed into his Christmas outfit and was wearing a navy blazer, light color chino pants, an Oxford white shirt and a red tie that had green Christmas trees on it. "I love your tie!"

As Annie glanced back at Ryan he still wore a very mischievous smirk on his face. David spotted it immediately. "What's with the grin dad?"

Ryan looked at his son for a second and then at Annie. His smile broadened and he winked at her. "Ask your aunt."

David directed his attention toward Annie. Annie shook her head slightly. "Watch out David. Your dad is in a crazy mood." She paused for a moment and looked at Ryan. "I have to get changed, so you better let me go."

"What if I don't?"

Annie laughed. "Then I'll be wearing old jeans and a worn out flannel shirt to church."

"Go, please." He waved his arm toward the stairs. Annie took off quickly glancing back once to make sure he wasn't coming after her. She couldn't help but smile. Even at her age, it was still fun to be chased around the house by a boy you liked. Some things never change.

After Annie had left the room David turned to his father. "Dad, when are you going to ask Annie to marry you? It's obvious that you two belong together."

Ryan grew serious. He went over and put his arm around his son. "David, I would have asked her to marry me a long time ago but she's not ready. She knows I'm going to ask her but she's not ready for me to...at least not yet."

"I'm sorry Dad. It must be hard for you."

Ryan nodded. "It is son. It's incredibly hard. I do a lot of praying and I hope God will keep me sane until Annie is ready." They hugged each other and then Ryan went off to get ready for church.

At four-fifteen, Annie made her way down the stairs. She was wearing her favorite formal outfit. A short red wool jacket came down to her hips and a white cotton shirt with a high lacy collar was underneath it. A long flowing full black Victorian skirt met the red jacket at the waist and went down all the way to her ankles. The end of the skirt was trimmed with in black lace and black velvet. She felt very festive and softly whistled Joy to the World as she came down the stairs and enter the great room.

Over by the huge Christmas tree, she spotted Ryan and stopped dead in her tracks. He was wearing a jet-black suit, white shirt, and narrow jet black tie. He looked breathtaking. When he saw Annie, he flashed his famous charming smile at her and she literally felt herself go weak in the knees. She was going to melt in a puddle right at his feet. Somehow, in the twinkling lights of the Christmas tree, his blue eyes seemed bluer, his smile seemed brighter and the love between them sizzled to the boiling point. Everything just seemed more extreme and concentrated. She sighed loudly and twisted her fingers nervously. Instinct kicked in and she took a step backwards. She felt thrown off balance and a little distance between them seemed wise. Very wise. The things this man did to her…. She just shook her head and glanced around.

"Looking for a crowd?" Ryan smirked knowingly.

Annie laughed nervously. "Maybe." She laughed again. She hated when she was so transparent.

"You look gorgeous." Ryan slowly walked toward Annie and gently took her hand.

The way he looked at her with so much love in his eyes made her feel like the most beautiful woman on the face of the earth. She simply felt loved and cherished. It was a wonderful warm feeling. As Annie gazed up into his deep blue eyes, she felt completely captivated. She could lose herself in them so easily. "You look great."

"Thanks, Sweetheart." He squeezed her hand. His touch was powerful and gentle.

Annie felt the intensity mounting between them to a level she didn't want to go to at this point in their relationship. Her heart was beating so loudly it echoed in her ears. The air between them thickened to the point where Annie felt she couldn't breathe. She was numb all over except for the feeling of him. It was all encompassing and washing over her like a tidal wave. She couldn't move or think. All she could do was feel the pressure of his hand on hers. It seemed so heavy yet so light at the same time. She was vaguely aware of the fact that her heart and her head were fighting for control over the moment. The heart had a set of rules all it's own that didn't necessarily have to make sense to her head. It wasn't a priority to make sense. Her head was strongly demanding that the existing rules stand firm while the heart was ruling in favor of a complete overhaul of anything preexisting. Times had changed. Or had they? Weren't these the very times for which she had set up the rules up for? Reason was in an all out battle against the deep surging desires that only love could stir up. As she looked into Ryan's eyes again, she knew she was about to be kissed. Her emotions were spinning out of control like someone had tossed them into a blender. She felt frightened and excited all at the same time. The passion between them at this moment was absolutely gripping. It bordered on pure obsession. It was stronger, hotter and more compelling than anything she'd ever felt before in her life. It was almost forceful in it's desire and she felt frightened that if things got going between them, even a simple kiss at this point, there would be no turning back. At this instant, she didn't trust herself to stop things and by the look in Ryan's smoldering eyes, she didn't trust him either. They were both consumed with each other almost to the point of beyond any reason.

It was at this very minute that the light went on for Annie. She abruptly became very alert and aware of the situation she was in. She knew, without a doubt, she was standing on the borderline of right and wrong. She was staring them both in the face and the picture was all of a sudden was very clear. She needed to make a choice and she needed to make it quickly. She knew if she crossed the line here, she'd end up going down a road that neither her heart nor her head would approve of. Maybe her heart was cheering her on now, but she knew tomorrow things would be different and not different in a good way. She knew she'd have to break the spell they were under before her brain totally shut down. This could only lead to one thing and that was major trouble. If she allowed things to progress, the memories of this time would haunt them forever and be a permanent stain on their future together. Even more than that, they would both be going against their strong desire to please God and do what is right in His eyes. She had to get him to stop looking at her like that. The adoring way he gazed at her only made things worse. Annie purposely yanked her hand from his. Ryan looked at her in shock for a minute and than slowly closed his eyes and shook his head. The fog was lifting for both of them and the reality of what had almost happened was extremely sobering.

"Annie," Ryan's voice was grieved and full of pain. "I'm sorry."

Annie's eyes welled up. "Me too. I was afraid. For the first time in my life I was afraid I wouldn't be able to stop."

Ryan sighed loudly and ran a hand through this hair. "I can't believe this." He dropped down into a chair near the Christmas tree; slumped over and let his head fall in his hands. "I'm so sorry. I thought I was stronger than this."

"I thought I was too," Annie whispered. "We need to be more careful."

"Yes." Ryan's voice was grave. "In all honestly, I didn't see this coming."

"I think it kind of snuck up on both of us."

Ryan slowly stood up. He turned and stared at Annie so intently that for a second she stared to squirm. "Annie, I need to get away from you for a few minutes and clear my head. I'm going to head outside. OK?"

Annie nodded. "I think one of us should. You might want to take your coat. You may need more than a moment. I know I do."

Ryan nodded. At that moment, as they looked at each other, they both knew the honest truth. They could not handle the physical temptations between them like they thought they could. Maybe they should have been able to. They were adults and all grown up but Annie knew that part of growing up was being able to really know yourself and admit your strengths and weakness. It didn't matter how grown up she was. She knew that if she couldn't handle something, she'd better run from it or she was going to crash and burn. If they were going to make it, and walk according to the way God had called them to, the boundaries had to be pulled in tighter- a lot tighter.

Annie sighed. It was amazing how easily and how quickly things could get out of control. Sometimes you didn't have a lot of warning or a lot of time to make a decision. Annie knew this was one incident that she was going to learn from. From now on, when a choice like this presented itself, she needed to make the decision quickly. If she took her time and thought about the situation, she knew she would fall. She thanked God for the rules that He had set in place. Those rules were her escape route and were going to help her not only to survive but to live this life for God.

"I'm going to go warm up the Suburban." Ryan sighed. It was obvious that he was still struggling with the fear of what almost happened. "Please tell the others to come out when they're ready." Annie nodded. "Annie," Ryan's voice was filled with turbulence, "do me a favor and don't come out until the others are with you. OK?" Once again, Annie nodded. Right now they needed more chaperones than two teenagers did. This had been their wake up call. If they let themselves fall asleep on this issue again, they might not get a second chance. They needed to be careful. Very careful.

$\mathcal{S}ix$

$\mathcal{W}$hen the whole crew was packed into the Suburban, they headed off for church. Bob started singing a loud and slightly off key version of Angel We have Heard On High and soon everyone joined in. As soon as one Christmas carol would end, someone would start another one.

When Ryan pulled into the church parking lot, Annie's eyes grew as big as saucers. Ryan laughed. "I knew you were expecting a small country church of about twenty-five. Am I right, Sweetheart?"

Annie had to laugh. "You're right. I was expecting a small church. Not exactly twenty five," Annie laughed again, "but definitely not as big as this place. How many people go here?"

"Oh," Ryan replied coyly, "I couldn't say for sure."

"Guess," Annie eyed Ryan carefully.

Ryan laughed. "Oh, probably three thousand."

"You have got to be kidding!" The panic rising in Annie's voice rang out loud and clear. "You mean to tell me that I'm going to have three thousand people staring at me, wondering who the chick sitting next to you is?"

Everyone in the Suburban roared with laughter. "Aren't you glad you didn't wear the old jeans and worn flannel shirt?" Ryan's winked at her. "Hey, I'm just a guy and not the best with fashion at times, but I figured the skirt thing that you're wearing is better. Am I right?"

Everyone laughed again. "You're a nut." Annie continued to stare at Ryan with a very level gaze. "I don't think I'm getting out of this car."

Ryan took Annie's hand and squeezed. "You have nothing to worry about. I'll protect you."

Annie sighed. "I think I have a lot to worry about and I don't know why I wasn't worrying about it before now."

"What do you mean?" Ryan was clueless.

Annie sighed. "You know exactly what I mean Mr. world-famous, handsome celebrity type." Annie narrowed her eyes at him. "You probably have every single female from eighteen through eighty chasing you. They're all trying to stake a claim on you. I'm a girl. I know how this works. Some chicks just go crazy. They think they're on some kind of wild African safari and you're the big game animal they're hunting."

Ryan blew out a loud breath. "Gee, from what you're saying, I think I should be afraid to go in there."

"We could always listen to a church service on the radio or TV."

"There may be a problem with that."

"What?"

"I'm supposed to play piano tonight. I can't do that if I don't show up." Ryan winked at her.

Annie laughed. "That sounds like a problem for you, not me!" Annie laughed again.

Ryan smiled and then went around and opened the door for Annie. "Come on Yank. Let's make the most of this. We'll stick together. It will be OK." Annie laughed and took his hand praying all the way into the church that God would help them.

Once they got inside the church, Annie had to fight off the waves of panic rising within her. The church that had looked big on the outside looked more like a cathedral on the inside. It was huge. There were balconies on either side of the church plus another one in the back. A quick glance around told Annie that the place could easily hold five thousand and there didn't seem to be an empty place in the house. It was jam-packed.

Ryan led the group upstairs to the left balcony. He managed to find ten seats, all basically in the same area. As Annie sat down next to him, willing herself not to shake, she noticed that Ryan was wearing newly polished black cowboy boots. She scanned the feet around her and then turned to Ryan. "Does every guy here wear cowboy boots?"

Ryan laughed quietly. "It's a mandatory policy if you're planning on joining the church. You gotta have boots."

"So, down here, if you're planning on joining a church you need to be saved and own a pair of cowboy boots."

Ryan smiled. "In that order."

"Where I come from," Annie grinned, "you need to be saved and own at least one Boston Red Sox hat. That's mandatory."

The pianist began playing the first hymn and Annie couldn't help but smile as the tune to Silent Night floated out over the church. She forced herself not to look in Beth direction because she knew she'd start laughing. She glanced quickly at Ryan and he winked at her. The big grin plastered across his face told her he knew exactly what she was thinking.

After a few more traditional Christmas carols, Ryan leaned over to her and told her he would be right back. She watched him curiously as he exited the balcony. Nikki, who was sitting next to her leaned over and whispered in her ear. "Dad always sings a song at the Christmas Eve service."

Annie smiled at her and nodded. When she looked down over the balcony railing, she could see Ryan already sitting at the piano. The piano was situated on the side of the church that Annie was on so she had a great view of Ryan and the keyboard.

Ryan's gifted hands glided across the keyboard in a powerful and masterful way. He performed a song he had written. It was a song about the baby Jesus and God's love for us and His son. Annie watched Ryan in awe as the words he had written reached the very depths of her soul. God always had used Ryan's songs to touch her and this occasion was no different. Tears clouded Annie's eyes as she dwelled on the words of the song. She always felt totally amazed when she thought about God's love toward us and how far He went so that we could have a relationship with Him.

As Ryan returned to his seat, amidst the thundering applause, he saw the tears in Annie's eyes and tenderly put her hand in his. "You OK?"

Annie nodded. "Yes."

"You're crying."

Annie smiled. "I'm not crying. It's allergies."

Ryan grinned. "I don't think so."

Annie smiled shyly. "You're songs usually make me cry. The words just touch my heart so deeply."

"Well," he squeezed her hand, "I guess if I'm helping you get closer to God you can go ahead and cry all you want." Annie smiled at him and he squeezed her hand again. He was so precious.

At the end of the service, Ryan rounded the crew together and quickly led them down a back staircase and out to the parking lot. When everyone had gotten into the Suburban, Ryan looked over at Annie protectively. "I knew I had to get you out of there fast or my church friends would be playing twenty questions with you. I figured it probably wasn't the way that you wanted to spend Christmas Eve."

Annie smiled. "You are so perceptive!" She laughed. "Thanks for the rescue! I really do appreciate it."

"Anytime!" He winked at her.

As they drove to the restaurant, Annie and Ryan talked quietly. "Thanks for singing that song. I love it. It's one of my all time favorites."

Ryan smiled. "I love to sing and write music. I feel like it is one way I can bring glory to God. It's a gift He has given me and I feel so close to Him when I'm using it. I can feel Him working through me." Ryan paused thoughtfully. "It's like I sit back and He creates this great song. I love to watch God work. I'm just the tool."

Annie nodded understandingly. "That's exactly how I feel about my writing. Some of the closest times I have had with God have been when I'm writing. I can really feel His presence and His hand on me. It's awesome and I feel completely humbled. He could have used a rock and done the same thing but for some reason He chose me. I know He doesn't need me but I need Him. I'm so thankful He uses me."

Ryan had tears in his eyes. "I understand exactly what you're saying. I feel the same way."

As they pulled into the restaurant parking lot, Tyler let out a loud cheer. "Chili's! I love this place!"

Ryan laughed. "I'm glad, Ty. It's one of our favorites."

The hostess seated them in a semi-private room and handed out ten menus. Heidi held hers proudly. She carefully examined the items on the menu even though she couldn't read. She was very glad to be included with the grown up people.

After the orders were taken, the hostess returned to the table with a small bucket of crayons. She placed them in front of Heidi and the little girl squealed with delight. The placemats were specially designed for kids. They had word games, crossword puzzles and lots of fun pictures on them to color. The activities would keep most adults busy for half an hour and most little kids busy for at least a solid three minutes.

Ryan snagged a red crayon out of the bucket and drew a small red heart on Annie's placemat. Inside he drew his initials on top and hers on the bottom. He added a 4-ever outside the heart and underlined it. It was a small, kind of grade school thing to do but Annie loved it. Ryan was a man who knew how to show a woman the tender side of love. He did it everyday in so many little ways. The touch of his hand on hers, his soft gentle kiss, holding doors for her and the protective way he would place an arm around her when she needed help all made her feel cherished. His love was so special and she knew it was something that she didn't want to live without. Ever.

Annie looked at the heart again that Ryan had drawn. She leaned against his shoulder and whispered into his ear. "Thank you. You always make me feel so special."

"That's because you are." He held her eyes lovingly with his own and smiled warmly. "I love you."

"Thanks." She was on cloud nine. If there were such a thing as cloud ten then she was on that. She was just riding high on his love and it felt great. No one else seemed to notice their quiet, tender words, but Annie knew she would never forget what Ryan said in words and deeds. She felt flooded with his love.

As the group enjoyed a variety of Chili's best, the conversation that surrounded the table was fun and lively. When Annie watched Ryan add Tabasco sauce to an already fiery dish, her eyes got big.

"You want to try some of this?" He waved a piece of hot, spicy chicken at her invitingly.

"No siree!" Annie waved a hand in front of her. "That's too hot for me. Yankees aren't used to the hot stuff you southerners eat. You see that right there?" Annie pointed to the chicken on Ryan's fork.

"That would kill me if I ate it and it would be a slow, painful death." Annie paused. "That's not the way I would choose to die. I'm a wimp. I put my order in for a quick and painless death." Annie wrinkled her nose at Ryan's food. "That's not quick or painless."

Ryan laughed. "Sometimes Cajun food does get a little hot."

"Sometimes?" Annie looked at him startled. "Are you kidding?" Annie laughed. "Listen, Pal, the word Cajun to my system is a code word for death by intensive first degree burns. It's going to burn going in and it's going to burn going out! It's not a pleasant experience at all. It's what I call a double torture!"

Ryan was laughing so hard that he choked on the spicy hot chicken that he had just swallowed. "You see," Annie quickly pointed out, "look what that Cajun chicken just did to you! Another Cajun casualty. Another victim bites the dust. I can't believe that you wanted me to eat some of that five-alarm fire. You're no friend at all. I can see that clearly now. Go away."

Everyone around them was laughing at their antics. Ryan drained his entire glass of soda trying to cool the fire burning down his throat. It didn't help. It never did, but he always tried. He turned to Annie, put an arm around her shoulder and spoke in an amused but firm tone. "Don't ever make me laugh like that when I've got a mouth full of food. I thought I was going to spit my food all over the table."

Annie pulled back from him and looked him squarely in the eye. "Now that really would have been gross. At your age, I'd think you could control yourself better." Annie shrugged her shoulders. "You should really try."

Bob was sitting across from Annie howling. "It's so nice to see her picking on someone else besides me. What a pleasure. Really."

Ryan shook his head and laughed. "Annie, "his voice was low as a grumble, "am I going to be able to eat my food here?"

She looked at him and shrugged her shoulders. "Well, that's really up to you now, isn't it? I don't see what it has to do with me."

Ryan laughed. "Stop telling funny stories so I can eat."

"Oh…" Annie exaggerated her tone, "so now you're blaming the choking, gagging, and spitting your food out on the table thing on me." Annie stared at him. "I honestly don't see why I should take responsibility for something that isn't my fault. If you want to blame anyone, blame the chicken. I did warn you about that before you ate it. Maybe next time you'll listen."

Ryan laughed and then leaned in closer to the culinary comedian. "You're going to want to listen closely to this because I'm not going to repeat myself."

Annie turned her head and looked at him. "OK…"

"Let's go back in time a little."

"How far?" Annie was curious where he was going.

"Do you remember last fall at Stony Brook Farm?"

"Of course I do. Do you?" She loved throwing his question back at him.

"I'm the one asking the questions here, Miss."

Annie laughed. He did a good impression of a police detective. "I know you're the one asking the questions. I just wanted to make sure you remembered."

"Why wouldn't I remember that?"

"Well, after all, you are getting old and you tend to be forgetful at times."

"What times?"

Annie laughed. "Do you really want me to make a list?"

Ryan laughed. He knew she was right. "No, I am the one doing the interrogating here, not you. Try to remember that."

"OK." Annie smiled politely. It was too politely and he knew she was being totally sarcastic just waiting patiently for a chance to jump him again. She was good at it but he knew the next words out of his mouth would stop her.

"Do you remember what I said I would do to you last fall if you didn't give my bus keys back?" The recollection of the memory flashed in Annie's eyes. She suddenly became very serious and stared at Ryan hard for a minute. Ryan laughed. Whoever said it was right. Having the last laugh really was the best.

"Yes," her voice became very quiet.

"Well," Ryan flirtatiously continued, "if you continue to make me choke on my food from laughter, I'm going to do the same thing to you right here." Annie's eyes widen in horror. "Right here. Right now. Do you understand what I'm saying?"

"You wouldn't," Annie whispered.

Ryan laughed harder. "Is that a challenge?"

Annie gasped. "No. Not at all." What Ryan had said back in the fall that she remembered so clearly was that if she didn't give the bus keys back to him he would kiss her long and passionately until she was breathless. Chili's was definitely not the place for it, but then again, she wouldn't put it entirely past him either.

"You would do that right here, in front of all the people in the restaurant?"

"You bet!" Ryan was grinning ear to ear. "On second thought," he turned Annie's face back toward his so he could look directly in her eyes, "tell another joke. I would really enjoy giving you what I'm threatening to give you."

"What's the threat?" Bob asked curiously.

"I can't reveal it right now," Ryan answered calmly.

"Listen, if you have a way to shut my sister up, I think I want to know about it."

Ryan laughed. "Trust me, Bob. This one wouldn't do you any good."

Annie's eyes narrowed. She felt a little fight coming back into her. "Bob would beat you up if you did that in a public place to me."

Ryan laughed. " Don't be so sure, Annie. I have a feeling he might applaud me."

Bob grinned. He was getting a good idea of what Ryan was talking about. "I have a feeling I might applaud you too." He laughed.

"Daddy, why are you going to plaud Auntie?" What was going on around the table had stirred enough commotion to make Heidi stop her coloring and question her daddy.

Bob laughed. "It's applaud, Honey. I was going to applaud Auntie because she is so funny."

"Liar," Annie grumbled.

Bob just smiled back at her. "Go ahead Ann, tell another joke. I want to see how this is all going to play out." Bob sighed. "I just love a good dinner theater."

"I'm not saying anything for the rest of the meal." Annie went back to playing with her pasta.

Ryan laughed loudly. "Aw, come on Annie. It would be fun!"

"No," she tried to control her laughter, "no more jokes."

Ryan smiled at her and went back to his hot, spicy chicken, having full peace of mind that he'd be able to eat it without choking on it. He turned his head slightly and smiled at Annie. He wished so much she'd make him choke one more time. He was dying to make good on his threat.

Annie was good for the rest of the meal. On the way out the door, Bob came up to her and put a big arm around her shoulders. When she looked up into face, the first thing she saw was a big obnoxious smile. "What?" she mumbled.

Bob laughed. "You really should listen to me more."

"And why is that?" Annie asked dryly.

"I'm not just older, I am wiser, too." Bob shrugged his shoulders. "I see it all so clearly now. I think it's a gift." He turned and looked Annie squarely in the eye. "You know, you really should be thanking me."

Annie went to jab Bob in the ribs, but he saw it coming and pulled away. "What am I supposed to be thanking you for now?

"My great wisdom."

Annie laughed. "I think I should be thanking you for your comedy. You make me laugh so much. You're very funny!"

"I'm not being funny. I'm serious."

"Bob," Annie smiled up at her big brother, "you are seriously funny!" Bob frowned.

"OK, I'll be good." Annie tried to swallow the laughter that was dying to escape. "What are we being serious about?"

"Me." Bob answered flatly.

"And the reason for that would be?" Annie looked at her brother with questioning eyes.

"We are being serious about my great wisdom and perspective into your love life."

Annie stopped walking and turned to face her brother. "Uh, we definitely are not. It's not a subject I'm going to discuss with you."

Bob laughed. "That's good. I like when I can do the talking and you listen. It's a rare time and I appreciate the quiet. I love when that happens."

Annie sighed. She knew it was inevitable. He was going to give his advice, his opinion, and his holy wisdom whether she wanted it or not. "OK. Talk. Just make it quick. Don't do any of that dragging out stuff that you like to do."

"I can't do any of the dragging out stuff?"

"We don't have time for it." Annie waved a hand toward the Suburban. Everyone was already inside and waiting for them.

"I see your point. OK. Here it goes." Bob took a deep breath and then plunged in. "You're completely, totally, head over heels in love with Ryan Jones. I told you that back in Boston. Remember?" Annie narrowed her eyes at him. "I'll take that as a yes. OK." Bob smiled at his little sister.

"How do you know this?"

He laughed and the sound of it annoyed Annie to no end. "I know you. I have always been able to read you like a book. You should know that by now."

Annie shrugged. "Maybe sometimes."

"Ann," Bob's voice became urgent, "he's the one for you." Bob paused and smiled. "I can't believe that God was actually able to make two men that could put up with you. Miracles do happen."

"Can we stay serious for a moment?"

Bob nodded. "Seriously? He's the one. Don't keep him waiting too long. It only makes it harder. Don't be afraid to tell him how you feel."

"I have." Annie hated being told what to do.

"Hum…you mean to tell me that you have told him that you love him?"

"Not in so many words," Annie stumbled through her answer. "He's a smart man. He knows how I feel."

Bob shook his head and smiled. "Ann, he needs to hear it from you."

"He will," Annie mumbled.

"In this lifetime?"

"Stop chewing on me Bob. I hate when you do this."

"Yeah, the truth sometimes hurts." Bob had to laugh. If Annie's stare could kill someone, he'd be six feet under by now.

"Listen," Bob said lovingly, "take some advice from your big brother. Tell him in three words. 'I love you' will get the message across just fine. They are three powerful little words packed with a great big meaning. Trust me. It works."

Annie sighed. "I don't know why I have so much trouble expressing myself."

Bob laughed. "You express yourself just fine except when it comes to telling a guy that you love him."

"That's what I meant."

"I wasn't sure. I was just trying to simplify and clarify the issues." Bob put his arm back around his little sister. He could see the struggle and turmoil she was going through. "Just tell him."

"Pray for me?" Annie sounded so vulnerable it broke Bob's heart.

"Always. I've never stopped."

"Thanks. I love you."

"Right back at you squirt."

When they got home that evening, they had their traditional tree lighting ceremony. Before they lit the tree, Ryan had everyone gather in the couches around the stone fireplace. He prayed and then read the story of Jesus's birth. Afterwards, they discussed the real meaning of Christmas and talked about some of the differences that Christ had made in their lives. Ryan said that he wanted to end the devotion with group prayer.

"Anyone who feels led to pray can go ahead and pray. Remember, prayers are from the heart. They don't need to be long, just sincere."

For the next fifteen minutes, one prayer after another was lifted up. Even Heidi felt comfortable enough to talk to her Heavenly Father in front of the group. When the prayers ended and the eyes were opened, it was evident to all that a special time had taken place before the Father's throne. His presence was so strong.

Ryan stood up slowly and looked at everyone. "It's time to light the tree!" Heidi squealed with delight. "Hey short stuff," Ryan winked at Heidi, "why don't you come over here and light the tree?"

Heidi didn't need prompting or a second invitation. She took the hand that Ryan offered her and walked over to where the switch was. He picked her up and held her up high so she could reach the lever." Go ahead," he encouraged her lovingly, "throw the switch."

When she did, the huge tree came to life with colored twinkling lights. Everyone stood around admiring the big tree. Ryan held Heidi up on his shoulders so she could see the higher parts of the tree better. She became chief inspector, examining the entire tree. The joy on her face reflected the happiness that was in her heart. The Sugar Plum fairies were having a ball in Heidi's head. Right at this moment, all the fairy tale stories were true. Cinderella had a Fairy Godmother, Snow White really did live with the Seven Dwarfs, Winnie the Pooh was alive and well in the Hundred Acre Forest, and Santa Claus was coming down her chimney with a sack of goodies.

"It's almost magical," Annie whispered to Ryan as she took his hand in hers. "I feel like I'm in a fairy tale world."

Ryan squeezed her hand. He liked when Annie took his hand. He felt glad that she was feeling more relaxed to do so. "I have been in a fairy tale world for the last four months!"

Annie smiled at him. It was true. Their time together had been just that. It seemed almost too good to be true. The last four months had been more of a storybook romance than real life. The blessing that Annie sensed on this relationship was so immediate and so strong it brought her back to the days when she had first met her husband Ryan Smith. They knew a few weeks after they met that they were going to get married. Annie knew that God's leading was the same in this relationship. The peace she was receiving from God about this relationship flooded her heart and soul. The Lord was slowly washing her clean from her past heartache and healing her. She could honestly feel it.

A slow smile escaped her lips. Ryan saw it and looked at her curiously. He pulled Heidi off his shoulders and she ran over to climb on Ty. Ryan put an arm around Annie. "What's going on in that pretty little head of yours?"

Annie's smile only widen. "Oh, just stuff." She shrugged her shoulders hoping to end the conversation.

Ryan waited and watched her tenderly. She glanced up at him feeling a little embarrassed. "I feel as though you can read my mind with those eyes of yours."

Ryan flashed a charming smile at her. "I can!" He squeezed her shoulders. "The more time we spend together, the better I get to know you and can read what's going on with you. I know you read me very well." Ryan leaned down and kissed her cheek quickly.

Annie smiled. "That's true. I think I've got your ticket."

Ryan squeezed her shoulders again. "I hope so because I'm a man completely in love with you, Darling."

Annie blushed and turned away from his tender gaze. It was just amazing to her what this man did to her heart. His loving eyes melted it with just one look.

"So, are you going to tell me what you were thinking a minute ago?" Ryan raised a questioning eyebrow at her.

Annie had to laugh. "Gee, if you can read my mind so well, then you already know what I'm thinking!" She giggled softly when a startled expression crossed Ryan's face. It was quickly replaced by a wide grin.

"I don't want to make too many assumptions here, Annie." Ryan's expression had grown thoughtful. "One thing I can say for sure is that God is working in your heart. I can see it."

Annie nodded and smiled up at him lovingly. "Yes, he is. God is healing my heart." Annie began to choke up. The Lord was overwhelming her with his goodness. He was healing a heart that she was convinced would never be healed again. Only He could do this. Annie glanced up at Ryan. "There are so many things that I want to say to you but I'm feeling unbelievably shy and awkward about it all."

"Annie," Ryan took both her hands and squeezed them encouragingly, "I know that sharing your feelings are hard for you. God will help you. In time, you'll be able to say what's on your heart and," Ryan winked at her, "I'll look forward to hearing it!" They smiled at each other lovingly. "For now, I'll keep reading your eyes. They tell me everything I need to know about what's going on in that heart of yours." They hugged and held each other for a few minutes. Annie felt so grateful that Ryan understood. Someday, she thought as she held him in a loving embrace, I'll be able to tell you how much I love you.

Ryan took Annie's hand and led her over to the piano. "Anyone want to sing?" A group quickly formed around the black piano. Ryan gently pulled Annie down beside him on the piano bench. "You get a front row seat," he teased. Annie smiled at him and then he playfully began banging out the tune for Jingle Bells.

"Oh, dad, no, please." Beth begged her dad for mercy. "I can't take any more of that song. The radios start playing it the day after Thanksgiving and by Christmas Eve I'm almost insane. Please, play anything else."

Everyone laughed and Ryan grinned and winked at his oldest child. Part of the fun of being a parent was teasing your kids. It was like the icing on the cake.

For the next hour, everyone joined in singing a wide variety of Christmas carols. David went and got his guitar and father and son led the group in singing the classic old favorites along with a bunch of modern silly ones. Ryan and David were an entertaining pair to watch as they played together. They liked to tease each other and add their own variations to many of the old classics. They had the group in stitches most of the time and Annie wondered if David would one day join his dad on stage. They had an obvious chemistry together that just clicked liked magic.

Around eleven, the crowd slowly started dispersing and heading toward bed. Annie and Ryan were soon the only ones left at the piano. He turned to her with a curious expression and asked her if there was anything she'd like to hear.

"Oh, is this request hour with the world famous singer Ryan Jones?" Annie giggled. She couldn't help it. It was getting late and she was growing tired and silly.

Ryan looked at her and grinned. "You're a piece of work Annie. You know that?"

Annie laughed again and let her head rest against Ryan's shoulders. "Thank you." She answered smugly. "I would love it if you would play that song about following God's path."

Ryan immediately started playing the request. Annie was mesmerized as she watched his fingers cross the keyboard. Yet as he began to sing, his words reached down to her soul. The intense yet sincere way he sang the song revealed his heart so clearly. Ryan had such a burden for others to come to know God. This song that he had written spoke of his desire for others to open their hearts up to God. He wanted people to personally experience God's love, forgiveness, grace and hope in their lives. When the song ended, Annie's eyes were full of tears. Ryan gently took her hand and led her to the couch near the stone fireplace.

"I love that song," Annie smiled as Ryan sat down next to her. "So many of the desires and burdens I have as a Christian are in that song."

Ryan nodded understandingly. "I am so burdened for people, of all ages, to come to know God. I want them to really know Him and not just for a few hours on a Sunday, ya know?" Annie nodded. She did know.

"The world is filled with so much pain and hopelessness and so often people try to deal with it all on their own. The problems are so heavy at times they can crush you. If only people would turn to God, He would give them the strength and power they need to get through life." Ryan sighed. "God can give them more strength and power then they ever knew existed."

Annie nodded. "God wants to help them, but so many people are blinded to it."

"That's why as Christians we need to pray for people and tell the world that God loves them. If they only really knew God, they'd run to Him. They wouldn't hesitate at all. They'd run to Him."

They sat quietly for the next few minutes enjoying each other's company and watching the flames dance in the fireplace. Ryan dropped and arm around Annie and she snuggled closer. "Annie, I haven't had my one-a-day yet."

Annie laughed quietly and turned her face toward his. "Well, what are you waiting for handsome?"

Ryan slowly leaned down and tenderly kissed Annie on her lips. Her lips were soft and warm and all together too inviting. The chemistry between them exploded instantly as if someone had set off a bomb. Emotions swarmed and desires surged. Ryan was taken back by the intensity of it all. Before he lost his head completely he gently pulled away. He stared at Annie for a minute and simply shook his head. Ryan slowly got up, like a man in a trance and sat in a chair that was next to the couch.

"I think I'll sit here for now."

"Good idea," Annie quickly agreed. She was struggling with her own emotions and waiting for her head to clear.

Ryan sighed loudly. "You have no idea what you do to me!"

Annie stared at him for a second. "If it's anything like what you do to me, then believe me, I have an idea."

"You," Ryan pointed a finger at Annie, "are driving me crazy. You have no idea the amount of discipline I'm exerting to maintain my high moral standards."

Annie sighed. "Ryan, I don't want to torture you."

"Too late. You already are."

"Listen, if it's any consolation, this is very hard on me, too."

Ryan smirked. "Good. I'm glad." Then he laughed nervously and ran a hand through his hair. "So, is it really hard on you, too, or are you just saying that to be nice?"

Annie smiled. "I believe the torture is about equal on both sides. You may think you're suffering more, but I seriously doubt it."

"Really?"

Annie nodded. "Really."

Ryan grinned. "Good!" He laughed loudly. "Somehow, probably in a sick way, that makes me feel better. You know, suffering alone isn't half as much fun as suffering with others. It's a group thing I guess."

Annie smiled. "I guess."

Ryan became very serious and stared at Annie intently. It didn't take long for her to start to squirm. Once again Annie was quite sure that the man could out stare a stone statue. She'd never met anyone like him. She laughed nervously. "Is something on your mind Dear? Maybe a little something that you want to share?"

That popped Ryan out of his staring contest and he laughed. "As a matter of fact, I do have something to share."

Annie smiled. "You know, for future reference, you don't have to stare me into squirming. If you have something to say, please just say it."

"I get intense at times. I'm sorry."

Annie smiled. "That's an understatement but you're forgiven. What's on your mind?"

Ryan smiled. "I am probably going to hold the world record for asking you to marry me," Ryan laughed softly, "but considering the way things are going, you know, the intensity of the situation, we might want to consider getting married soon."

Annie laughed. "What kind of proposal is that? You didn't even get down on your knees or anything."

Ryan smiled. "I'm trying to vary the way I propose to you so one of these times you say yes." Ryan laughed. "Is it working?"

Annie smiled. "Ryan, I want to marry you but I just can't marry you yet. Do you understand? I'm not saying no to you, I'm only asking that you wait...a little while." Annie paused. "Do you think you can do that?"

Ryan smiled. "Honey, I'm trying. I'm really trying."

Seven

Christmas morning the house woke up to snow flurries gently falling from the Tennessee sky. Heidi shrieked excitedly when she saw them. "Daddy, can we go out in the snow and play? Please!"

Bob picked up his little bundle of energy in his arms. "Listen Sweet Pea, we'll go out later in the day. I promise. OK?"

Heidi reluctantly nodded. Everyone filed into the kitchen to feast on muffins, donuts and croissants for breakfast. Afterwards, they went into the great room to open presents. David played host and cheerfully handed out one gift at a time. "We like to open the gifts one at a time. That way," David addressed the group, "we get to watch everyone and it makes the presents last longer." Everyone laughed.

"OK, Heidi," David handed a package to the little girl who was almost bursting with excitement, "you go first!"

No argument came from the curly, blonde-haired girl as she enthusiastically ripped the paper off her package. She shouted with delight as she saw a collection of toy horses. "Thanks, Auntie, Ty and Amy.

I love horses!" Heidi threw her arms around each one of them and hugged them as she thanked them again.

As the gifts were slowly opened, a variety of presents were revealed. There were clothes, jewelry, toys, music, videos, CDs, hats and food. As Ryan opened his gift from the Smith family, Annie held her breath a little. He opened a big box to reveal a new pair of black cowboy boots.

"Thanks guys!" The smile on his face clearly indicated he liked the boots. He got up and gave each of them a big hug. "My boots are getting pretty worn. This here is a welcomed sight. Thank you."

Ryan went over to the tree and picked up a large box that was gift-wrapped in red with a green bow. "OK, Annie," Ryan smiled excitedly, "it's your turn." As he handed her the box he kissed her softly on the cheek.

To Annie's shock and delight, she opened the box to find a black pair of ladies cowboy boots inside. "These are great!" Annie held the boots in her lap touching the soft leather. "I can't believe we picked out the same gift. What are the chances of that?"

Ryan had a wide grin on his face. "Great minds think alike! Besides, I wanted you to be able to join the church down here. Remember, having cowboy boots is one of the requirements for membership!"

Annie smacked Ryan in the arm and he only grinned wider. He had sort of a sinister smile, but in a good way. She got up and gave him a big hug. "Thank you so much! I love the boots!"

"I love you!" Ryan whispered in her ear. Annie smiled up at him tenderly.

"Hey, you've got to try your boots on. I want to make sure they fit alright."

As Annie slide into them, her right foot suddenly stopped. "Something's in my boot." She pulled it off and put her hand down into it. As she pulled her hand back up again she stared in shock at a little maroon jewelers box. "It's a box," Annie stated to no one in particular.

Ryan was grinning like a fool. "Why yes it is a box. Don't you think that you should open it?"

Annie smiled at him while everyone around them laughed. As all eyes waited on her expectantly, she suddenly began to feel a little nervous. Ryan wouldn't dare give her an engagement ring right now, would he? Annie looked back at Ryan and he was stilling grinning like he'd won the World Series or something. "What is it?" Annie mumbled out, watching Ryan closely for his reaction.

Ryan laughed. "Well, the best way to solve that mystery is to open the box."

Annie stared at him. What if she opened the box to something she didn't want to see. Well, she wanted to see a ring in her future with Ryan, just not right now. Annie scrunched her forehead in thought. "Is this something that is appropriate for me to open in front of everyone?"

Ryan finally understood what she was getting at. "Annie, you're going to love it. Trust me, will ya? Open the box."

Annie nodded and looked at the box. Slowly she lifted the soft velvet lid. Relief washed over her as she saw a delicate, small gold cross necklace staring back at her. "It's beautiful!" Emotion was crowding Annie's voice out.

Ryan took it out of the box for her, undid the clasp and fastened it around her neck. As everyone else went back to their Christmas treasures, Ryan leaned close to Annie's ear. "It symbolizes our faith and our love." Annie nodded. "I just want to make one thing clear to you." Annie looked at him expectantly. "You don't need to be afraid to open jewelry boxes from me. I promise you that I won't give you an engagement ring until you're ready to be engaged. Deal?"

Annie smiled. She was so glad that he understood. "That's a deal. Thanks."

Ryan laughed. "Most girls I know would be dying to get a ring on their finger."

"I'm not most girls."

Ryan smirked. "Yeah, I noticed that right away. I like the way you are. Don't change a thing."

"That's a deal too!"

As Ryan pulled Annie into a big hug, she saw tears in his eyes. "I love you Annie. You are so precious to me. Don't ever change."

Annie hugged him and laid her head on his chest. "You mean more to me than I could ever express, Ryan. Don't you ever change either."

At hearing her words, he pulled her back from himself and lovingly searched her eyes. It was the closest she had come to telling him she loved him. "Thank you, Honey. Your words mean more to me than you'll ever know."

After a big ham dinner, with all the fixings, Ryan asked if anyone would be interested in a friendly game of ice hockey. "I've collected skates for everyone in the barn except for Ty." Ryan glanced at the young man's feet disappointedly. "Sorry."

"Don't worry about it." Tyler laughed. "I don't even think they make skates to fit these big boats!" He lifted one of his large sneakers to prove his point.

Soon everyone was heading out into the snow. Even though there were only a couple of inches on the ground, the outdoors looked enchanting. As Ryan helped people into their skates, David skated around the large pond, with a wide broom clearing the light fluffy snow off the ice.

Annie pulled her big brother to the side and spoke to him quickly. "Bob, don't tell Ryan that I skate or know how to play hockey. I want the element of surprise working for us."

Bob grinned wickedly. "No problem, Sis. Pick me on your team, and we'll show that country boy how to really play!" They laughed quietly, and Annie agreed.

Bob leaned down to help Annie with her skates. "Hey, I can do this."

Bob smiled. "He doesn't know that and I don't think you want him to!"

The light went on quickly for Annie. "Right..."

"By the way," Bob's voice grew serious, "we need to talk."

"Now?"

"Hey, there's no time like the present. Besides," Bob tugged on her laces, "I kind of have you captive for a moment." Annie groaned. "I just want you to know that I'm watching you and Ryan."

Annie laughed. "Big surprise. I knew you'd have us under surveillance from the start."

"Yeah, well, just doing my job." Bob winked at her. "Anyways, I just wanted to tell you from a guys point of view that Ryan is really nuts about you. He's got it bad."

"Thank you for your manly insight," Annie replied sarcastically, "but I think I already figured that out." Annie paused. "I thought you had too."

"I did figured it out, but what I'm trying to tell you, is he has it worst than I thought. He's crazy for you Ann."

"Why do I feel like a speech is coming?"

Bob laughed. "Because it is, but you'll like this one. I'm making it multiple choice."

"Oh goodie." Annie rolled her eyes at Bob.

"As I see it," Bob went on smoothly, "you've got a few choices here." Bob stopped and smiled at her. "You see, this is the multiple choice part that I promised." Annie groaned. "You can accept his love, send him packing, or keep stringing him on for the rest of your life and totally make the man nuts and break his heart."

Annie narrowed her eyes at him. "I don't like any of your choices. Go away Bob."

"Think about it, Ann."

"I think I'd rather think about shooting a hockey puck into that annoying mouth of yours."

Bob grinned like he had been handed a compliment. "Good luck trying. Let's go play hockey."

Annie and Ryan were team captains for the north verses south hockey match. After the teams were picked, Ryan turned and smiled at Annie. A confident, proud expression covered his face. "Annie, these teams don't exactly seem fair. If you want to trade, I'm open to it."

Annie eyed him innocently with her big brown eyes. "What do you mean? They seem fine to me." Ryan's smug expression was almost too much for her. She fought hard to hold back the laughter that was dying to escape.

"Well," he looked at the teams hesitantly, "I've got all my kids and basically you've got Bob and Amy. Tyler can't help much without skates. It doesn't quite seem balanced, if you know what I mean."

"Oh, do your kids play hockey well?" Annie asked, continuing the innocent act.

"David and I are pretty good," Ryan admitted confidently.

"Well, to even it up a little, why don't we put Ty and David in as goalies."

"Still," Ryan put an arm around Annie, "you're going to get creamed. You know that, don't you?"

Annie bit her tongue to keep from laughing. "I thought you said this was a friendly game."

Ryan winked at her. There was no mistaking the distinct competitive look in his eye. Annie eagerly accepted the silent challenge. "Listen," Annie fumbled out onto the ice, "if you'll help me to the center of the pond, I think I'll be OK."

Ryan nodded and Annie hung unto his arm, letting him pull her to the center of the pond while she acted completely helpless. She even pretended to slip a few times. "Gosh, this ice is really slick." Annie laughed. "It would be easier to stand up if it weren't so slippery."

"Annie," Ryan's voice held concern, "I don't feel right about this. It's definitely not fair. I'm afraid you're going to get hurt."

Annie looked up bravely into Ryan's eyes. "Oh, it's just a little game Ryan. Come on. Let's play."

"OK," Ryan eyed her compassionately, "but your team gets the puck first. If at anytime you want to change teams, we will. OK?"

Annie nodded sheepishly as she leaned clumsily forward on her hockey stick. Ryan skated backwards away from her as Bob skated over. "Sis, you should have been an actor," Bob whispered into Annie's ear. "That was one of the greatest performances that I've ever seen!"

Annie fell into Bob's chest so she could hide her big smile. "He's a little too confident, don't you think?" Annie looked up at Bob and grinned broadly. "It's going to be fun to knock the cocky grin off his overconfident face." Annie chuckled quietly. "Pride comes before a great fall...."

"Should be fun!" Bob pretended to help Annie stand up straight. As he skated a few feet away, Annie clung to the hockey stick like a lifeline, letting her backend slide far out.

"You ready?" Annie almost laughed at the sympathetic expression on Ryan's face. She nodded to him apprehensively and Ryan blew the whistle, dropping the puck unto the ice right in front of her.

That was all the encouragement she needed. She sprung into action, attacking the puck, hitting it competently side to side on the stick a few times before she passed it off to Bob. Bob returned her pass skillfully, putting the puck right back at her stick. In a matter of seconds, the brother/sister dynamic duo duped Ryan and his team scoring an easy shot off an unsuspecting David.

Annie skated towards Bob and they gently high fived their sticks. They were both laughing so hard that they leaned over, putting their hands on their knees so they wouldn't fall over.

Out of the corner of her eye, Annie saw Ryan skating quickly over to her. Bob saw him coming too. "Showdown, Sis." Both Annie and Bob couldn't stop laughing. The look on Ryan's face was one of utter shock and disbelief. It was priceless, and she wished she had a video camera with her to capture the moment.

Annie instinctively started skating backwards away from Ryan. She wanted to keep a certain distance between her and her rapidly approaching attacker.

"Oh, no, you don't!" Ryan shouted at her as he quickly pursued her. "You don't think that I'm just going to let you skate off innocently, Annie." She laughed but kept skating backwards away from him.

"You never mentioned that you could skate well, much less play hockey with the speed and accuracy of a professional!"

"You never asked!" Annie giggled back at him.

"Where did you learn to drive the puck like that?" Ryan asked, still chasing her across the pond.

"Oh, I used to play hockey on a town team with Bob. I'm sure I mentioned it, didn't I?" Annie's expression was wide-eyed and completely innocent.

"You most certainly did not!" Ryan laughed loudly. "How many seasons did you play?"

Bob skated over and answered for Annie. "She's been playing hockey since she was four. She still plays on a woman's team in Boston. She a co-captain!" Bob roared with laughter.

Ryan's face fell. "You're kidding! You're a co-captain?"

"Girls do play hockey, you know."

"You're living proof of that Annie."

Annie looked at him and just laughed. "So, Sport," she teased, "does that really bother you?"

Ryan laughed loudly. "Not at all. The only thing that bothers me is that I wasn't on your tail the minute that you had the puck! I figured I had to give you a head start because I foolishly thought you couldn't play!"

"Very foolish!" Annie laughed again. She dropped her stick to the ice and raced ahead of Ryan, losing him quickly.

As she glanced back, she could see that Ryan had also dropped his stick and was racing after her, swinging his arms like a professional speed skater. Annie immediately noticed that Ryan was very fast and skillful on the ice. The next minute, he had her around the waist and dropped them both into bails of hay at the end of the pond.

They sat up laughing, trying to catch their breath. "You're doing time for that one Pal!" Annie threw an accusing finger at Ryan. "Hit the penalty box!" Ryan laughed and fell into an exhausted heap against the hay.

"Annie, you are such an incredible stinker!"

"Thank you!" Annie received the jab as though it were a great compliment.

Ryan reached out and ticked her in the side. Annie roared with laughter and rolled away. "Life is going to be fun with you, Annie!"

Annie smiled at Ryan and offered him a hand up. As he made a grab for her hand, she skated backwards, just out of reach, and Ryan fell backwards against the bails of hay. Annie laughed so hard she almost fell over. She really did enjoy teasing him.

"OK, Sister," he got up without any help from her, "you're a dead woman now!" Ryan scooped some snow up from the side of the pond and made a snowball. He threw it, hitting Annie squarely in her backside. She turned around, pretending to be angry but couldn't pull it off. She couldn't stop laughing. She turned and skated backwards as she watched Ryan approach her.

He wrapped an arm around her and laughed himself as he looked at her amused face. He quickly kissed his impish girlfriend on the cheek. "Shall we resume the game?"

"Absolutely!" Annie grinned confidently. "Oh, did you still want to change the teams? I want to make sure you think they're fair?"

"Go away!" Ryan barked.

"Just checking…"

"Go!" He pointed to the other side of the ice. Annie smiled and then skated off.

David came out of the goalie position, and Beth went in for him. They played an active game for the next hour. In the end, the "City Slickers" beat the "Country Boys" five to three.

As the unlaced their skates, Ryan looked over curiously at Annie. "Do you have any other accomplishments that I should know about?" Ryan laughed good-naturedly.

"I think I'd rather just surprise you."

Ryan sighed. "I was afraid you might say that!"

"Don't worry, Cowboy," Annie ran a hand through his hair playfully, "I promise to go easy on you!"

Ryan looked skeptically at her. "Oh, yeah," he laughed, "just like you did with the hockey game!"

"Just like it, Cowboy!" Annie laughed. "Just like it! Besides, it keeps life interesting, ya know?"

Ryan looked at her, and then laughed. "I don't think I need my life to be that interesting, Annie."

"Sure you do. A little spice in life is good for everyone."

"Even you?" Ryan challenged.

Annie laughed. "Even me!"

Eight

On the twenty seventh of December, Ryan, Beth, Nikki, and David brought the Smith family to the airport. On the trip to town, Annie sat next to Ryan holding his hand tightly. Everyone was unusually quiet. The visit had been great but as always, the time went by way too fast.

"You sure you can't stay another few days?" Ryan's voice was choked up and Annie couldn't look at him for fear she'd burst out crying.

"I wish we could," Annie replied softly. "I wish I could stop life for a while, but it keeps marching on. Tyler has to get back to the Coast Guard base in New London, Connecticut, Bob has to get back to his job in Maine and Amy has a school basketball tournament she's playing in."

"I know," Ryan sighed heavily. "I just want you to stay longer."

"Me too." Annie leaned against his shoulder. "You know something? I don't think our good byes are ever going to be easy."

"That's definitely true." Ryan paused for a second and then leaned down and whispered in Annie's ear. "Why don't you stay forever?"

Annie covered her eyes with a hand as hot tears flooded her face. How she wished she could just say yes to him now and never leave him. She wanted that more than anything, but she knew that her heart wasn't totally ready for that yet. She was still healing from the death of her husband. She had come a long way but she knew she still had a lot of ground to cover before she could fully commit to Ryan. She needed to be fair to both of them and she knew that until she could fully commit to Ryan, and be totally his, she couldn't marry him. It frustrated her to no end but she took hope in that fact that she knew God was healing her. He wasn't done with her. He would make her heart whole again. She was sure of it and that was a miracle in itself because a few months ago she thought it would be impossible.

"I'm sorry, Annie," Ryan said gently. "I shouldn't have asked you that. I know that you're not quite ready. I guess I just get impatient at times." He smiled at Annie. "Someday you will be ready, and what a day that will be!"

Annie looked at him with tears in her eyes and nodded so slightly that at first Ryan thought he had just imagine it. A smile began to spread across his face. "I saw that Annie. I saw that nod. That is progress and proof to me that God really is healing you Honey. We have to hang in there and let God do His thing." Annie nodded again. "I love you Sweetie!" Annie smiled at him and then laid her weary head against his shoulder for the rest of the ride.

At the airport, when the two families said good-bye, it was so tearful that it resembled a funeral. The visit had been good. It had bonded the kids closer together, given Bob a first hand chance to check out Ryan, and confirmed to Annie, even more, that she didn't want to live without this man.

As the others boarded, Ryan told his kids to go for a walk. "I want to be alone with Annie for a minute. Beat it!" They kids laughed and so did Annie. She admired the way Ryan was so frank with everyone. You always knew where he stood and Annie found comfort in that. She never had to second-guess him on anything.

"I'm already missing you so badly that my heart's breaking into a thousand pieces." Ryan took her hand tenderly. "This is the worse feeling in the world."

"I know. I feel like that too. I've been dreading saying good bye for days now."

Ryan smiled. "Good. I'm starting to grow on you. That's a good sign."

Annie smacked his arm. "You started to grow on me from the beginning. You're very easy to get attached to."

"It's because of my ruggedly handsome good looks and warm and irresistible personality." Ryan smiled charmingly.

"No," Annie laughed. "That's not it."

"No?" Ryan acted puzzled. "What could it be? Most babes fall for that."

"I'm not most babes." Annie laughed again. He was so funny.

"Yeah, I know and that's why I love you. You have that discerning way about yourself that you can look past all my good looks and charm and see right to my loving, tender, sensitive heart."

Annie smacked him again. "Kind of full of yourself today, aren't you?"

Ryan laughed. "You know that I'm only teasing." Annie nodded. "I figured it was better to tease you at this departure than have us both standing here crying our eyes out."

"Good choice." Annie smiled. "You are right about one thing."

"Only one thing? I thought I was better than that. I've tried to put aside my usually manly macho self and get in touch with my softer, feminine side." Ryan grinned at Annie. "I think I have succeeded and that's the reason I'm so tender and compassionate. What do you think?"

Annie smacked him again. He was right. She'd rather be laughing at his corny jokes than bawling her eyes out. "I think you are a very handsome man, but that's not what drew me to you. You have the most tender, kind, loving heart of anyone I've ever met before. Once I got a glimpse of it, there was no turning back for me."

"Really?" Ryan's eyes welled up and tears began to spill down his checks. The silliness was over, and they knew they were both going to cry.

"Really." Annie wiped her own tears away.

Ryan leaned down and kissed her lightly at first, but it soon grew into an all- out, consuming passionate kiss that left Annie completely breathless. "Man, you really know how to kiss a girl!"

Ryan smiled impishly. "It's been awhile and I'm a little out of practice. Let me try it again to make sure I got it right."

Annie laughed. "Trust me. You got it right. You did just fine."

They both laughed. As Annie heard the final boarding call for her plane, she hugged Ryan tightly. "Thank you for the wonderful time. I will never forget it."

"You're welcome."

"Ryan," Annie waited until he looked down into her eyes, "I want you to know that I love you. I love you with all my heart." She broke away from Ryan quickly and ran down the hallway toward her plane.

Ryan was still standing there in shock when his kids returned several minutes later. "Are you OK, Dad?" Beth asked staring at her father in concern.

Ryan slowly nodded his head. In a quiet but awed voice he turned to his kids and whispered, "Annie loves me! She finally said she loves me!" His kids surrounded him with hugs and cheers.

As Annie literally ran aboard the plane and down the aisle to her seat, Bob grabbed her arm as she passed him. "Cutting it kind of close there, aren't you?"

Annie just smiled at him. "Wait a minute," Bob stood up next to his sister. He looked her in the eyes for a moment and then one of the biggest smiles that Annie had ever seen on spread across Bob's face like wildfire. "You told him, didn't you?"

All Annie could do was smile and nod. Bob embraced her in a big bear hug. "Way to go kid. I knew you could do it. You're going to be all right." Bob's eyes clouded over with tears. "You're going to be all right."

Nine

The month of January, Annie and Ryan stayed in touch daily. They talked on the phone every day and sent each other cards and emails. Ryan even sent Annie cassette tapes of songs that he wanted to play for her, and their love continued to blossom and grow.

January was a big work month for both of them. The doctor had given Ryan the OK to start touring again. Tests showed that his heart surgery for HOCM had been a success and his heart had healed one hundred percent. Ryan got to work right away putting together his spring tour. Annie never realized all the planning that went into touring. It was almost an overwhelming amount of work between getting a band together, choreographing dance steps, scheduling all the concert dates, and so much more. Annie was thankful that Ryan had a great staff to lean on. They organized him and took very good care of him.

Annie was also very busy during January. She was finishing up her twenty-fifth novel and racing to meet her February deadline. She always felt a mixture of joy and sadness as she finished each book. Having the story completed as a whole was very satisfying but she always felt a bit sad as she sent it off to the publisher. She always felt that she was saying good-bye to some very special friends.

One evening, when Annie and Ryan were talking on the phone, she asked him if he was going to play in the annual "Christian Writers vs Christian Singers" softball game. It was held every February at an indoor arena in Denver, Colorado. All proceeds of the game went to fight world hunger, domestic and foreign, adults and kids. It was a great cause.

"You bet I'll be there!" Ryan answered excitedly. "I never miss it."

Annie laughed. "Good, because I'm going to be playing this year too!"

"Really?" Ryan sounded surprised. "I didn't think you played softball. I've never seen you there in the past."

"I was never able to make the date before. Something always came up but I've wanted to play for years." Annie paused and her voice grew heavy. "It really bothers me that I never went before. I mean, if I had gone, my family would have come with me and you would have gotten to meet your brother."

"Annie," Ryan sighed, "you can't blame yourself. One thing that I've learned, the hard way, I might add, is that you can't look back and second-guess life and the decisions that you made. If God had wanted me to find my brother before he died, I would have. For some reason He kept us apart. God had a purpose for it Annie." Ryan paused. "I'm just so thankful that I got to meet you and you could tell me all about him. I've taken great comfort and peace in that Annie. I know my brother was a Christian and that I'll see him in heaven. It's a wonderful feeling."

"You're right."

"There you go again." Ryan laughed and Annie had to join him. She knew what was coming. "Why do you ever doubt me? I am right!"

"Sometimes…"

"Uh, I think my track record is pretty good."

"About some things."

Ryan laughed. "About a lot of things and you know it!" All Annie could do was laugh. He was honestly funny and knew how to make her smile.

"So," Ryan's playful tone continued, "are you any good?"

"Excuse me?"

Ryan laughed. "In softball-are you any good?""

Here we go, Annie thought shaking her head. She absentmindedly patted Ranger. The big dog loved any attention he could get. "Not really, but I think it's a great cause, and I've wanted to participate in it for years."

Ryan let out such a loud laugh that Annie had to hold the phone away from her head for a minute. "Yeah! I bet you're not any good!" He laughed again. "Just like you're not any good at ice hockey! I've got your number, Sister!"

"Ryan," Annie tried to keep her voice low key, "you've never seen me play softball. Don't jump to any conclusions."

Ryan laughed loudly again. "Annie, I'm a quick learner. I got trounced by you once. This time," he laughed again, "I will be ready for you!"

Annie started to object but Ryan cut her off. "Sweetheart," he was still laughing, "you're right. I've never seen you play but one thing I know is you! Whenever you start playing that 'Little Miss Innocent' routine, I'd better be prepared or I'm going to get clobber!" Ryan laughed loudly. "I'm not one to be twice burned if I can help it!"

Annie couldn't help herself. She laughed loudly and the sound sent both her big dogs, Scout and Ranger, scrambling to their feet. They looked at her with startled expressions, as if they were waiting for her to explain herself. She patted the gentle giants and they soon dropped to the floor again.

"Ryan, you really are too funny for words! I don't know what to say here, except, well, you're assuming a lot!"

"Hum…" Ryan sounded analytical, "are you saying that you don't play softball at all?" He cleared his throat loudly. "I want to remind you that you are under oath here."

Annie laughed. "I play but I'm really not that good. I play hockey much better than I play softball. Really."

Ryan laughed. "I'm sorry. I didn't hear anything after you said that you played. So you do play! I knew!"

"Not that well."

Ryan laughed. "Sure…like I believe that. Sorry, I'm not buying it. No Oscar for your performance this time Babe. You're going down."

"Ryan…" Annie grumbled out between clenched teeth, "you're not listening to me."

Ryan laughed. "Actually, I'm listening very well to you. I hear everything you're saying and everything you're not saying. The stuff you're not saying is even more important here."

"You're a pest."

"That's all been covered before, Dear." Ryan laughed. He was enjoying himself.

"You're bringing the pest thing to a new level."

Ryan ignored her. "OK, answer a few questions for me."

"Shoot." Annie tried to appear confident. She was quite sure that whatever he was going to ask she wasn't going to want to answer. Her mind was already running in overtime trying to think of a way to end this conversation. She knew when she was about to sink and the water around her was rising quickly.

"Did you, or did you not play softball in high school or college?"

Annie sighed. Here it came, the CNN interviewer side of Ryan. The probing, snooping, general pain in the neck side of him that always put her on edge. She wanted to let this issue die and he wasn't about to. "Well," Annie answered vaguely, "I'm sure I've played some during those years. I'm mean, almost everyone I know has hit a softball or two during their high school and college years."

OK…" Ryan answered slowly, "I'll take that as a yes."

"Ryan, it's not what you think."

Ryan laughed loudly. "It's definitely what I think and probably a whole lot more. I have the home court advantage of really knowing you Annie."

Annie laughed. "Oh, yeah? And what does your home court advantage tell you?"

"You're lying big time, Honey!" he howled into the phone.

Annie tired to remain serious. "I am not lying. I don't lie."

"Let me rephrase what I just said."

"I think you'd better."

"How can I put this delicately? Hum…you're not lying, but you're not telling me all the truth. Does that sound fair?"

Annie knew if she admitted to it, she would just open up a can of worms. If she admitted she was telling him everything, she'd end up on the phone for three days discussing every softball game she had ever watched or played in. "Let's drop this subject. It's getting worn out."

"Oh, I see," Ryan said smugly. "You want to drop it because I'm getting too close to the truth." Ryan paused. "I'm so good at investigative reporting I think I've missed my calling."

"Listen, Mr. CNN, bag your questions. I'm sick of them."

"Annie," Ryan stated quietly, "I really only asked one question." Ryan laughed. "We've done a lot of talking here, but you never really answered my one, simple, little question."

"What was your question?" Annie was stalling and Ryan sniffed her out like a bloodhound.

"Did you play softball during your high school or college years?"

"I did answer that. I said that I was sure at some point in time I had played. Most every kid in the country has."

"You're being too vague."

"You're being too nosy!"

Ryan laughed. "I'm always nosy. It's the part of my personality that you love the most."

"Not!"

"Listen, just tell me did you ever play on a team in high school or college?"

"That, Mr. Nosy CNN, is privileged information."

"HA! I knew it. You played."

"I never said that. I said the information you wanted was privileged."

"Why?"

Annie laughed. "Because…you and I are on opposite teams. You're the competition. I shouldn't be talking anymore with you about this subject. Drop it."

"Not likely." Ryan laughed. "I always like to check out the competition. I find that a little homework in this area really pays off."

"Well, Mister, you have done enough checking. You'd better close the case soon."

"Annie," Ryan whispered in a low suspicious voice, "I smell a story."

"I smell a rat!"

Ryan laughed. "Oh, Annie," his voice dripped with feigned misery, "that really hurt. You cut me deep there."

"Drop this subject or I'm hanging up the phone."

"You won't!"

Annie smiled. "Good bye!"

"No, no wait!"

"You promise to be good?"

"Define good."

Annie laughed. "Ryan, if I have to define good then you don't stand a chance of achieving it."

"Uh, Annie, I think you better make me promise to be good just about one subject at a time. To ask me to be good in every area is a little extreme. Don't you think?"

"Are you going to stop being a pest about softball?"

"Yes! I can do that. See, aren't I cooperative?"

"You'd better not be crossing your fingers."

Ryan laughed. "Hey, would I ever stoop to doing anything so juvenile?"

It was Annie's turn to laugh. "You stoop to doing juvenile things all the time. You do it so much that you probably think this behavior is perfectly normal for an adult."

"I'm insulted." Ryan pretended to pout.

"Did you cross your fingers?"

"I had an itch. They're not really crossed."

"You are impossible."

"Not totally." Ryan smiled. "You see, it just may seem like that at times."

They agreed to call a truce and for the next hour talked about everything but softball. Yet for Ryan, the conversation that he had with Annie about softball was never very far from his mind. Annie was trying to dupe him again and he knew it. He wrote a note to remind him to call his mom after he got off the phone. His mom was still the Head Librarian in a small Pennsylvania town where Ryan had grown up. Her specialty was research and she was the best person that Ryan had ever met for digging up all kinds of abstruse facts. She was great at getting all those little informational things on a topic, that were commonly overlooked, that made the story so interesting, and put the icing on the cake. This time the topic was Annie and softball. All Ryan would have to do was provide his mom with a few facts like Annie's age and where she had grown up. If the local newspapers had carried any sports related stories on her, mom was sure to find them. Ryan smiled. He just knew his mom would find something, and he knew it was going to be really good.

Annie was busy making her own plans. After she got off the phone with Ryan, she immediately called Maine. "Bob," Annie's tone was nothing short of desperate, "I need your help." Annie quickly explained the situation to her big brother and then listened to him laugh loudly into the phone.

"Annie, you are still so competitive after all these years. You shouldn't have anything to worry about. You have been playing softball every season on your church team for years. Your skills are still pretty sharp."

Annie shook her head firmly sending her short brown hair flying madly. "Bob, Ryan is onto me this time. I have no element of surprise."

Bob laughed. "Ann, after what we did to him playing ice hockey, you may never have an element of surprise with him as long as you live. He's going to suspect everything. If you're playing a sport, especially opposite his team, he's just naturally going to assume you're a pro at it and he's going to get creamed if he doesn't be careful." Bob laughed. "Annie, your record for softball is almost as good as your record for ice hockey. I really don't know why you're worried."

"I haven't played ball since last summer. I really need to brush up on my skills."

Bob smiled to himself. "OK, Squirt, I know how you love to make me an accomplice with your scheming plans. What do you want me to do?"

Annie sighed in relief. Bob was starting pitcher for his baseball team in both high school and college. He had an unbelievable arm that wouldn't quit. His records were still unbroken at Boston College, and Annie felt quite sure that they would be for a very long time. He had been scouted right out of high school to go pro but declined the offers because he felt God calling him into the business world. Many around him had laughed at his decision, but Bob stayed true to his calling from the Lord. That was the most important thing to him, and he never looked back. Annie knew that with Bob helping her, she just might be able to get her act together in time. She wanted to give this game her best. Anything short of that just wasn't acceptable to her. "Listen, Bob, I need your help. If you can come down and pitch to me, well, I'd owe you big time."

Bob laughed. "You already owe me big time, Squirt! I have bailed you out of so many jams it isn't even funny."

Annie laughed. "That's what big brothers are for!"

"You're a stinker." He paused thoughtfully. "OK, listen, I can come down every Saturday until the game. I'll throw you two hundred balls a day if you want. But," his voice took on a familiar warning sound that always made Annie cringe inside, "just remember, Ann, you are playing for fun. That's the most important thing. You don't have to pressure yourself to win."

Annie had to laugh. He always gave her the same speech and she always pressured herself into having not that much fun. She had never succeeded in finding the right balance between winning and having fun. Often times they didn't coexist for her. She didn't know if sports were ever going to be fun for her because of the expectations she placed on herself and the expectations of those around her. She hated to let people down and anytime her team lost, that's exactly how she felt. It was an awful feeling to look around the crowd and see the disappointment in their eyes. She knew she had a problem taking the defeats too personally but it had always been that way for her and she often wondered why she still played. This game was to raise money for charity. It was a great cause and she knew it should be fun, but she had her doubts about the whole fun factor immediately after she had signed up to play. Regret flooded through her but she had already signed on.

"Bob," Annie's voice was heavy, "you know me better than to say something like that. I have to go out there and know that I've given my best."

"That's fine, Ann," Bob encouraged her, "just be happy with your best and don't take the mistakes and defeats so personally. A team never loses or wins because of one person. You always had trouble remembering that."

"Listen, let's not get into all that not. I'm sure when you come down here there will be plenty of time to lecture me. When you get on the pitcher's mound, it's like you're on your own soapbox. I'm trapped, and you love it."

Bob laughed. "That's part of the price for asking me to pitch to you!"

Annie let a low growl rumbled across the phone line. "Make yourself useful here, will ya?"

"I thought I was." Bob loved teasing his little sister.

"Being useful would be getting your friend at the Boston Arena to let us come in and hit a few balls."

Bob laughed. "You didn't think that I was going to pitch to you in the field behind the red barn, did you? It's January and there's got to be two feet of snow on the ground. I'm not a glutton for punishment."

"HA! You're from Maine. What's a few feet of snow to you! That's hardly a dusting from where you come from. I don't think they'd even close the school for that. According to Heidi, they don't close school unless there's ten feet of snow!"

Bob howled. "It seems like that to her! She sees a few snowflakes and wants the state shut down so everyone can go out and play in the snow. That's the mind of a five-year-old for you."

"She'll probably feel that way even when she's in high school."

Bob laughed. "You did! You were always so disappointed when they didn't cancel school. To see a teen girl cry breaks my heart."

"Oh, be quiet, Bob. You conveniently have a way of remembering my sob stories and not yours. I bet I can refresh your memory pretty quickly."

"No thanks. I'll pass."

Annie laughed. "I bet you will. Oh, I just had a thought."

"Better tell me quick before you lose it."

"I'm going to let that go. Listen, what I was wondering is if the Red Sox are practicing at the Boston Arena yet?"

"The boys of summer usually don't come in until February. We should be all right."

"Good, I don't want them in our way!"

Bob howled. "I can't believe it! After all these years you're still ticked off that the Red Sox don't allow girls to play. Man, do you hold a grudge."

Annie grinned into the phone. "It's not a grudge, it's a simple fact. If I can play better than the guy in center field, then why shouldn't I have the job? It should be based on the person's ability to perform in their job and not about whether they're a girl or boy. Maybe if the Sox let a few girls play they'd have won a World Series in my lifetime."

"Ann, I'm not bringing you into the Arena unless you promise not to pick on any the players. I think some of them are still afraid of you."

"That's ridiculous. They're grown men." She paused for a moment. "Besides, didn't you just say that the Sox didn't show up until February?"

"Sometimes earlier…" Bob mumbled. "Either way, I don't think Kenny Wells appreciated the baseball tips you gave him."

"That's too bad. It was good advice."

"Promise me, Ann, or I'm not taking you through the doors. I mean it."

"You're such a Scrooge."

"At times, and this is one of those times."

Annie sighed. "OK, I'll be good but only because you've backed me into a corner." She smiled as she looked at her fingers that were crossed. If it still worked for Ryan, then it could work for her, too.

"Would it be within the guidelines of your strict rules to get a few autographs? I think Ryan would really love it."

"He's not a Boston Red Sox fan. Doesn't he root for the Atlanta Braves?"

"Hey, he's a baseball fan. He'll love the signatures of a few pros."

"I'll get them for you."

"I wanted to get them."

Bob laughed. "No way. You bother the guys and pick on them too much. I think Kenny Wells would run from you if he saw you coming."

"You know, for a professional, he really is such a baby at times. He doesn't appreciate my good advice. I feel hurt." Annie laughed. She loved to pick on Kenny because he, in her opinion, had her job. If she could play center field for the Sox, it would not only be a dream come true, she was pretty sure she could do it better than him and she didn't hesitate to tell him.

"Bob, you've got to let me pick on Kenny a little. You know I live for it."

Bob sighed. "Maybe under supervision, I'll let you pick on him a little." He paused again. Annie and Kenny were very funny together and he was quite sure the center fielder enjoyed picking on his sister as much as she did him. They'd throw the lines back and forth until Kenny couldn't think of anything else to say but "You're a girl." Annie always ended her attack with, "It's a good thing that I'm a girl or I'd have your job and you'd be bat boy in the minor leagues." As long as the playing field was fair, he didn't see any harm.

"I'll be down Saturday with Jude and Heidi. Does the same deal still stand?"

"Always. You know I love baby sitting for your little chatterbox. Bring them every Saturday you come down and I'll baby-sit every evening. While you guys go out on your date, Heidi brings me up to speed with what's been happening in your life."

"Don't pump her for too much information."

Annie laughed. " I don't have to. She volunteers all kinds of interesting little tidbits. It's always a good time."

"You're making me have second thoughts about this arrangement."

Annie laughed. "Relax. Your secrets are safe with me. It's not like I'm tape recording her or anything." Bob and Annie laughed. They both knew Heidi and what she was capable of. "Hey, I can't wait to see you all this weekend. Give Jude and Heidi a kiss for me."

"Now that's a job I love to do. See ya later, Squirt!"

Annie's next call was to Rock down at the town's indoor batting cages. She spent more time there as a teenager, slugging at fast pitch softballs than she could remember. It was like a second home to her. She asked Rock to pencil her in for an hour every morning. That would help her to get back in her groove.

"You're starting up a little early, aren't you?" The grandfatherly man asked her curiously.

Annie had known Rock for all her life. He was like a second father to her. He faithfully attended all her high school and college softball games. He was there to celebrate the victories and offered his shoulder to cry on during the defeats. Everyone who knew Rock immediately adopted him into their lives. He was a rare gem and the type of person who was a blessing just to be around.

As she let Rock in on her plan, the old man let out a low whistle. He knew the competitive teenager had turned into a competitive adult. She competed more with herself than anyone on the field, and it always worried Rock how hard Annie was on herself. She never gave herself a break.

"I'll put you in the lineup Annie," Rock's voice had a soothing effect on her. "If you want, I'll hang around the batting cages and give you tips on your swing."

Annie recognized the gift that she was being offered and quickly accepted it. Rock used to be a batting coach for the Boston Red Sox. He was one of the best at what he did, and even after years of retirement, he was still a legend in the baseball world. His insightful comments were always taken seriously. He had a way of bringing out the best in a player and bringing back their confidence.

The next morning, when Annie showed up at Rock's batting cages, Rock was waiting for her with open arms. She hugged her grandfatherly friend tightly and then dropped into a chair in his office so they could catch up on all the news in each other's lives.

Rock smiled as he handed Annie a cup of coffee. "So," he asked curiously, "are you going to tell me about Ryan Jones?"

"How do you know about him?"

Rock smiled that gentle grandfather type smile that Annie loved. He was adorable. He always reminded her of Robert Young, who used to play Marcus Welby on TV. He was tall and slender, with a full head of silver hair, and carried himself with a

sense of style that was just plain graceful and elegant. The man had class not only on the outside but
on the inside as well. He had been a believer for over
fifty years and married to his high school sweetheart for over sixty. His life was a witness for God
and he had led more people to the Lord than Annie
could remember. He was a man of God that walked
the walk.

"So," Rock smiled at her, "you're not going to
hold out on me, are you? I want to hear the news
on the celebrity."

Annie laughed. "As soon as you tell me your
source. How did you find out?"

Rock laughed. "Now how do you think?"

"Bob." Annie replied flatly.

Rock smiled and winked at her. "Now tell me
about Ryan."

"I'm going to kill him."

Rock laughed. "Ryan or Bob?"

Annie had to smile. You just couldn't stay mad
around Rock. He was too upbeat and cheerful. "Bob
is the one I'm thinking of killing. When did you talk
to him?"

"Yesterday after you called, and if I were you, I
wouldn't kill him until after he pitches for you."

"Thanks for the tip."

"Also, don't pick on Kenny Wells too much."

"Why? He picks on me?"

"You rattle him. It's not the best way to start a season."

"Are you serious?"

"Annie, you've got a lot of talent and he knows it. An encouraging word from you could go along way."

Annie laughed. "If I said something encouraging to Kenny Wells, he wouldn't believe me."

"Try. See what happens."

Annie smiled. "Rock, for you I'll try. But," Annie waved a hand at him, "if he gets mouthy with me, I'm not responsible for what I might say."

"That's a deal. If he gets mouthy with you, let him have it!"

The both laughed. Annie loved talking baseball with Rock. They always ended up talking about so many of life's important issues after the baseball talk broke the ice. Right now, Annie knew that Rock was trying to break the ice for her to talk about Ryan, or the celebrity as he put it.

"Ryan's nice. You'll like him."

"So, does that mean that I'm going to get to meet him?"

Annie laughed. "I hope so, Rock. I'm planning on marrying him someday."

Rock smiled. "Then I'd better get to meet this young man."

"I want your approval Rock."

"That's good and if I disapprove, you'd better send him packing." They both laughed.

"You'll like him. He's very special, and he likes baseball."

"He can't be that bad then. I'll give him one point." They smiled at each other. "So, is he really Ryan Smith's long lost twin brother?"

Annie narrowed her eyes. "Just how long did you and Bob talk yesterday?"

Rock laughed. "Quite a while. Long enough to fill me in on everything that I needed to know." He paused and his eyes started to fill up. "I may be getting old Annie but I still watch your back."

Annie's eyes teared up. Her conversations with Rock usually involved tears at some point or another because her conversations with Rock always went straight to the heart. "Thanks Rock. I love you."

Rock smiled lovingly. "I love you too and I'd like to remind you that I am still an active Associate Pastor at the Park Street Church here in Boston." Park Street Church was one of Boston's biggest. It was located right off the Boston Common and had a membership that was well into the thousands. They had a staff of excellent pastors and they were fortunate enough to have Rock as one of their associates. He was a blessing wherever he went.

Annie smiled. She knew what Rock was hinting at. He would be the perfect man to perform their wedding. "I'm not sure where we'll be getting married. We may get married in Boston or it may be Tennessee. Wherever it is, it's going to be small and fast."

"Bob explained that, too."

"Bob has a big mouth."

Rock laughed. "He loves you, Annie."

"I know, but he still has a big mouth at times. I know where Heidi gets it from."

Rock laughed again. "That little tot is a ticket."

"That's one way to describe her."

"Getting back to the wedding… I'd love to help out if you need me."

"Like I said before, it may be in Tennessee."

"I have been known to make house calls, Annie." The twinkle in his eyes made Annie smile.

"Really? You'd go all the way to Tennessee for me?"

"Honey, you're like my own child. I'd go to the moon for you."

Annie's eyes teared up again. He always did this to her. "Rock," her voice was choked up, "I'll let you know when and where."

"Your fellow won't mind me performing the ceremony?

"My fellow wants to get married so badly that he wouldn't mind if someone from the Yankees performs the ceremony."

"That's bad. We don't say that word around here."
Annie laughed. The competition between the Yankees
and the Red Sox was still as fierce as it always had
been. Rock was a die-hard Red Sox fan and didn't
like to talk about the Yankees at all.

Rock and Annie walked over to the batting cages.
"Set the speed at Slow Pitch. The game will be played
in Slow Pitch and I want my timing to be right."

"Yes Ma'am, you're the boss."

"I wish all men saw it that way."

Rock laughed. "Annie, don't go down that road
with me. Take it out on Kenny Wells."

"I thought you told me not to pick on him. "

"Didn't mean it." Rock smiled. "As long as you
leave things good between both of you, my advice,
strictly off the record, is to let him have it. He gets so
much publicity. Someone's got to keep him humble."

"And you think I'm the one for the job?"

"Definitely." Rock laughed. "You're definitely the one
for the job. Knowing that a girl could give him serious
competition really eats him up. Hey," he straightened
up, "let me know when you're going to the Arena and
I'll tag along. I love to watch a good show."

"Will do." Annie smiled. She had brought her duf-
fle bag of bats and went through it to find her favorite
bat. She concentrated on the pitches coming at her
and connected solidly with each one. Rock tossed
her occasional tips and she adjusted accordingly. It

was the routine practice that they'd been through a million times before and both of them fell right into step. They worked together like a well-oiled machine.

By lunchtime, Annie was beginning to feel a little sore. "Rock, I'm packing it in for today but I'll be back tomorrow at the same time."

"I'll look forward to it. I'll also look forward to learning more about your new fellow." Annie smiled and went over and gave him a hug. "See you tomorrow, Sweetpea."

"Thanks for everything Rock." Annie smiled at the old nickname that Rock had given her as a little kid. It had stuck and because of Rock more than half of Boston still called her Sweetpea. "See you around ten?"

Rock nodded and then winked at her. "I'll be waiting."

Ten

Several days later, as Annie followed Bob and Rock into the Boston arena, she thanked Bob for the hundredth time. "I really appreciate this so much, Bob. I can't thank you enough."

Bob laughed loudly. "Annie, you have thanked me enough. You'd better stop because quite honestly, I'm getting sick and tired of you thanking me. OK?" He turned and looked at his sister. Annie nodded. "Besides, all the free baby sitting that you've trading me is totally worth every ball I throw to you. Heidi doesn't stay with babysitters well but she stays with you and that gives Jude and I peace on mind when we go out. I should really be thanking you."

Annie laughed. "OK, thank me!" Bob went to jab her in the ribs but Annie saw him and jumped away.

"On second thought, I don't think I'll thank you for anything. You're a little bug!"

Annie scanned the arena and noticed that all the Red Sox were finishing with practice and gathering their gear to head off to the showers. There was only one lone figure in the batter's box at home plate. As her eyes zoomed in on the player, a wide smile crossed her face. "Well, if that isn't the man himself!" Annie laughed loudly.

"You said you'd be nice, "Bob warned.

"Oh, now that I'm through the doors I guess I should tell you the truth."

Bob glanced at her skeptically. "And that would be?"

"I had my fingers crossed when I said I wouldn't pick on Kenny Wells."

Rock's laughter floated off the ceiling. "That's my girl." He patted Annie on the back.

"Tell me you didn't?" Bob demanded through clenched teeth.

Annie burst out laughing. "Actually, I did. I was desperate to get into the arena."

Bob shook his head. "I never thought you'd stoop to such low tactics."

"Oh come on now, sure you did."

"If you pick on Kenny too much I'm going to haul you out of here over my shoulder."

Annie smiled at him. "You'd have to catch me first."

Annie made a beeline for the bleachers directly behind home plate. She arrived just in time to watch Kenny Wells swing hard and come up with a whole lot of nothing. "Strike!" Annie yelled as loud as she could.

Kenny turned around and spotted her immediately. "How did you get in here?"

"Good to see you too, Kenny." Annie gave him a big, exaggerated toothy smile. "I see some things haven't changed since last year. You're still swinging that lumber and coming up with air." Kenny scowled at her. "You know that's not going to help the Sox, Kenny. Your timing is all wrong. Help me help you."

"Security!" Kenny yelled at the top of his lungs.

"Oh, don't be such a baby. I can help."

"You're a girl."

"And two points to you for noticing Mr. Major League. Now let's get back to that swing of yours. Your timing is way off. This isn't Little League ball, ya know."

Kenny turned and saw Rock and Bob smiling at the conversation. "Man, aren't you going to haul her out of here?"

Bob and Rock both laughed. "I'm too old," Rock admitted quickly. "I can't haul Annie anywhere."

"I was talking to the girl's brother. You," he pointed his bat at Bob like a dagger, "take her away."

"Now Kenny, maybe she's right. You could learn a thing or two from her. Now even though she's a girl, she knows baseball." Bob smiled at the ball player. "You're a professional. You should be able to get past that point."

Kenny was trying hard to hide the smile that was tugging at the corners of his mouth. "If you don't take her out of here, I'm going to ask to be traded far away to a team on the west coast."

"Is that a promise?" Annie asked hopefully. "Maybe then I'll get to play!"

"Girls don't play baseball!"

"Well, this girl does!" Annie grabbed her glove and ran unto the field. "If Bob pitches to you, do you think you can hit anything my way?"

"Of course I can hit it your way!" Kenny smiled at the spunky outfielder. "You get ready now. You ain't seen nothing yet!"

"That's right, Kenny! I ain't seen nothing yet! You think you might actually hit that ball?"

"Girl, you got a mouth on you!" He pointed the bat at Annie. "Get into the outfield!"

"Should I go further out than shortstop? I mean," Annie asked in a puzzled tone, " are you feeling lucky today?"

Kenny growled at her. "I'm going to slam this ball over your head!"

As Annie made her way to Kenny's position in deep center field she simply shrugged. "We'll see. Personally, I think you're over paid and a little over-weight. You'd better hit it far so you can make it around all the bases."

Kenny turned to Bob. "Throw me something to shut her up with."

Bob laughed. "Kenny, when she gets like this, nothing shuts her up!"

Kenny smiled. He liked Annie and Bob a lot. They were his biggest fans even if they did drive him crazy at times. Bob threw a few warm-up pitches across the plate. When Kenny stepped into the batter's box, Bob sailed a fastball by Kenny and Rock called the strike.

"Man, what did you do to that thing, Superman? I didn't even see it."

Bob laughed. "You want me to throw you another one?"

"You're stinking right I want you to throw me another one. No guy that's not even in the majors is going to strike me out." Kenny stared at Bob. "Throw another one," he demanded fiercely.

Bob did and Kenny connected with it, sending a pop fly right up the middle of the field toward Annie. She was waiting for it, ran in and made the easy catch. Kenny pretended to act shocked. "You were just lucky. That was an easy play."

Annie jogged in with the ball in her glove. "Listen, I won't tell anyone what happened here if you take this ball in and get the other players to sign it."

"No one would believe you," he said taking the ball from her.

"The tabloid papers love stuff like this!" Annie laughed at Kenny's shocked expression.

"I'll be right back." He headed to the locked room listening to the laughter behind him fill the air.

Annie spent the next twenty minutes swinging at pitches Bob threw. As she got her timing down, connected solidly with the ball, it went further and further into center field. Kenny quietly came out of the locker room and watched Annie batting. He walked over Rock. "She hits real good for a girl."

Rock smiled. "She hits real good period. Lucky for you the Sox don't let her play. I heard after your slump last season they were actually considering it." Rock laughed and Kenny threw an arm around his good friend.

"So, how's Sweetpea doing? I'm still feeling torn up about her husband."

Rock smiled gently. "Good news on that front. Looks like she's going to be getting married again."

"Stop talking about me behind home plate. I can't concentrate," Annie growled at them.

"You can concentrate all you want but that's not going to help you." Kenny laughed loudly and Annie laid her bat down and came over to him.

"I'll forgive you for saying that if you have my ball signed."

"I don't mean to make an issue out of it, but that ball is the property of the Red Sox. You didn't buy it, they did."

Annie laughed. "You make enough money- you pay for it."

"First you make me get the ball signed, now you're making me pay for it? You're so demanding!"

Annie smiled as he handed her the signed ball. "It looks like all the players signed this."

"They did. I even waited for guys to get out of the shower so they could sign this." He narrowed his eyes at her. "So, what are you going to do with it?"

"Sell it on Ebay. I figure I could make a small fortune. Thanks."

Kenny's mouth dropped open and Annie roared with laughter. She loved picking on the big, brown haired, brown-eyed ballplayer. He looked enough like Bob to be her brother. "I think you need a spanking!"

"She's needed a spanking for a long time." Bob smiled proudly. He enjoyed watching Annie beating up on Kenny.

"I'm going to give the ball to a friend of mine. He's a big baseball fan."

"Not a Yankee fan I hope. I don't sign for Yankee fans." Kenny winked at Annie.

"No, he's a Braves fan but he'll love getting this ball."

"He'd better not sell it on Ebay."

"I'm sure he'll treasure it, Kenny. Thanks a bunch."

"This wouldn't be the guy you're dating, would it?"

"How did you know I was dating someone?" Annie watched him carefully.

Kenny smiled proudly. "Now wouldn't you like to know."

"Yeah, I would."

"I have my sources. Anyways, from what I hear, the guy seems pretty serious about you. If he makes you an offer, I think you should go for it."

"And just why is that?" Annie demanded.

"Annie," Kenny grinned, "it's not every day a guy is going to come along that's able to put up with you. If he makes a valid offer, take the deal." Kenny laughed loudly.

"Shows what you know. I've probably had more offers than you!"

"How much did Bob pay them?" Kenny shot back quickly.

"I should clobber you for that!"

"Now, Annie," Kenny put an arm around her shoulders, "you know I'm just having a little fun with you. You're like my own sister, and I pick on her all the time."

"I bet she hates you!" Annie laughed.

"She adores me!" Kenny replied smugly.

"Don't be so sure you don't find her rooting for the opposing team."

"That would never happen."

"Do you pick on her like you pick on me?" Kenny nodded. "Then it just may happen."

They teased each other for a few more minutes before Kenny had to go. "Listen, Sweetpea, I hope this guy is good for you. If he's the one, marry him. He will be getting a real good lady."

Annie hugged Kenny. "Thanks. You give Jeanie a hug for me. OK?"

"You bet." He hugged her again and then made his way to the locker room. Annie and Bob practiced another hour before they called it a day.

True to his word, Bob came down from Maine to Boston every Saturday to help Annie get ready for the big game. Both of their families enjoyed the time they got to spend together and Bob was a wonderful coach at getting Annie's softball skills fine-tuned.

Before they knew it, it was February third, and Bob and Annie were standing in the United Airlines terminal, in Boston's Logan airport, waiting for their flight to Denver, where the celebrity softball game would be held. As Annie absent-mindedly scanned the terminal, she suddenly spotted Rock coming toward them. She quickly went to greet him. "I can't believe you came all the way down here to see us off!"

Rock laughed. "Annie, I didn't come down here to see you off, I came down here to go off with you!"

"Really?" Annie squeaked in excitement.

Rock smiled and nodded. "Bob talked me into last night. I was going to call you and make sure it was OK, but Bob assured me it was and said I should surprise you."

Annie hugged Rock. "This is a wonderful surprise and you're going to get to meet Ryan too!"

Rock grinned. "Now, gee, that hadn't occurred to me. Is he playing in this game as well?"

Annie laughed. "You know he is! And by the way, you don't make a very good liar!"

Rock laughed. "Probably because I haven't had much practice at it."

Annie shook her head and smiled at him. "I'm so glad you're coming. You can bunk with Bob."

"Aren't you two sharing a room?"

Annie laughed. "Not on your life! He snores really, really, really bad." Annie paused. "I'm sure we've had this conversation before."

Rock smiled. "Probably, we've talked about so many things."

Annie's eyes narrowed. "You might want to get a room of your own. Bob does snore really bad. It's no joke. After listening to him drone on, hour after hour in the middle of the night, you find yourself on your knees, desperately praying to God, pleading with Him to make the snoring stop. It just about drives me insane."

"I'm not that bad, Ann. You're exaggerating." Bob finally came to his own defense.

"You're worse. Even when we were in Tennessee, I could hear your snoring all the way down the hall. You're awful."

"I was snoring then because I had a cold. It couldn't be helped."

"Uh huh. Sure. Yeah right."

"It's true."

Annie laughed and then turned to Rock. "I don't know what bugs me more when I'm having to bunk with Bob. The fact that he's snoring and keeping me awake, or the fact that it's the middle of the night, and he's sleeping and I'm not because he's snoring like a lumberjack sawing wood. I guess my animosity here is mixed and stems from both things. Sometimes, his own snoring actually wakes him up and that is pretty funny. The thing is, he rolls over and not only goes back to sleep but back to snoring as well. It's so irritating."

Rock turned to face Bob. "Hey, Buddy, no offense but I'm getting my own room."

"Traitor," Bob mumbled.

Rock smiled at Bob. "You can call me what you want but after listening to your sister here I've decided not only to get my own room but get my own room in another hotel." Annie and Rock roared with laughter.

"If I had known you were going to take her side, I wouldn't have talked you into coming."

Rock's eyes twinkled. "You didn't talk me into coming. I wanted to come all along. I was just looking for the right opportunity to tell you two!"

Annie was sandwiched between Rock and Bob on the plane, which suited her just fine. She was able to steal Bob's complimentary nuts, sip his juice after hers was all gone, borrow Rock's earphones long enough to decide she didn't like the movie, and then borrow Rock's book. It was a perfect situation –for her.

Annie explained to her companions that each softball team was given two practices. Their first practice session would begin Thursday night and then a second one on Friday afternoon. Annie was looking forward to meeting the rest of her teammates.

Annie finally caught up with Ryan Thursday night after her first practice. After he gave her a big hug he stood back for a second and Annie could see the man was grinning proudly like a Cheshire cat.

"What?" Annie mumbled cautiously.

"Oh, nothing," Ryan replied vaguely.

Annie narrowed her eyes. "That grin definitely does not mean nothing mister. I know that grin. When I'm grinning like that at Bob, it means I've got something good on him and I'm about to cash it in."

Ryan laughed. "You're too suspicious."

Annie laughed. "I am not. I just have the uncanny ability to spot trouble coming at me." Annie took a step closer to Ryan. "I smell trouble."

Ryan laughed. "That's not trouble, it's that corn beef and cabbage I had for lunch. It's been giving me a little gas. I apologize. I'll try to stay downwind from you."

Annie smacked his arm. "You are so gross. By the way, you're not sidetracking me here. I know you and I know you're up to something." Ryan smiled at her but wouldn't say another word.

"Are you going to introduce me to your friend?" Rock had been observing the situation long enough to see that Annie had quite possibly met her match with Ryan Jones.

"Ryan, I'd like to introduce you to a great friend of mine, Rock Bennington." Annie turned and face Rock for a moment. "I honestly don't know who this guy is," she whispered loudly. "He's been following me around here and I can't seem to get rid of him. Maybe you should call security."

Ryan laughed and shook Rock's hand. "Don't mind her."

Rock smiled and shook Ryan's hand. "I usually don't."

Ryan laughed and winked at Annie. "I have heard so much about you. It's such a pleasure to finally meet you."

"Same here, young man."

"He's a pastor, so you'd better be nice to him," Annie insisted.

"That's right," Ryan nodded. "Hey Annie, that could come in handy for us."

Annie smiled at Rock. "I told you he wouldn't mind you marrying us. He's so anxious to get married, he'd probably agree to you marrying us in the coffee shop over there."

Ryan smiled. "The place really isn't important to me Annie. If you want to get married in that coffee shop, I'll follow you in."

Annie smacked Ryan on the arm. "I can't wait for the game. I'm really looking forward to it. It should be so much fun."

"I'm sure it will be," Ryan smirked widely.

"What is with you?"

Ryan laughed. "You'll find out tomorrow."

"Why do I get the feeling that your little surprise is not going to be a good surprise?"

Ryan winked at her. "All surprises are good."

Annie snorted. "That is so not true. I have lived long enough to know, for a fact, that most surprises that come my way are not good."

"You're kind of a cup half empty type of girl, aren't you?"

Annie smiled. "I'm kind of a, let's not throw myself into an embarrassing situation type girl. I'm not big on public humiliation, especially, when I'm the one getting publicly humiliated. If I can avoid that, I definitely will."

"You'll like this."

"Don't be so sure."

"Let's change the subject."

"I'd rather not but if you're not going to tell me what you're up to, maybe you'll tell me what position you're playing tomorrow?"

"I can't tell you that! Remember, you're the competition!"

Annie glanced at her watch. "Well, if you're not going to tell me anything interesting, I'd better head to my hotel. We have a ten o'clock curfew."

Ryan grinned. "Annie, I can tell you plenty of interesting things."

"I mean about the game."

"Why limit the topic to the game? There are so many other interesting things we could discuss."

Annie pushed him away and laughed. "Not tonight."

Ryan smiled. "OK. Some other time we'll talk about interesting things. By the way, are you rooming with Bob?"

Annie laughed as Bob came next to her and slid a hand across her mouth. "Ann and I will not be rooming together because we have irreconcilable differences."

Ryan looked knowingly at Bob. "You snore, don't you?"

"Did she tell you?"

Ryan laughed. "She didn't have to. I know the look in her eyes. There's a guy on my team that snores so bad he peels the paint off the walls. No one will room with him either."

Annie laughed. "I'd like to put him and Bob together and see if they keep each other awake snoring."

"This is not an experiment, Ann." Bob sighed loudly.

"Maybe not for you but I bet it would provide hours of entertainment for the rest of us."

"Go away," Bob grumbled.

"You're still grumpy because I ate your complimentary nuts on the plane."

A look of shock crossed Bob's face. "You ate my peanuts? I was wondering where those went."

Annie smiled at him. "They were good too."

"You'll eat anything that's not nailed down. You're pathetic."

"Hey, in my own defense, the peanuts were sitting on your tray forever. I didn't think you wanted them."

"Forever?" Bob questioned his little sister.

Annie nodded. "Forever and a day."

Bob laughed and turned to Ryan. "In Annie time that comes out to about five minutes. Watch your food around her. She has quick hands."

"I'll keep that in mind." Ryan smiled at Annie. "Now off to bed with you. I don't want you saying that your team lost because you were tired from me keeping you up. No excuses here."

"Why would I give an excuse? Winners don't give excuses, they give acceptance speeches!"

Ryan laughed. "If I don't see you before the game, I want to wish you luck."

Annie laughed. "Winners don't need luck either!"

"See you tomorrow."

"Not if I see you first!"

The next day, the teams arrived in the arena by nine o'clock. The game was scheduled to start at ten and the team members were busy warming up. At ten o'clock, after a short prayer, the game began. Annie's team took the field first and she was able to play her favorite position, centerfield.

As she was jogging out to the outfield, an announcer was introducing all the players to the audience. When he got to Annie's name, he introduced her as a contemporary Christian writer and then paused. Annie stared toward the announcer feeling a strange dread creep over her. The announcer then added in an amused voice that he had a few extra tidbits to share about Annie Smith. Annie cringed inside. This must have been the surprise that Ryan had spoken of. She instinctively knew she wasn't going to like it. She could just tell. She was about to get dumped on.

"Annie Smith is probably the closest thing we've ever had to a professional softball player," the announcer's voice floated across the stadium that was growing quieter by the second. "Annie comes with a long line of softball accomplishments, including a row of state championships in high school and two national championships in college. Annie has been awarded the most valuable player a total of six times throughout high school and college. Currently, Annie plays on a church softball team in Boston. Welcome aboard, Annie."

Annie was gripping her glove so tightly that her hand hurt. How did Ryan find that out? She knew it had to be him because it was just the type of thing that he'd sink to doing. Well, she thought quickly, it was just the type of thing that she'd sink to doing but this time it was different because the shoe was on the other foot and it didn't feel so good at all. Annie found recognition awkward and embarrassing. She always had.

As the announcer went on to introduce the other team players, Annie quickly jogged off the field toward Ryan. He was grinning so widely that Annie could see every tooth in his mouth. His face was bathed in amusement without a single bit of remorse showing. He didn't even attempt to fake it.

"You!" Annie poked a firm finger in his chest. "I know you did that. Don't even try to deny it because I know you did it."

Ryan laughed. "I wasn't about to deny it."

"How did you find out about all that stuff?"

"I'm sure I mentioned to you that my mom is a research librarian. She's very good at what she does."

"You pulled your poor mother into this? Shame on you."

Ryan smiled. "Yeah, just like what you do to Bob all the time. You pull him into your little conspiracies."

Annie smiled. "I don't have to pull him that hard. He's a willing participant."

"So was Mom. I knew that when you said you weren't that great of a player, that well, you were under estimating your abilities. You are so modest!" Ryan burst out laughing.

Annie narrowed her eyes at him. "We'll talk about this later. I have a game to play."

"Good luck."

"Yeah right."

Little did Ryan know, but he had actually done Annie a huge favor. Before the introductions, she was extremely nervous. After what Ryan had just done, the anger of it fired her up. She was ready to play and ready to give it her best. That also meant that she was ready to try to get Ryan out every time he was at bat if he hit anything her way. She would try her hardest to make sure that the ball ended up in her glove. It was the very least she could do for him.

As the game got under way, the first player struck out. The second player hit a single. The third player up hit the ball right up the middle to second base. That was unfortunate for the player forced to go to second, because he was immediately tagged out. With one man on first, Ryan got up and hit the ball deep into right field. Annie watched in dismay as the ball sailed right out of the park. Ryan ran the bases smiling and waving like he'd just won a gold metal. Annie had to laugh. The man knew how to pump his team up. The next player hit the ball deep to center field. Annie was waiting for it and made the easy out effortlessly. Her team was up. It was time for a little vindication.

As Annie jogged toward the dugout, she tried hard to keep her head in the game. She found it quite a challenge because she'd never seen so many Christian celebrities in one place at one time. It was a bit overwhelming.

As she methodically looked through her bag of bats, her second favorite Christian singer came over to her. Glenn Mason was a favorite of hers from childhood. It was a thrill to see him in person. Annie tried not to be intimidated by his ruggedly handsome good looks or his captivatingly charming smile. He was stunning, and something in the back of her head warned her that he knew he was. Something about him just seemed too smooth and polished.

As Glenn extended his hand to her, she shook it, eyeing him carefully. "Good luck with the game, Annie." His slow, southern drawl washed over her gently like a soothing comfort and she found it almost mesmerizing. Other words began to flash through her mind about the magnetic singer. He was charming, attractive, poised, confident, well mannered, charismatic, fascinating and altogether too appealing. Warning bells went off loud and clear. Something was up. He was acting just a little too friendly.

"Ryan Jones sure is one lucky guy," Glenn went on smoothly. He smiled at her charmingly and her head filled with fog. She couldn't think. She knew, subconsciously, he was trying to mess with her and she also knew, subconsciously, that he was succeeding. There didn't seem to be anything she could do about it and the small amount of self-respect that she had left was extremely annoyed with her.

At that moment, Jim Dunn, her team's captain, came running up to them. "Glenn," Jim's voice was filled with disgust, "you take yourself and that sweet talking accent of yours out of here." Annie looked at Jim with clear shock written across her face. The fog in her brain was beginning to lift. "He's trying to mess with your mind Annie. Without a doubt, I think that entire team is out to submarine you. If I were you," Jim leaned in closer to her, "I wouldn't talk with any of them until after the game. They're a bunch of rotten scoundrels. They'll stoop to anything to try to win."

Glenn smiled at her shamelessly. "Well, that being that case and all, I guess I'll just mosey on over to right field. You have a good game there, Annie, ya hear?"

At that moment she did hear. Jim was right. They were trying to mess with her so she wouldn't be able to concentrate and play well. Amazing. She never pictured Christians using this tactic.

"I thought this game was supposed to be fun." Annie looked warily at Jim.

"Are you having fun yet?" Jim asked sarcastically as he walked back to the dugout.

"Not really," Annie mumbled to herself. As she idly scanned the field, it didn't take her long to spot Ryan. He was proudly standing on the pitcher's mound, gently tossing a ball into his glove. Her mouth dropped open in shock. For some reason, she had never considered that Ryan would be pitching. She groaned inwardly realizing how hard it would be to hit off the confident, smug smiling pitcher. He was in his element. The pitcher's mound was his throne and the field was his kingdom.

When they made eye contact, his grin only broadened. She knew that he'd seen the exchange between her and Glenn and now she also knew that he was probably the one that had set the whole thing up. She wouldn't put it past Ryan to parade every singer on his team in front of her, just to distract her and make her lose her concentration. Annie's eyes narrowed. Two could play this game and when she played games, she played to win.

She decided to hang out behind home plate to watch Ryan pitch. Since she was batting in the number four spot, it gave her a little time to check out his style and get a feel for what she might be facing. Immediately she noticed two things. Ryan's pitches were right over the plate time and time again. He was consistently good. The other thing she noticed was that Ryan was working his hardest to try to rattle every batter. He could be such a charming distraction, and he was, without a doubt, pulling out all the stops. He'd playfully tease each batter, smile charmingly at them, wink at them and try to distract them in any way he could.

At that moment, Jim Dunn strolled over. "He's infuriating!" Annie complained.

Jim laughed. "Not only is he infuriating, he's very good at being infuriating!"

"That's not fair!"

"Annie," Jim put a hand on her shoulder, "this isn't pro ball. It's just a fun game. Part of the job of the pitcher is to rattle the batter."

"Are you doing that when you're pitching?"

Jim grinned. "To the best of my ability, though I personally think that Ryan Jones is more gifted in this area than most."

Annie smiled. "So why don't the batter's try to rattle the pitcher? I think Ryan needs a good taste of his own medicine!"

"Go for it, Annie. I think you're just the girl for the job. Good luck!"

Annie smiled. As she walked confidently to the plate, she knew the only way to deal with the flirting, charming, infuriating pitcher was to throw his own sweet talking words right back at him. "Hey, Sweetie Pie," Annie called to Ryan as she entered the batter's box, "you're kind of cute!" Ryan was taken off guard only for a second. He winked at Annie, grinning broadly as he silently accepted her challenge.

"Your arm must be getting a little tired, Ryan," Annie stated with feigned compassion. "Your first pitch went pretty wide there. Don't hit anyone in the dug- out. Maybe you should sit down for a few innings. You aren't as young as you used to be!"

Ryan laughed loudly but kept his composure as charming as ever. "You're all talk Annie!"

The next pitch went wide and Annie burst out laughing. She was successfully rattling this blue-eyed charmer and nothing could have made her happier. She turned and looked at Ryan. "Honey, did you forget to take your Gerotol today?"

Behind her she could hear the dugout roaring with laughter. "Hey, big shot," Ryan shouted back, "why don't you hit that ball and show us what you've got?"

Annie smiled. "Why don't you throw me something that I can hit? You're pitching is all over the place. If you throw me something even close to the plate, I promise I'll hit it!"

The crowd, as well as the teams was enjoying the banter between Annie and Ryan. Ryan's next pitch went right up the middle and Annie slammed it over the centerfielder's head. Annie took off like a shot and was heading for second base before the girl playing centerfield even got to the ball. The outfielder tossed the ball toward third base as Annie was rounding third. At the third base coach's instructions, Annie threw herself into high gear and headed for home plate. She crossed the line a full minute before the ball did and was declared safe by the home plate umpire.

Annie turned and flashed Ryan a big, toothy, victorious smile. "Nice pitch, Jones."

"That was a lucky hit!" Ryan shouted to her. The crowd burst out laughing at his comment. It was obvious that no one believed him.

"You throw me a pitch like that again and I'll do the same thing to it," Annie replied in a sassy voice. "I guess you like seeing your pitches go to the moon!"

Ryan grinned. "You just wait until the next time you're up. Than we'll see what you think about my pitches."

Annie dramatically placed a hand across her chest. "I'm looking forward to it with all my heart!"

"Get out of here!" Ryan barked.

"The agony of defeat stings a little, doesn't it!" Annie laughed loudly.

"Go!" Ryan instructed. Annie winked at him and then slowly strolled back to the dugout. Victory never tasted sweeter.

Annie's team scored four runs before they had to return to the field. Ryan did have a very athletic team and they proved it in the next inning. The first three batters all got on base. You could feel the tension mounting as Ryan stepped to the plate. Annie quickly decided to trade positions with the shortstop. She wanted to be close enough to Ryan to hassle him. Somebody had to after all he put the batters through.

He was ruthless. She smiled. She could be ruthless too. She's had a lot of practice with Bob.

"Hey good looking," Annie's voice was sugar coated, "let's see if you can hit any better than you can pitch!"

Ryan looked at her and relaxed his batting stance slightly. "I'm on to you Annie! You can't rattle me. I've got nerves of steel!"

Everyone broke up laughing. Just before Jim fired a pitch right across home plate, Annie shouted out to Ryan. "I hope you can hit better than you can play hockey!" That did it. Ryan froze long enough to miss his pitch. It sailed across the middle of the plate and the Ump loudly called the strike. Annie stood her ground proudly smiling at Ryan.

"That was very funny Annie!" Ryan grinned.

"Thank you. I thought so."

"This one is going out of the park so you'd better say good bye to it now."

Annie decided, out of the kindness of her heart, to lay off Ryan. True to his word, he sent the ball sailing over the head of the left fielder and out of the park. Ryan jogged around the bases triumphantly. When he reached the position that Annie was playing, his smile grew so wide it was almost blinding.

"Great shot, Slugger!" Annie smacked him on the arm.

"Thank you!" he replied pompously. "You're right. The taste of victory is pretty sweet!" Annie smiled. Even though he was on the opposite team, she couldn't help but feel proud of her man.

A little over two hours later, the game ended, nine to eight in favor of the Singers. Annie felt pleased with the outcome because she knew she had done her best. For the first time in her life she had fun in a game and wasn't devastated by losing. The joy of the game out weighed the agony of defeat. It was a wonderful feeling.

As she was jogging over to Ryan, Glenn Mason stopped her and put a friendly arm around her shoulders. "You sure played a great game Annie." Once again his southern sweetness washed over her. There was definitely something about that accent. "I never saw a girl hit the ball like that. You're mighty good."

Ryan came running over and pulled Annie away from Glenn and put an arm protectively around her. "Glenn get your filthy hands off my woman! This is my girl. If I see you making moves on my girl again I'll kick your sorry tail all the away back to Tennessee."

"Hey, man, sorry," Glenn held up his hands in front of his face defensively. "I didn't know you and Annie were an item."

The look Ryan gave Glenn could have melted steel. It was clear that he didn't believe a word that man said. "Well, now you know." His voice was a little too even and Annie could tell Ryan was working hard to control his temper. "She's my girl. Do the world a favor and get a woman of your own. This one," Ryan eyed Glenn hard, "is already taken."

Glenn looked at Annie. "She's a good one Ryan."

"Yes, she is, and she's mine." Ryan tightened his grip around Annie's shoulders.

"You're very lucky."

"Yes, I am."

"OK, Ryan," Glenn sounded insincere, "I hear you loud and clear."

"You'd better," Ryan said quickly.

Glenn turned to face Annie. "Listen Sweetheart, if he ever gives you any grief, you come and find me." Annie laughed and Glen walked away.

"Annie," Ryan's voice held an edge to it, "if you ever go find him, I'll give you grief. Our business is our business."

Annie laughed. "Ryan, I'd never go to him. The man refers to me like cattle. She's a good one. I don't like men doing that. Men that do that are too likely to put you out to pasture. Besides," Annie smiled coyly, "he's a sweet talking charmer. Oh wait a minute," Annie scratched her head, "so are you!" Annie grinned up at him.

"Yeah, but I'm your sweet talking charmer."

"That's right,and believe me, I won't forget it. You're too big and obnoxious to ignore!"

Ryan went to poke Annie and she jumped aside. "Ya know, you were kind of hard on Glenn."

"Are you kidding?" Ryan's forehead wrinkled in disbelief.

"You don't think you were hard on him?"

"If I gave in to my strong desire to pound him into oblivion, then I would have been too hard on him."

"I definitely agree with that."

"Listen, Annie," Ryan sounded frustrated, "Glenn Mason has quite a reputation with the ladies. He goes through women like a kid goes through candy."

"Really?"

"I think he has a heart for the Lord, but he has a major weakness for the ladies. He's hurt a lot of women by using them and losing them. It's awful. When I saw him making moves on you, I got so mad I was seeing red."

"Ryan," Annie said gently, "first of all, I am committed to you. You don't have to worry about that. And," Annie had to laugh, "even if you and I weren't an item, I would never, in a million years, fall for a guy like that. He's not my type. You," she poked him in the side, "are exactly my type."

"Good," Ryan nodded seriously. Ryan squeezed her. "I love you. A guy like Glenn just lusts you. There's a huge difference, ya know?"

"Yes, I do know. And," Annie squeezed Ryan's hand hard, I love you too!"

Ryan beamed. "Now that's enough to take away my bad temper. I love hearing you say those words, Annie."

"I love saying them." Annie looked tenderly at Ryan. "I really love you so much."

"And I love you."

As they continued making their way out of the stadium to the place they were going to meet Bob and Rock, they talked easily with each other, enjoying one another's company.

"You did great out there, especially," Ryan cut her a sideways glance, "for someone who isn't that good at softball."

Annie laughed. "Hey, I'm just a modest individual who doesn't like to brag."

Ryan howled. "That's definitely not it."

"Yeah, what is it?"

"You like to whip my hide through the element of surprise. You've done that already."

"It keeps life jumping, ya know?" Ryan agreed. "Hey, you really know how to handle yourself on the field. I was very proud of you. I cheered for you on the inside a lot."

"I cheered for you too Annie. I'm glad you came. It was a fun game."

"Yeah, you play softball much better than you play hockey!"

Ryan laughed. "You're such a tease."

"Nothing new to you."

"I hope you never change."

Annie laughed. "I don't think you'll have to worry about that."

Outside the stadium, they caught up with Bob and Rock. "That was a very good game. It was very entertaining." Rock smiled at Annie.

"Yeah, you two should take your act on the road." Bob winked at his little sister. "You two are very funny."

"I'm glad you enjoyed it," Annie smiled again at Bob.

"Did you enjoy it?" Bob eyed her questioningly.

Annie laughed. "Yeah, ya know, I really did." Bob's mouth hung open. "You should close that cave. You might get a bug in there."

Bob shook his head. "I'm just so surprised to hear you say that you enjoyed the game even though you didn't win."

"I think I'm making progress." Annie winked at Rock.

"I honestly never thought I'd live to hear you say that." Bob gave Annie a big hug. "I'm so proud of you Squirt. You've come a long way."

Annie shook her head. "And I know I've got a long way to go."

"God walks with you Annie," Rock said gently.

Annie nodded. "That's the reason I'm still here today Rock. God has carried me through valleys that I thought were impossible for me to get out of."

"He's the God that specializes in impossible situations." Ryan squeezed her hand tenderly. "We both are living proof of that."

Just then Bob's stomach growled loudly. "It wasn't me, it was him." Rock laughed and pointed a finger at Bob. "Are you hungry there, Bob?"

Bob grinned. "I'm almost always hungry."

"What do you say we meet at that little Italian restaurant around the corner from the hotel?" Ryan asked the group. "Does an hour seem like enough time?"

"Sounds good," Annie nodded.

An hour later, they were all seated in the quaint little restaurant. Red-and white-checkered tablecloths were on every little table and Italian opera music played in the background. Even the men making pizza and other foods all talked to each other in Italian. Bob frowned and then sighed loudly.

"What?" Annie asked curiously.

"I don't like it when I can't understand the language." Bob frowned again.

"What's the big deal?" Annie shrugged. "They're probably talking guy talk, you know, the same boring things that you talk about."

"And that would be?" Bob stared at his little sister.

"Power tools, cars and home improvement projects." Annie rolled her eyes at him. "The language is different, but not the subject. Blah, blah, blah. I could die from the boredom of it all."

Bob smiled. "Yeah, well what if they're talking about the food they're serving us. What if they're saying stuff like, it's garbage, and instead of throwing it away, they have us to pay for it. Maybe we're all going to die from food poisoning or something all because we don't speak Italian."

Annie laughed. "You have such an imagination. But if this was going to be my last meal, I'd forget the diet and order one of everything on the menu. When I'm done with the main course, I'd head straight into dessert without ever looking back. If I'm going to die, my diet is definitely getting chucked."

Everyone laughed and then the waitress came up to take their order. She was a pleasant Italian teen girl and Annie decided, from one woman to another, she was going to ask her the mystery question. "Can you tell what the men are talking about back there? It's all Italian and I don't speak any of it."

The girl smiled at Annie. "My uncle Tony just put a new addition on his house and that's all they've been talking about for days." The girl shook her head. "His addition, his power tools, his clever abilities to use his power tools. They are making me nuts!"

"Boy do I understand what you're saying. Right now, I'm glad I don't understand Italian. It doesn't matter what language it is, men talk about the same subjects."

As the girl left to place their order, Annie smiled at Bob. "See, we're not going to die. I guess I'll have to be content with the salad I ordered and not switch over to the lasagna."

"She could be in on the conspiracy," Bob grumped.

"You don't give up, do you?"

"You know that I never give up. It's in our blood." Bob made a silly face at her. "I don't want to be the one to remind you of this, no wait," Bob grin, "of course I want to be the one to remind you of this. What was I thinking? You never quit either. We come from a long line of stubborn people."

Annie blew her straw wrapper at him and hit him right in the nose. "Good shot," Ryan smiled at her.

"Hey, I had a big target!" Everyone laughed.

The conversation continued like this for the next hour. As they finished their meal, and settled into their coffee time, Ryan grew quiet. Annie stared at him over her coffee cup rim for a second. "What's up?"

"What time do ya'll fly out?"

She loved when his accent got heavy. "Our plane leaves at six. We should get to the airport by four or so."

"I wish you could stay longer."

Annie bit her lip to keep from crying. "So do I."

"Do you want to come down to the ranch for a while?" Ryan's eyes silently begged her.

Annie smiled lovingly. "Ryan, as much as I'd like to say yes, I know that wouldn't be a good idea." Ryan raised questioning eyebrows at her. "I don't think that we should be alone."

Ryan nodded understandingly. "Annie, I understand what you're saying but you've got to realize that we wouldn't be alone. David, Tag, Sadie and Banjo are always lurking somewhere nearby."

"You're putting your dog in the lineup here?" Annie laughed. "Gee, are you desperate."

Ryan grinned. "I was trying to make it sound like more people."

"You're dog doesn't count."

"OK," he nodded, "the others do. They'd always be around."

Annie smiled. Ryan was making this hard on her, but she felt like she had to stick to her gut feelings.

"I don't think they'd be around enough. Last time, things got a little too interesting."

Ryan nodded seriously. "I know what you're saying, I just miss you so much."

"I know this is hard. I miss you too."

Ryan leaned over and whispered in her ear. "Are you any closer to being ready for the alter?"

"Actually, I am." She smiled at him and he could feel her peace at the subject.

"Are you totally ready? I mean," Ryan smirked, "I'll get down on my knees right here and," he grinned again, "we do have a minister present." Ryan looked over at Rock and smiled and nodded. "Isn't this all so convenient?"

"It's convenient," Annie replied seriously, 'but my timing is still off. I'm getting closer Ryan. I'm sorry to put you through this. I really am. If you can just hang in there a little longer, I know I'm going to get through the past and be ready for a bright future with you." Ryan squeezed her hand and nodded understandingly.

"Here son," Rock handed Ryan his business card, "take this and call me when it's the right time. I already told Annie that I make house calls. I don't care where you two decide to get married. I'd just be very honored if you'd let me perform the service."

Ryan looked at Rock through tearful eyes. He had known the man for such a short time but had come to care for him and respect him a great deal. "The job is yours Rock," Ryan's voice had grown tight, "and I hope I'll be calling you soon."

"Me too," Rock smiled at Annie. "You're almost there, Honey. I can feel it. Let God finish His work in you. You're almost there."

Annie smiled at him through tearful eyes. "I know that you're right Rock. It's just that it's been so frustrating at times."

"Of course it's frustrating," Rock smiled gently. "Look at the path that you've had to walk down."

"Not an easy road," Annie mumbled.

"Never is," Rock agreed. "Yet the Father is bringing you through this dark tunnel, Annie." He placed his big hand on hers. " You're going to make it. I know you are."

"Thanks, Rock. I appreciate your support so much."

"Anytime, Sweetpea," he looked at her compassionately, and then glanced at Bob and Ryan. "That goes for the rest of you too. I am here for all of you, twenty four/seven. Do you understand?"

"Yes," they responded in unison.

"Good," Rock nodded thoughtfully. "I mean, someone has got to look out for the bunch of you!"

"And you think you're the man for the job?" Annie asked quietly.

"I know I am, Dear. The Father's direct orders. I've been assigned to help you through this and if you'll let me, I'd like to."

"Thanks Rock," Bob fiddled with his watch. "We all love you."

"Well, it's a mutual feeling. I assure you."

Eleven

$\mathcal{A}$s Annie stared at the tickets in her hand, a big smile crept across her face. Ryan had sent her tickets and airfare to attend his first concert of the season in Nashville, Tennessee.

Amy came flying around the corner and curiously looked over her mom's shoulder. "What did you get?"

Annie held up the concert tickets for Amy to see. "We got tickets from Ryan."

"Oh, Mom," Amy jumped around the room excitedly, "we're going to go, aren't we?"

Annie nodded her head and Amy let out a loud scream. "I need to start planning my wardrobe. I don't think I have a thing to wear."

"Your closet is full of stuff."

"Not good stuff. I need to go shopping."

"We'll talk later about that." Annie studied the tickets in her hand again. "Ryan says that we'll be sitting front row, center, with Beth, Nikki, and David. It sounds like a lot of fun."

"This is going to be so cool Mom but I need to go shopping." Amy couldn't hide the desperation in her voice. "This is a major event for a teenager and I need to look good."

Annie stared at her daughter for a second. "Just how much is this 'good look' of yours going to cost me?"

Amy laughed. "Not a lot. Just a few key essentials."

"Do you think you could finance a few essentials yourself?"

"Sure Mom, anything. Just get me to the mall. Oh," Amy ran a hand through her hair, "I may have to have my hair done too."

"No hair," Annie said adamantly. "Clothes we'll do. Not hair. Your hair looks great."

Amy smiled. "I think it could look greater."

Annie smiled. "Don't mess with perfection. Let the hair be. We'll do the mall this afternoon."

"It's a deal," Amy nodded. "Oh, are we going to get to stay at the ranch? I love that place."

Annie nodded. "Yes, we've been invited to. Ryan says, if we'd like, we can stay the week. I thought you could bring all your schoolwork with you. What do you think?"

Amy squealed with excitement. "Mom, this is going to be so awesome! I can't wait!"

"Well, it's not until May 20, Am, so don't pop."

"I wish Tyler could go with us."

"Me too," the disappointment in Annie's voice was keen. "His ship is scheduled to be out at sea during that time."

Amy nodded and put a loving arm around her mom. "We can take lots of pictures and send them to him. It will make him feel a part of things."

"I hope it doesn't make him feel left out and show him what he missed. It's a fine line trying to include him and making him feel left out."

"Mom," Amy went over to the sink to grab a glass of water, "Tyler loves what he's doing. He knows it involves consequences but he feels strongly he's where the Lord wants him to be."

Annie shook her head. "When did you grow up so much?"

Amy smiled. "I'm not a little girl any more, Mom."

"I know." Annie sighed. "It just seems like you've shot into adulthood over night." Amy smiled. "Don't grow up too quickly. You have all your life to grow up and only a short time to be a kid."

"Don't worry Mom. I'll always be your kid."

Annie smiled at her daughter and then thought of Ty again. She always cherished the times that her family could be together. It seemed, as they got older, the together times got less and less. Annie knew that her kids were becoming adults and getting on with their lives. She sighed. Sometimes she just longed for the days when they were little and they would crawl up in her lap for stories and cuddling times. She was usually able to fix the problems of their world with a Band Aid and a kiss and hug. Those days were gone but a supportive hug and listening ear still worked well. She prayed for her children all the time and would give anything to take away the hard times they had to go through. She knew it was part of life to go through the tough times, it just wasn't easy for a mom to watch her children experience them. Annie sighed again. Being a mom was the best job and the worst. It could fill your heart with wonderful joy or break your heart into a million pieces. Life was cruel sometimes and a mom never took a back seat to the hardache her kids went through. You rode through it with them as if it was your own problem. Annie laughed because it was her problem if her kids had a problem. Nothing touched your heart more.

On May 20, Annie and Amy boarded a plane in Boston to take them to Tennessee. Ryan had arranged for them to fly in on a Friday afternoon so they could spend some time together before the Saturday evening concert.

At the Nashville airport, Ryan and his three kids met Annie and Amy. As soon as Annie came into the terminal, Ryan hopped the waiting room railing and took Annie in his arms. He gave her a big hug and then brought her back to the rest of the group in the terminal.

"I have missed you so much!" Ryan took Annie in his arms again and spun her around.

"I've missed you too!" Annie's eyes were spilling over with tears.

Ryan leaned down and brushed a soft kiss across Annie's lips. Then he turned to Amy. "Come here, girl! I didn't get my hug yet!"

Amy laughed and lovingly gave Ryan a hug and Annie went to greet Beth, Nikki and David with hugs. The welcome couldn't have been more loving.

After the luggage and all the people were seated in Ryan's Suburban, Annie leaned against Ryan's shoulder. Soon she was lost in serious thought. She knew, as she had known for a while, that she wanted Ryan with her forever. As she lovingly glanced up at Ryan, tears filled her eyes. Her love had grown steadily for him over the months to the point where she knew she couldn't live without him. She needed him.

Ryan glanced down and saw the look in Annie's eyes. When he stopped at a traffic light a few seconds later; he took the opportunity to take a deeper look into her eyes. He felt like he could see all the way down to her heart. A knowing smile quickly spread across his face and Annie knew he had read her heart. They didn't say a thing. They didn't have to. They both knew what was on each other's minds and hearts and it wasn't a conversation that they wanted to in front of a carload of kids. Ryan had been waiting months to have this conversation with Annie and it was one that they needed to have in private. It was a conversation that would change their lives forever. Ryan smiled. He really looked forward to talking to her later.

Once they got back to the ranch and everything was unloaded, Ryan suggested to his kids that they bring Amy for a horseback ride before it got too dark. As the kids excitedly left for the barn, Ryan stopped David and took him aside for a moment.

"Son," Ryan spoke quickly, "bring them up the old mountain road to the notch."

"Dad," David replied surprised, "that's a two hour round trip."

"I know," Ryan grinned and then winked at his son.

"Oh…" David smiled at his father, "you're going to ask her, aren't you?"

Ryan's smile was all the confirmation that David needed. Ryan pulled David into a quick hug. "Keep this between us, OK? I'd like Annie to hear the words from me first."

David smiled. "You've got it Dad."

As Annie walked into the great room ten minutes later, she found Ryan at his black piano practicing a song she'd never heard. He looked up and stopped as soon as he noticed her. "Hey," he asked invitingly, "do you want to play a duet with me tomorrow night?"

"No way!" Annie shuddered. "Ryan, I could have a heart attack just thinking about being up on stage. Don't even joke about it."

"OK," Ryan winked at her, "I guess I'll take that as a no."

Annie laughed. "You'd better believe that's a no. End of discussion."

"Come sit over here next to me," Ryan patted the black piano bench. "I've written a song for you."

Astonishment covered Annie's face. "You've written a song for me?"

Ryan grinned. "Do you want to hear it?"

Annie nodded looking more like a little schoolgirl than the woman she really was. No one had ever written a song for her. The idea of it touched her deeply.

Annie sat down next to Ryan, and he leaned over and kissed her softly on the cheek. "You don't have any music or words," Annie observed.

Ryan smiled. "Sweetheart," he said tenderly, "this song is from the heart. I don't need any music or words."

Annie smiled at Ryan and he began to play his song. She loved to watch his fingers glide gracefully across the keys. It almost mesmerized her. As he began to sing in a quiet sweet voice, Annie immediately recognized the heartfelt words as a love song. She bit her lip to keep from crying but she knew it wasn't going to work for long. She was going to bawl like a baby whether she bit her lip or not.

Ryan's song was filled with promises and heartfelt desires for the future. He had a way of taking the simplest words and giving them such deep meaning. Holding onto each other as they follow the Lord, the song told of a bright and happy future for two people who were being given a second chance at love. They both were and both thanked the Lord for His blessings.

After Ryan finished singing, Annie turned tearful eyes toward him and had to smile when she saw his eyes were flooding with tears. It was such an emotional song. It could make the toughest person tear up and flood over.

Ryan slowly stood up from his piano bench, took Annie's hands and knelt on one knee before her. Looking lovingly into Annie's eyes, he whispered tenderly, "Annie, I have loved you since the first time I saw you. You hit me straight in the heart and I still can't think straight around you." He paused for a moment and swallowed hard. "From that first day, my love for you has continually grown deeper and stronger." He paused again to wipe some tears off Annie's cheek. "I love you with all my heart. I never want to be apart from you again." He smiled at her in a way that made her feel cherished. "Annie," he looked deeply into her brown eyes, "I want you to be my wife. Will you marry me?"

Annie's face was covered in tears. In a choked up voice she softly but confidently replied, "Yes. I love you, Ryan."

Ryan lifted Annie off the piano bench and held her tightly in his arms. They held each other for several minutes. When they parted, Ryan covered her lips with small soft kisses. As things began to heat up, he gently drew away.

"I am forgetting something very important here." Ryan took Annie's hand and led her over to the couch. "As she sat down, Ryan reached into his jean pocket and pulled out a sparkling diamond engagement ring. "I took the liberty of picking out an engagement ring Sweetheart." He slid it on her finger slowly. "If it's not the style that you had in mind, you can pick out another one."

Annie stared down at her ring. "It's beautiful." Her voice was breathless. "It's absolutely perfect." Annie jumped off the couch and gave Ryan a big hug. "Thank you so much! It's exactly what I would have picked out for myself. Thank you!"

They hugged each other again and then sat down on the couch. Ryan put his arm snuggly around Annie. "So, Sweetie, when do you want to get married?"

Annie turned and looked at him lovingly. "I guess tomorrow is out because of the concert." She laughed at Ryan's surprised expression. "I told you when I was ready, I would be ready. I don't want long engagement. I want to get married soon."

Ryan smiled. "That's fine with me, Honey. The sooner the better."

Ryan's eyes narrowed in concentration. "So, tomorrow is out because of the concert, but Sunday afternoon is a definite possibility."

Annie laughed. "Ryan, there are so many decisions that you and I have to make. Sunday seems too soon. All the preparations kind of get me bogged down. They can make everything so complicated." Annie sighed. "I want to simplify. I don't want things to be too complicated."

"OK," Ryan nodded, "simple sounds good. How about me, you and the preacher? Is that simple enough?"

Annie laughed. "A little too simple. I can handle more than that. I was referring to simple as in the plans not the people."

Ryan smiled. "OK. How about this?" He looked like a man on a mission. "First tell me what seems complicated to you. Let's start there."

"Well," Annie rolled her eyes at him, "for starters, I live in Boston and you live in Tennessee." Annie laughed. "Maybe we could buy a house in

Pennsylvania and just commute every day to our states."

Ryan stared at her for a second. "That does not sound practical."

"I was only kidding."

"Good thing. I was doing a precheck of all the coffee and bathroom stops in between." Ryan smiled. "I just don't think that would work. I'd probably gain fifty pounds eating my way across each state just trying to stay awake." He grinned at her. "What other plan to you have in mind?"

Annie sighed. "I'm not sure. See, things are already getting complicated."

Ryan smiled. "Annie, this is not that complicated. Getting you to say yes was the complicated part. I think I asked you to marry me about a million times." Ryan grinned. "I really think that has to be some sort of a record. Don't you?"

Annie smiled. He always knew how to put things into perspective. "You did ask a lot."

Ryan grinned again. "Hey, I figured one of these times you had to say yes. You know, even if it was just out of self-pity. If pity gets you to say yes, well, then that works for me."

"I just want you to be clear on one fact."

"OK…" Ryan smiled, "what fact is that?"

"I did not accept your proposal of marriage out of pity for you." Annie laughed.

Ryan made a funny face. "Aw, come on, you didn't feel even the least bit sorry for me?"

Annie laughed. "Oh, I felt sorry for you from the beginning. You're one sorry man." Annie laughed again at Ryan's shocked expression. "Your sorry state wasn't what got me to say yes."

Ryan smiled wildly. "It was my charming personality? The chicks love it."

"No," Annie answered flatly. "It wasn't that."

"My good looks? Chicks seem to love that too."

"No."

"The way I sing?"

"Nope. Do the chicks love that too?" Annie roared with laughter.

"Yes, they do. OK, how about my tender heart?" Ryan asked hopefully.

"Uh, no. Not that, either."

"Annie," Ryan said exasperatedly, "I'm running out of attributes. "There's got be to some reason you're agreeing to wear that engagement ring."

"It's a nice ring," Annie admitted.

"So, if I had given you some cheap dime store ring, you would have turned me down flat?"

"Maybe..." Annie tried to stay serious, but she couldn't.

"Come on. Help my ego. What was it that made you fall for me?"

"Man, are you desperate for a compliment!"

"So throw a drowning man something!"

"OK," Annie appeared in deep thought. "can I get back to you on this? It might take some time."

"Annie…" Ryan growled.

"OK, it wasn't the looks, the charm, or the personality. It wasn't the singing, the songs, or the way you play piano. It wasn't your fame or riches." Annie turned and gave Ryan a startled look. "Gee, what was it then?"

"Annie…" Ryan was growling again.

"Wait, wait a second here. It had to be something." Annie scratched her head. "You know, for the life of me I can't seem to think of anything. I'm coming up empty here."

That did it. Ryan started tickled her and Annie retreated behind a chair. "I think we did this before."

"I want you to tell me why you're marrying me."

Annie burst out laughing. "I got it. It's your humility. You're so humble about your attributes!" Annie rolled over in laughter. Ryan was so fun to tease.

Ryan looked like a tiger ready to pounce. "Listen there big guy, if I answer honestly, do you promise not to eat me?"

"I think you'd be fun to eat." He licked his chops.

Annie smiled. "Then I'm not opening my heart up to you!"

"OK," Ryan stuck his lower lip out, "I promise not to eat you."

"Ryan Jones," Annie threw her hands on her hips, "if you don't know why I'm marrying you, then I'm not sure I should."

Ryan looked sheepish. "Annie, I know," he admitted reluctantly, "it's just that a guy like to hear the words…"

"I love you," Annie said sincerely.

"Those are the words." Ryan smiled. "I love you too. Now let's stop the clowning around and see if we can get this wedding date set."

"There's so much to think about," Annie became serious and quiet again.

"Listen, I don't have a problem relocating to Boston. It's a nice place and I think my southern accent will blend right in. I can learn to say things like lobsta, instead of lobster and Linder and Anner instead of Linda and Anna. See how quickly I learn?"

Annie smiled at his humor but shook her head firmly. "You can't leave Tennessee. The music industry is here and this ranch is the closest thing to heaven I've seen on earth."

"Yeah, the music industry is here, but guess what? There are planes that take you everywhere today. When I need to be down here, I could hop on a plane."

"I don't like it."

"Annie," Ryan was starting to sound frustrated, "I just want to be with you. I don't care where I live."

Annie nodded and then leaned over and kissed him softly on the cheek. "You are so sweet."

"That's the reason you fell in love with me. I forgot. I'm sweet!"

Annie laughed. "And very funny. You make me laugh."

"Another thing. How could I forget that? I am very funny! Thank you for reminding me, Dear."

Annie smiled. She knew their life together was going to be great. Ryan had a way of poking fun at himself that always made her laugh. "Listen, let's try to be serious here for a moment."

"I can do that," Ryan said eagerly.

"Good, I'll give you some M&M's later. In the meantime, I've been wondering about some things…"

"What things?"

"Would it be to hard on you to have me living in Chatfield Hollow as your wife?"

"No." Ryan answered quickly.

"Do you want to expand on that?"

"Uh, no, not at all?" Ryan winked. "Were you looking for more than that?"

Annie nodded. "Yes. I need to make sure that if I move down here it's not going to be too difficult with memories of Kay and all."

"Annie," Ryan took her hand gently, "my heart is with you. I don't want you having any doubts about that."

"I don't."

"Good." Ryan paused. "A better question would be, is it too difficult for you to come down here?"

Annie slowly shook her head. The confidence in her eyes was all Ryan needed to see. "I love this place. It's come to feel like home to me." Annie sighed. "Being at the farm in Boston has been tough for me and the kids. I know that Tyler is always glad to escape back to his ship and Amy is looking forward to going away to college just to get away from the farm. There are too many memories that we can't seem to shake. I think we all need a change."

Ryan looked concerned. "I don't want you ever to regret your choice of leaving the farm or feel any resentment toward me. This has to be your choice Annie. Take your time with it."

Annie smiled. "I have been taking my time. Since your brother died a few years ago I've wanted to sell the farm. I promised myself that I'd wait long enough to know that my decision was the best thing." Annie sighed. "I've thought about this a lot Ryan. I can't tell you how much I've been praying about this. I feel like God gave me a wonderful answer a few days ago."

"What was that?"

"Bob is being transferred back to Boston. I know he and Jude would jump at the chance to own Stony Brook Farm. Bob really deserved the farm all along.

It just kind of fell in my lap because he was settled up in Maine. I would feel really good about giving him the farm."

"I can see that you've given this a lot of thought."

Annie nodded. "All those nights that I couldn't sleep gave me a lot of time to think and pray. Tyler, Amy and I need to make a fresh start. This seems like the perfect time to do so."

"How do the kids feel about it?"

"They completely support the idea."

"Really?" Ryan seemed surprised.

"Really," Annie smiled in relief. It was good to get decisions made. "The good thing about Bob owning Stony Brook Farm is that the kids and I can go back anytime we want to. I think this is a great situation for everyone."

"It does sound good," Ryan nodded thoughtfully.

"So, can we move in with you after the wedding?"

Ryan smiled a smile that warmed Annie's heart. "I'd be honored to have ya'll move in with me. I only have one condition."

"You have a condition?" Annie asked curiously.

Ryan nodded. "Just one. You would need to redecorate the entire inside of the house."

"Why?" Annie seemed startled. "I love the way the ranch house looks."

"I'm afraid I need to insist Sweetheart." Ryan squeezed her hand lovingly. "We need to make this place our own."

Annie knew by the serious expression that covered Ryan's face that he felt very adamant about the issue. As she thought about it for a minute, she nodded understandingly. Things needed to be changed more for him than for her. "Well, I see your point; but if we're going to change things, I'd really like the kids to all be in on it. It's their home too. I think if we make this a joint effort, it with help everyone feel like they belong. Ya know what I mean?"

Ryan nodded. "Good idea." He fiddled with Annie's engagement ring. "Now that we have the problem of location solved, we need to work on the date. If I recall, the only thing we settled on was that Saturday wasn't good because of the concert."

"Well, we have another problem."

"What?"

"Amy graduates the middle of June. I could never ask her to leave her school a month before graduation." Annie grinned. "On the other hand, I want to get married now. I don't want to wait until after she graduates."

"I agree. Let's think on that one. There has to be something we can do." Ryan kissed Annie's check. "I think I hear the kids coming into the house. Why don't we tell them the wonderful news and then try to hammer out a date later?"

"Sounds good to me."

When the kids came into the house, Ryan broke the news to them right away. "I've asked Annie to be my wife and she's accepted!" Cheers went up that were quickly followed by lots of hugs.

"When's the date?" Amy asked excitedly. "I hope it's soon!"

"Am, we haven't figured that one out yet." Annie went on to explain to her daughter about the possibility of moving to the ranch full time.

"Mom! That's a great idea!" Amy threw her arms around her mother. "I was looking forward to going away to college to get away from the farm."

"I had thought as much," Annie admitted.

"Mom," Amy said urgently, "it's not because of you. It's because of Daddy. It's just too hard, ya know? Every time I look around the farm I see all the memories. It's just too much for me. I look over by the red barn and see the path where Daddy taught me to ride my bike or the dirt road where he taught Ty and I how to ride the four-wheelers." Amy paused and intently studied the floor for a second. "We have great memories Mom," she paused again. "I just can't seem to handle living at the farm right now." She sighed deeply. " I can't stand to go into the kitchen. After Daddy died there…I just," Amy struggled to control the emotion in her voice, " well, I hate to go in there. I still see him lying there. I know it sounds kind of stupid. I used to love the kitchen, now I hate it. I don't know what else to say."

Annie embraced her daughter in a hug. "You don't have to say anything, Sweetheart. You don't sound stupid. I understand better than you think I do."

"Really?" Amy asked awkwardly.

Annie nodded. "Really. I hate the kitchen too." Mother and daughter hugged again. There was something so comforting and therapeutic about being hugged by someone you loved. It was simply healing to the soul.

When their hug ended, Amy stepped back from her mom. "Honest Mom, I wouldn't have any trouble leaving the farm. I'm not sure I ever want to go back. Well," Amy admitted thoughtfully, "at least not for a very long time."

Annie smiled and squeezed her daughter's hand. Ryan's death was something that was going to take her and the kids a long to deal with. They wouldn't ever get over it. She was sure of that now but she did see that they were all beginning to heal. The healing process was happening but it sure was slow. Annie sighed. She didn't think there could be anything tougher for them to deal with than this. Ryan had been such a special man. He was a wonderful husband and father. Time, Annie whispered to herself. They needed time and the Lord's healing touch.

Annie focused her mind on her daughter again. "Amy, you're going to graduate next month. I'm honestly not sure what to do until then."

"Mom," Amy's voice was confident, " I don't want to go back to Boston or the farm. I can't," Amy sighed, "at least not now."

Annie exhaled loudly and glanced curiously at Ryan. He smiled and winked at her. "Honey," Annie looked at her daughter, "I'm going to tell you something that Ryan and I have talked about. I want your input here but," Annie waved a finger at Amy, " I want you to be totally honest. OK?"

"Mom, I'm always honest with you. What up?"

"Sweetheart, Ryan and I are ready to get married right now. We would set up a small wedding for family and a few close friends for next week." Amy squealed in excitement. "But," Annie continued on seriously, "there are a few complications. If we did that, what would we do about your schooling? You still have a month to finish up high school in Boston." Annie paused. "I'm not sure what to do."

Amy thought for a minute. "Well, most of my classes are finished. I still have my English term paper and my finals in History and Spanish." She paused again going through things in her head. "Maybe Mr. Porter, he's the headmaster," Amy informed Ryan, "would let me write my term paper down here and take my exams at a school in Tennessee." Amy smiled at her mom. "I have a great GPA mom, and I think Mr. Porter would consider it. It's worth a try. Why don't you call him?"

"Wouldn't you miss your friends?" Annie eyed her daughter compassionately. "I mean, you have all those special senior activities coming up. You have the graduation, the senior skip day and the prom. I don't want you to miss that."

"When do all these events happen?" Ryan asked curiously.

"Two days before graduation. It all starts the beginning of June," Amy informed Ryan.

"Well," Ryan looked at Annie and then Amy, "if Porter says that you can finish your work down here, we could all fly back for your graduation early. That way you could attend all the events. You wouldn't miss a thing. You could go do all your senior stuff while I help your mom pack up the farm."

"That's a great idea!" Amy ran over and almost knocked Ryan over with a hug.

Annie stared at Ryan thoughtfully. "That might work."

"See, I'm good at uncomplicating life."

Annie smiled. "Yes you are."

"Mom, call Mr. Porter. Please!"

Annie looked at her daughter and nodded. "I'll give him a call and see what he thinks."

To Annie's surprise and relief, Mr. Porter was actually home. After she explained the situation to him, he immediately agreed but he did have two conditions. "I would like Amy to take her senior tests at the local Christian high school there in Nashville. I know the headmaster at New Life and I'm sure he would agree to this."

"That's fine, John," Annie agreed quickly.

"Also, this request is more of a personal favor." Annie laughed when she listened to John Porter's favor.

"Hang on, John. He's here now. Let me ask him."

Annie's eyes zoomed in on Ryan. "He says Amy can take all her tests at New Life Christian School but he has one more request." Annie smiled. "This one directly involves you."

Ryan grinned. "What?"

"He wants you to sing at graduation. I don't want you to feel forced, Ryan. I know you have a busy spring with the tour gearing up and all. Don't feel pressured."

Ryan laughed. "Annie, tell the man it's a deal. I would do anything to marry you now!"

Annie smiled. "You sure?"

"Absolutely. Ask him if he has any request."

Annie laughed. "Knowing John Porter, I'm sure he will."

Annie wrapped up the conversation with John Porter, made a few notes about things she needed to do and then turned to Ryan. " Hey, big guy, when do you want to get married?"

Ryan pulled her gently into his arms. "How about Wednesday? That would give us plenty of time to make the arrangements and pick our honeymoon spot."

"It's not cutting it too close?"

"What do we have to do?" Ryan winked at her. "Show up at the church and make sure the preacher's there. Doesn't seem like a lot to me."

Annie smacked Ryan's arm. "We need to make arrangements."

"Get specific," Ryan crossed his arms. "What exactly do we need to do?"

"Well," Annie closed her eyes for a second, "clothes for one."

"I think we should wear them." Ryan burst of laughing.

Annie grinned. "I wasn't implying that we shouldn't." She laughed again. "What I meant to say is that should we go informal or formal?"

Ryan's eyes twinkled. "Glad we're wearing clothes. I feel more comfortable in them."

"Ryan…" Annie tone was full of warning.

"Oh yeah, formal or informal. Let's see. What do you want to do? I really don't care."

"Well, I already did the gown thing once. You know, I'd just as soon wear a dress or suit or something like that."

"That sounds perfect to me. Hey, "Ryan said excitedly, "I love that cream colored suit that you brought with you. Why don't you wear that?"

"Mom," Amy came and sat down next to her mother, "I think you should buy a really nice wedding gown, you know, something special that you really love. Remember when you got married you said that you and daddy didn't have any money to buy a dress?"

Annie nodded and glanced at Ryan. "I wore my mother's wedding dress."

"Yeah, and you hated it," Amy said quickly.

Annie laughed. "That's because it didn't fit me well. It was faded and the design was just plain ugly."

Ryan looked at Annie thoughtfully. "You never mentioned the dress thing."

Annie shrugged. "I didn't have a reason to. Your brother and I just wanted to get married. All the outfits and frills were secondary." Annie laughed. "The frills definitely become secondary when you don't have the money."

Ryan shoved his hands in his pockets and paced before her. "Listen, we have the money now. You should get the dress of your dreams. We can make you look like Cinderella."

Annie laughed. "Uh, is that Cinderella before the ball or Cinderella after the ball? There's a huge difference."

Ryan smiled. "I was thinking Cinderella going to the ball."

Annie tried to look serious. "You mean, you want me to arrive at the wedding in a pumpkin." Annie paused. "I don't think that's going to work."

Ryan smiled and knelt down before her. "You know what I mean. We should get all decked out for this. You know," he swung a hand in the air, "the whole nine yards."

Annie smiled. "You're so sweet but I think at this point in my life it's just too much money."

"Listen, when you were young, you didn't have the money. Now that you do, we should do this right."

Annie looked at him and smiled. "It is every girl's dream to get all dressed up. There's something so special about it but there may be a problem."

"I am the problem fixer. Tell me your problems."

"Well," Annie's voice was skeptical, "if we want to get married in a few days there's no way we're going to be able to pull off a big wedding. That takes a lot of time. People plan these events for months and months."

Ryan grinned at her. "Oh ye of little faith…all you have to do is know the right people and get the wheels turning."

"And you know the right people?"

"As a matter of fact," Ryan wiggled his eyebrows at her, "I do. Being in the entertainment business gets you connected. I think if we get the kids helping us on the phones, we could actually pull this off."

Annie's eyes sparkled. "Really?"

"Really and truly."

"Then I have one more request."

"Your wish is my command," Ryan bowed before her.

"Wow, really?" Ryan nodded. "Well, if that's the case, I may want to take a little more time with my wish. I mean, hey, the sky's the limit. Right?"

Ryan grinned. "That's not exactly what I was thinking when I said your wish is my command."

Annie's eyes narrowed. "I thought so. You're a Genie with limitations." Annie laughed and Ryan. "What did you do, flunk out of Genie school?"

"You're such a pest sometimes."

"I know. Listen, this is what I had in mind. If you and I are getting all decked out, I'd like the kids to be in the wedding party and get all decked out too. I think it would be so much fun."

Cheers went up from all the girls but David just groaned. "You're going to make me wear a tie? That's like putting a noose around a man's neck."

"Even worse," Annie laughed, "I was picturing you in a tux with a top hat."

"Really? A top hat," David smiled. "That could be cool. Kind of like the old movies." David looked at his dad. "If you throw in the top hat, I'll wear the monkey suit."

"Just so you know, the top hat isn't going to have a bunny to pull out of it," Ryan smiled at his son.

"Gee Dad," David pouted, "that won't be nearly as much fun. The bunny in the hat is what makes the outfit."

"Deal with it," Ryan mumbled.

"Yeah, I guess I'll have to. Life really is tough."

"We should get back to the planning," Annie looked at Ryan. "Do you have any bridal shops nearby?"

In unison, Ryan, Beth and Nikki shouted, "Beverly's!"

Ryan went on to explain. "Beverly's is the biggest bridal shop in the state. The place is huge. It's the size of three football fields We should be able to find everything in there from dresses, to tuxes to shoes. That place is great." Ryan narrowed his eyes. "Do you know that you can even rent socks?"

"I can see that. You want to make sure they match your tux," Annie stated matter of fact.

"I was just going to wear my white jock socks." Annie looked skeptically at him. "What?" Ryan asked shrugged his shoulders. "They're white. White goes with everything."

"Athletic socks do not go with a tux."

"They're white," Ryan pretended he didn't understand the problem.

"You're renting socks, Buster," Annie laughed at him.

"It seems strange to rent socks."

Annie laughed. "It seems even stranger to wear white athletic socks with a black tux."

"You think so?"

"I know so. Rent the socks."

"What if some guy with stinky feet has worn them before me?" Ryan scrunched his nose up. "That would be kind of gross."

Annie laughed. "They do wash their socks before they rent them out ya know."

Ryan's mouth formed a big O. "Well, I guess if they wash them it would be OK. I mean, I'm more comfortable in my athletic socks but for you, I'll wear the rented socks."

"Thank you," Annie smiled at him.

Ryan shook his head. "The things I do for love."

"So, when are we going to Beverly's?" Nikki asked excitedly. "I love weddings!"

"How about I call them now and see if we can be scheduled in first thing Saturday morning. I bet by noon we'll have everything we need." Ryan looked at Annie.

"Really?"

"Annie," Ryan threw his arms wide, "they have a million dresses in there. I'm sure we can turn you into Cinderella."

"Without the pumpkin," Annie crossed her arms. "I'm not doing the pumpkin thing."

"Don't worry. I wouldn't ask you to." Ryan paused. "I'm going to go call Beverly's now. I'll be back a minute."

Ryan was back within five minutes. "We have an eight o'clock appointment. They're going to give us three salespeople." Ryan smiled. "This is going to be great."

"This is unbelievable," Annie felt like she was dreaming.

Ryan winked at her. "Believe it, Babe. Fairy tales do come true."

"I am starting to believe it." Annie sighed. "OK, what else do we have to do?"

"I should call and book the church." Ryan picked his cell phone up again.

"Uh, Ryan," Annie hesitated.

"What?" He came to stand in front of her.

"You're church is so huge. I'd feel like I'm getting married in a coliseum. Is there any place smaller?"

Ryan nodded thoughtfully. "Yeah, lots of places. What do you have in mind? Are you thinking inside places or outside places?"

Annie looked stunned. "Outside places? I hadn't even thought of that option."

"Dad!" David shouted excitedly, "You could get married at the Victorian Park. They use it all the time for weddings and it has that really cool gazebo."

"Ooh," Nikki cooed excitedly, "if you get married at dusk the little white light outlining the gazebo would be all twinkles. It would look so beautiful."

"That sounds beautiful," Annie's voice was awed.

"Yeah, the twinkle lights get me every time." Ryan laughed.

"Oh, and because it's the end of May the roses around the park and all the flowers will be in bloom! It would be perfect!" Beth looked like she was going to explode in excitement.

"Do you want to book it?" Ryan asked Annie.

"Definitely. It sounds perfect. Book it for seven o'clock."

"I'll call Dad," Nikki grabbed her cell phone from her purse. "I know the head groundskeeper."

"Didn't you go on a date with him last week?" Beth asked.

Nikki laughed. "Like I said, I know the head groundskeeper. I'll go call now."

"OK," Ryan nodded, "another thing to cross off the list. See how easy it is when you have your own personal army of kids? I love a big family!"

"Me too!" Annie reached over and squeezed his hand.

"OK," Ryan winked at her, "What else do we need to do?"

"Well, we probably want chairs for our guests to sit on." Ryan paused. "You know, I think it would be kind of rude to ask them to stand up for the entire service."

Annie laughed. "Yes, I agree. Chairs would be good."

"Hey, I've seen weddings there before and they use wooden white chairs." David smiled at Annie. "They look nice."

"That does sound nice," Annie looked at David. "You wouldn't happen to know a guy that rents chairs like that, would you?"

David smiled. "I know a guy. I am one well connected teen."

"Doesn't Mr. Jerries at your school rent stuff like that?" Ryan asked his son.

"That's my connection," David smiled. "Do you want me to call him?"

Ryan looked at Annie and she nodded. "Go ahead son." Ryan turned back to Annie. "How many chairs do you think we're going to need?"

"Well, I'd say probably fifty from my side," Annie closed her eyes for a minute counting the people she needed to invite in her head. "Yeah, fifty should do it."

"OK, and another fifty on my side." Ryan turned to David. "Tell Mr. Jerries we need one hundred chairs."

"I'm on it Dad," David left the room quickly.

"What do you guys have in mind for flowers?" Beth looked at both of them. "I've spent the last three summers working at Flowerland. I'm sure they would help us put together whatever we needed."

"That's a great idea Beth!" Ryan snapped his fingers. He turned to Annie. "That place is really good. I'd highly recommend them."

"Is that where the flowers came from that you sent me?"

Ryan nodded." Yeah, that's right. You've gotten a bunch of things from them."

"Let's put them to work," Annie smiled at Beth.

"What kind of flowers do you have in mind?" Beth asked.

"Well, I love white roses," Annie said dreamily. "They're my favorite. If I could have a bouquet of white roses I'd be in heaven."

"OK," Ryan smiled at Annie, "heaven it is. Beth, start making a list. White roses for Annie's bouquet and," Ryan turned and looked at Annie, "you want the guys to have a white rose pinned to their lapel?"

"That would be great!"

"OK," Ryan looked back at Beth, "white roses for the guys. How about around the gazebo? I've seen Flowerland decorate that gazebo with garland greens and those twinkling lights. We could have them add some white roses to the garland greens. Does that sound good?"

"That sounds wonderful," Annie smiled at him. "You're going to spoil me."

Ryan winked at her. "You could use a little spoiling." He turned to Beth. " Go make the call and tell them to be generous with the flowers. I want things to look really nice."

"OK Dad, "Beth grabbed her cell phone. "I'll call them now."

"I love delegating responsibilities!" Ryan smirked. "It makes me feel so powerful!" He laughed as Annie shook her head. "Hey," he pointed a finger at her, "we're going to need a car."

"You mean it's too far to walk?" Annie asked teasingly.

"Yes," he eyed her closely. "Don't get sassy with me and when I say we need a car I'm not talking about a VW Bug." Ryan threw his hands in the air. "I mean a limo."

"I've never been in a limo before," Annie replied quietly.

Ryan smiled. "Think of it as your modern day pumpkin. I think if Cinderella could, she would have opted for the limo over the pumpkin."

Annie smiled. "I think you're right."

"I know the limo guy," Ryan was already popping open his cell phone. "Let me make a call." He called right from the living room. Part way through the conversation, he put a hand over the phone and turned to Annie. "Do you want a white limo or a black limo?"

"What do you want?"

"Listen, because of my career, I've ridden in limos a million times-both black and white. This is your call. What does Cinderella want?"

"White!" Annie smiled. Ryan was making her feel like a princess.

Ryan wrapped up his conversation with the limo man and put his cell phone away. "That was easy. The limo will be here at six thirty. The park is only fifteen minutes away, so that should work out good."

"Wow, everything is falling into place." Annie felt the relief washing over her.

Just then Nikki walked into he room. "OK, we've got the park reserved."

"What took so long?" Ryan asked curiously.

"Oh, Jason asked me out for next week and we were trying to work our schedules out."

"Did you?" Ryan smirked.

"Of course," Nikki laughed. "Where there's a will, there's a way." Nikki smiled at Annie. "So, what else is on the list?"

"Honeymoon," Annie purred. "Where do you want to go?" She looked at Ryan excitedly.

"If you could go anywhere in the world, where would you go?" Ryan looked at her seriously. "I want it to be someplace special, not the Budget Hotel or anything."

"Well," Annie sighed, "anywhere but Boston is fine with me."

Ryan laughed. "That's not narrowing it down a whole lot. Can you be a little more specific?"

Annie laughed. "Ryan, I don't care where we go, I just want to be with you."

Ryan winked at her. "I can guarantee I'll be there!" Ryan grinned, "Come on, tell me where you want to go."

"I've never been to Hawaii," Annie whispered more to herself than to him. "Have you?"

Ryan smiled. "Being in the singing business brings me to a lot of places. I have been to Hawaii. It's a beautiful place and I'd love to go back."

"You're not just saying that to be nice, are you?"

Ryan laughed. "Annie, you know me better than that. Besides, we're talking Hawaii here. Who wouldn't want to go to Hawaii?"

"OK," Annie nodded, "what other plans do we have to make for our wedding?"

"Well, let's see. How about the reception? It would probably be nice of us if we fed the crowd." Ryan smirked. "You know, toss them a grilled cheese or something."

Annie laughed. "That's where I draw the line. No grilled cheese sandwiches at our wedding."

Ryan acted insulted. "You are so fussy."

Annie laughed. "Sometimes… do you have any concrete suggestions in this area?"

"Of course I do!" Ryan laughed. "I'm full of wonderful suggestions."

"Let's hear one."

"There's a nice place in town called the Covered Bridge. They have excellent food and a great ambiance. I bet we could rent out one of their banquet rooms."

"At this short notice?"

"Hey, I sang at the manager's wedding last year. I'm sure he will work out something for us."

"That sounds great." Annie crossed another item off the list she had made in her head. " So, what else?"

"There doesn't seem to be that much to do," Ryan grinned. "We need to call some friends and family."

"We can't forget about Rock."

Ryan took his card out of his wallet. "I have been carrying his card with me so I'd have it handy. Do you want to call him or should I?"

"Would you mind if I did? I'd really love to say hi to him."

"Not at all."

Annie smiled. "So, the planning went quicker than I thought."

"See, it's all working out Sweetheart?"

Annie nodded. "You're right."

"Oh, please don't go there. You know I'm always right!" Annie shook her head and groaned.

Ryan pulled her into a big hug. "Listen, I'll use my cell phone and you can use the phone in the kitchen. We can wrap up the rest of the calls."

"Sounds great. Who do you want to call?"

"Let me call the restaurant and you call the travel agency."

"OK," Annie nodded, "I'll call Bob and Rock and the rest of my family and you call your family and friends."

They took off running for the phones with the sound of the kid's laughter trailing them. In an hour, they both returned to the great room, hand and hand, mission accomplished. The wedding was set for Wednesday, May 25, at seven P.M. All the important family members and friends could come. The reception and the honeymoon were all planned.

"Only five more days!" Ryan hugged Annie tightly. "I can't wait!"

"Neither can I!" Annie knew the smile on her face couldn't be any bigger then it was. "Bob and Jude were so excited. Oh, I asked Heidi to be a flower girl. Is that OK?"

Ryan beamed. "Annie, anything is OK with me. I just want to get married." Ryan paused. "Little Heidi is a ticket. She will look so cute as a flower girl."

"Too bad we don't have someone to be a ring bearer," Annie looked at David.

"Uh, no way. I mean, I will support you guys in whatever way I can but don't think I'm going to walk down the aisle with Heidi as a ring bearer." David stared at his dad. "That's not going to happen."

Annie laughed. "I wasn't going to ask you."

"Good thing because I wouldn't do it. That's a job for a little kid. I'm a man." David flexed his muscles. "Hey, ask Tyler. I'm sure he'd look cute at 6'9" or whatever the giant man is, walking with Heidi carrying a little ring sown to a lacy pillow."

Annie sighed. That was the only hard thing about the wedding. She knew Tyler wouldn't be able to make it. His ship was scheduled to be out to sea for three months. She sighed and then chewed her lip. She wished so much he could be there.

"Hey," Ryan put an arm around her, "I'm sorry about Ty. I really am. I wish things were different."

"So do I." Annie thought she was going to cry. Her son was so special to her that she couldn't imagine not having him at her wedding.

"Any chance that they would let him come?" Ryan asked hopefully.

"No. Once he's on the ship they've got him until he comes back. The Coast Guard is very strict that way." Annie laughed. "Probably the President of the United States is the only one that could get him permission to leave."

Ryan didn't say anything but pulled Annie closer to him. "I'm sorry Hon. If you want to wait, we can. I mean, I've waited this long."

Annie shook her head. "Ryan, we really have to get married. We're long overdue."

"I'll agree with that but are you going to be OK with Ty not being here?"

"I think I have to be."

"One good thing about you becoming my wife is that I won't need to stick to the one-a-day rule." Ryan laughed. "I'll be able to kiss you a million times a day."

"Isn't a million kisses a day a little extreme?"

"Actually," Ryan grinned, "I think I may have underestimated it. I think I should make it two million!"

Soon everyone started shuffling off to bed. Sleep came hard that night for Annie. Her mind was still spinning with all the details of everything going on. The wedding planning had gone off without a hitch except for Tyler. Annie felt the tears sting her eyes and slide down her face and onto her pillow. She wished so much her son could be there. He had been such a huge support through everything. Not having him there would definitely put a damper on the day. "Please, God," Annie prayed silently, "if there's any way to get Tyler there, please arrange it. I want him there to give me away. Please, Father, please make a way."

Twelve

Saturday morning, bright and early, everyone loaded into the Suburban to go to Beverly's. The atmosphere was almost as festive as Christmastime. Annie never knew planning a wedding could be so much fun.

As they pulled into the parking lot at Beverly's, Annie mouth dropped open in shock. "This place is huge."

Ryan laughed. "I wasn't exaggerating. It really is the size of three football fields."

"Their selection must be incredible."

"It is," Ryan smiled at his bride-to-be. "That's why I was so confident that we could find everything we need here." Ryan glanced at Annie. "If they don't have it, we probably don't need it."

When they walked into the bridal shop, the sales clerks were waiting for them. "Hi, you must be Annie." A tall slender blonde lady extended her hand to Annie. "I'm Michelle, and this is Christy and Marie. We're going to be your sales clerks today. Why don't you come with us?"

Annie paused. "Ryan and the kids are going to need help too. Shouldn't we divide up?"

Michelle smiled. "The three of us are here to help you. We have other sales clerks waiting to help them. Come on. I have so much to show you. This is going to be fun."

Annie kissed Ryan good-bye and turned to Amy, Beth, and Nikki. "Listen, I want you guys to pick out the outfits that you're going to wear."

"Really?" They all squealed.

Annie smiled and nodded. "I want you to have fun with this. Just make sure the dresses match and they're on the traditional side. I'll be picking a traditional style gown so we should match nicely."

Annie then turned and went off with her three helpers. After just a few minutes, she realized they were right. This was going to be fun. They had rows and rows of dresses in Annie's size all set out for her.

"Now," Michelle said excitedly, "we were given strict orders by Ryan that you are not to look at prices. You should pick out what you like and not worry about anything else. OK?"

Annie nodded. "What if they dress I pick out needs altering?"

Michelle smiled. "Don't worry. We have seamstresses right on location. That's no problem. Why don't you start looking through the racks? The traditional styles are to the right and the contemporary styles are to the left."

"Thanks." Annie went immediately to the traditional styles. Every gown looked so beautiful. She felt like she had entered Cinderella's closet. It was fairy tale land at its best.

The next dress in line caught Annie's eye. It was Victorian in style with a high lacy neckline, full skirt, and petite satin buttons that ran halfway down the back. It was simple but elegant, understated but extravagant. The more Annie looked at it; the more she fell in love with it.

"I think you should try this one on," Michelle took the dress and led Annie to a changing room. "I think you'd look very good in this style. It's very popular."

After Annie put the dress on, she turned around slowly and looked into the long set of wall mirrors. She gasped. The dress looked even better on her than it did on the rack. It had a whimsical, airy kind of flow that she didn't see before. It made her feel like a storybook fairy princess. It was simply enchanting.

"There's a larger set of mirrors in the hall. Why don't you come this way." Michelle led her down the hall to the mirrors. As she looked at the dress again, she fell in love with it. "This is the one," she smiled at Michelle.

"You look beautiful," Michelle commented sincerely. "It's charming."

Just then, Annie saw Ryan's reflection in the mirror. She turned slowly to face him. His mouth hung open and he looked completely dazed. "Do you like it?" He didn't respond. "Ryan," Annie asked louder this time, "do you like the dress?"

The girls helping Annie laughed and then walked away to give them some privacy.

Annie walked toward Ryan. "What do you think?"

The slow smile that spread across Ryan's face was precious. He took Annie's hand and squeezed it gently. "Sweetheart, Cinderella's got nothing on you. You look absolutely gorgeous. I just mean, like wow. The dress is so beautiful Honey, but not nearly as beautiful as you. You make the dress."

Annie thought she was going to cry. "Thank you," she squeaked out in a tight voice. "You make me feel like a princess every day."

Ryan's eyes welled up. "That's because you are to me."

"Thank you. I love you."

"I love you, too."

"Thank you for making this dream come true. The wedding is going to be such a special time."

Ryan nodded. He was still staring at Annie like she was the most beautiful girl on the face of the earth. He made her feel so cherished and loved. "Listen, I'm going to change out of this and then I want to see how all of you made out."

Ryan smiled. "I'll be waiting for you."

Annie was very pleased with the guy's outfits. They chose the traditional black tux, with long tails and white shirts. Unfortunately, she didn't get to see them all decked out because they had already changed out of them.

David still had his top hat in his hand. "I love this thing!" He waved it at Annie. "I always thought I had to be a magician or in some Shakespeare play to wear one. This is great." He put the hat on for Annie and strutted around.

"You look great!" Annie smiled. "The black top hat made him look very distinguished.

"Dad says we can even carry these fancy wooden canes if I promise not to hit anyone or trip them."

"Did you promise?" Annie asked.

"Not yet," David whispered, "I was kind of hoping that he'd forget about that part. I can think of several cousins coming that I'd love to clobber!"

"I heard that!" Ryan said stiffly. "No promise, no cane."

"Aw Dad, can't I at least smack Willie around a little bit? You know he deserves a good clobbering!"

Ryan smiled at his son. "You're right. He does. I'll make a deal with you. You can whack him after the ceremony. OK?"

David smiled. "Now you're talking!"

"I'm not giving you permission to hurt him," Ryan warned.

"Dad, the threat of harm is better than harm itself. Willie's such a little weasel." David turned to Annie. "This is payback time."

Just then the girls strolled out. They were wearing matching mauve colored dresses that were Victorian, lacy, and looked beautiful on them. They suddenly looked so grown up that Annie felt a lump growing in her throat.

"Don't you love them?" Amy asked.

"You look beautiful," Annie was already dabbing at her eyes.

"What's wrong Aunt Annie?" Nikki asked.

"You all look so grown up!" Everyone laughed.

"Mom," Amy walked next to her, "look at this flower girl's dress we found for Heidi. Isn't it perfect?"

Annie looked at it and smiled. It was perfect. It was a shade darker than their dresses and had a big bow on the back that was just too cute. "She's going to love that."

As the girls went back to change out of their dresses, Annie slipped her hand into Ryan's. "I think we're finished here."

Ryan smiled. "Yeah, and it's not even noon."

Annie narrowed her eyes at him. "Did you get the socks?"

Ryan laughed. "Yeah, I got the socks. I'm making everyone wear them. I figure if I have to wear rented socks, so do they."

Annie laughed and hugged her prince charming. As they left Beverly's, she marveled at how easily everything had come together. Now if we could only get Ty here, she silently prayed, everything would be perfect.

Thirteen

The night of the big concert had finally arrived. While Annie waited with the others for Ryan to come on stage, she scanned the huge coliseum. She had managed to talk Ryan into letting her trade her front row seat in for a balcony seat. She wanted to be far enough back from the stage to really take in the scene around her. David and Beth were talking on one side of her and Amy and Nikki on the other. She hardly heard them. She was so excited.

As Annie's eyes scanned the audience, she smiled at the diversity in age. There was a mom holding a young tot, while right next to them an older couple sat holding hands and smiling at each other. The first floor of the coliseum was the rowdy section. It was filled with energetic teenagers that appeared to be having a party of their own. At a quick glance, Annie noticed that their food selection was impressive. She spotted popcorn, nachos with cheese sauce, candy bars and soft drinks. The kids knew how to have a good time.

A movement on stage drew Annie's eyes there. The stage crew was still making a few adjustments. Annie took a minute to study the stage area before the show started. It was a very large stage filled with a lot of instruments. There was a big drum set sitting center stage but put toward the back. Sitting directly on the center stage mark was a black piano. Annie smiled as she thought of Ryan playing it. As she scanned the stage, she saw at least four electric guitars and a few acoustic ones as well. The horn section was unbelievable. Annie spotted trumpets, saxophones, trombones, French horns and even a tuba. The instruments had been set up between ramps and walkways. It all looked so fun. Annie smiled as she pictured an energetic Ryan Jones running around them. She couldn't wait for the show to begin.

She didn't have to wait long. A moment later the lights dimmed and Ryan's band came running unto the stage. They began playing the first song and then Ryan ran onto the stage with a cordless mic and started singing. The crowd exploded in applause and jumped to their feet just as Annie knew they would. She stood up as well trying to enjoy the show as a fan and not as Ryan's soon to be bride.

Annie noticed that Ryan had the crowd in the palm of his hand right from the moment he jumped on stage. Their love for him was evident. Even the teenagers had stopped eating and were standing in front of their seats following Ryan's every move as though he were the Piped Piper. She smiled as she thought about Ryan's witness for the Lord. He was a wonderful, godly example for people to look up to and if they were going to follow him like the Piped Piper, then she knew he would lead them directly to the Father. He was a light for Jesus and he wanted his songs to draw people closer to God. That's why he got up on stage and sang night after night. He had a tender heart for the people who came out to see him and a strong desire to make sure that throughout his concert they came to know God better.

Annie smiled as she watched Ryan on stage. He was quick and energetic and interacted with his band members and fans along the way. He was fun to watch yet throughout all the excitement you could not miss the clear gospel message. It was obvious that Ryan's faith was the most important thing in his life. His songs and actions clearly reflected that to his audience.

He would often stop between songs and talk with his audience like he was talking to a group of old friends. He didn't have to try hard to connect with his fans. They loved him and their hearts were open to him in a very trusting way. Time and time again Ryan took that trust and pointed them to God. Ryan helped his audience center on God's message of love, salvation, forgiveness, hope and peace. He helped his audience see that they were priceless in God's eyes. Ryan had a gift for getting people fired up for God and to live for Him. It was obvious that Ryan wanted God to have the glory in his concert and not himself. Ryan stuck to his priorities and that was always putting God first.

As Annie continued to watch Ryan, she really gained a new insight into the ministry that he had. Ryan loved God so deeply and he loved his fans too. He had a deep desire to help people make that godly connection. He was clearly reaching out to them, standing in the gap, trying to pull them closer to God.

After ninety minutes, the concert ended. When Ryan exited the stage after two encores, the crowd was still going crazy. The teenage girls were the worst. They screamed at the top of their lungs declaring their steadfast love for him. The stage became scattered with roses. Once again, Annie noticed that the majority of the flowers came from the teenage girls in the front row. It was clear that they were smitten with him. Annie laughed. They really had it bad. She didn't mind their devotion to Ryan as long as things cooled down after they left the coliseum. After all, he was her man and she felt pretty strongly about that. She didn't mind sharing him for the concerts as long as every single female fan in the auditorium realized he was her man.

As Annie left the concert hall with the kids, she felt completely drained but felt her heart so much closer to God. The words of Ryan's songs had touched her heart and she knew that she would carry them with her forever.

Annie listened to the kids talk about the concert on the ride home. Ryan was making a separate get a way and would join the family a few hours later at home. It was important for him to leave the concert hall immediately so his devoted fans didn't trample him.

David was sitting next to Annie on the ride home and asked her what she thought about the concert. Annie smiled. "I loved it. It was great."

"How did you feel about the chicks screaming their brains out at my dad?"

Annie laughed. "Well, they were pretty loud. I'm sure he heard them."

"Stuff like that always happens to Dad. He has to have security so the female fans don't storm the stage."

"I think some of them get a little carried away."

"A little?" David looked at her in astonishment. "Some of those chicks are downright nuts. I mean," he sounded exasperated, "that's my dad up there. I want to yell to them to get a grip. Ya know?"

Annie nodded. "Yeah, I know but I don't think they'd hear you. They're too busy shouting how much they love him."

"It's all part of the business. I think Dad handles it very well. He never lets their praise go to his head. He doesn't take that stuff too seriously."

"I'm glad," Annie laughed. "If he did he'd have an ego the size of Montana."

At home, the kids made a beeline for the kitchen to raid the frig. Annie smiled. They were teenagers and they were clearly starving. She was not starving but she was exhausted. She headed for the great room and collapsed on a couch. Annie snagged an afghan that was draped over the back of the couch and pulled it over her. As she settled in she thought about the concert. She had no idea that Ryan was such a huge celebrity. She always had known he was famous but the status that he had with his fans tonight bordered on super stardom. It was a little overwhelming for her. The young female fans were obviously smitten with him and for more reasons than just his songs. It was a strange feeling to hear others describe her future husband as a hunk and a totally gorgeous hunk.

Annie understood that the teens needed someone to look up to and idolize in their own teenage way. If they weren't admiring Ryan, they might be looking up to someone who didn't love God and someone who might lead them the wrong way. Annie fell asleep thinking it was going to take some getting used to being Ryan the celebrity's wife. She knew God would help her adjust but just the same, she knew it would be an adjustment.

Annie woke up some time later to something tickling her nose. As she tried to brush the irritating object away, without opening her eyes, a low laugh rumbled near her ear. Her eyes flew open immediately and through a sleepy gaze she saw Ryan kneeling next to her.

"Sweetheart, I hope you're not going to brush all my kisses away like that!" Ryan was smiling charmingly at her. It always melted her heart when he did that.

Annie pulled herself up to a sitting position. Ryan wrapped the afghan around her and then sat down next to her. "I guess I must have fallen asleep." Annie covered a huge yawn with her hand.

Ryan laughed. He gently ran a hand through his future bride's hair. "No doubt about it Babe. You were off in dreamland."

Annie smiled at him. "The concert was great. You really have a gift for connecting with your audience." Annie took Ryan's hand and held it gently. "You have a way of making people feel special to God and special to you. That's a gift Ryan."

"That's what it's all about Honey. I want them to know how important they are to the Father and how much He loves them." Ryan smiled. "I'm just a lighthouse."

Annie smiled. "You have a great way of conveying that to your audience."

"Thanks Hon," he leaned over and kissed her on the cheek.

"You must be exhausted! I got worn out just watching you!"

Ryan laughed. "It's starting to hit me a little right now."

Can I do anything for you?"

"No Sweetie," he held her hand tightly. "Just having you next to me is wonderful. I love you Annie."

Annie smiled. "I love you too."

Ryan looked into Annie's eyes. "You have no idea how good it is to hear you say those words. My heart feels like it's going to explode with happiness."

Annie leaned over and kissed Ryan gently on the cheek. "I love you, I love you, I love you!"

As their eyes started to fill with tears, Annie whispered, "I'm so sorry that I couldn't say those words to you before when you said them to me." Annie wiped the tears out of her eyes. "I promise I'll make it up to you. I'll say I love you so much that you'll get sick of hearing it!"

Ryan smiled. "Hon, I'll never get sick of hearing you say those words."

Ryan leaned over and kissed Annie smack on the lips. It was a quick kiss but filled with a lot of love. "I can't wait until you're my wife."

"Me too!"

"Annie," Ryan sighed loudly, "it's going to seem like an eternity until our wedding. I think the next few days are going to the longest days of my life!"

"I know what you mean. I think we should plan to stay incredibly busy and make sure we're always around other people."

Ryan nodded seriously. "That's a good plan. I don't want to blow it right before the wedding day. I mean, I've been so good this far, what's a few more hours."

"These next few hours are going to be the toughest for us to get through."

"I agree. We will keep busy and stay in a big group. I don't want to be alone with you after tonight. I don't trust myself. In a moment of weakness I don't want to make a mistake. Ya know?"

"Same with me."

"We can pack for our honeymoon and tie up loose ends. Oh, are Sadie and Tag going to stay with the kids while we're gone?"

Ryan nodded. "Yes, that's all settled. Sadie runs a real tight ship so you don't need to worry about a thing. She's a regular drill sergeant."

"Good," Annie agreed. "I think they may need that kind of structure."

They sat quietly for a moment and then Ryan turned so he could see Annie's face clearly. "I need to ask you something and I want you to be completely honest with me."

Annie nodded. "OK, shoot."

"Well, we talked about the concert but you never said anything about the fans."

"They were great!" Annie replied quickly.

"Annie," Ryan's voice became very serious, "I mean, more specifically, the teenage girls' reaction to me." He paused for a moment looking utterly embarrassed. "I don't know what to do about it so I basically ignore them. Personally, I find it very embarrassing."

Annie smiled. "Oh, those fans!" She slapped the side of her head absentmindedly. "You mean the yelling, foot stomping, screaming at the top of their lungs, rose throwing fans." She looked at him and he nodded. "I didn't notice them at all."

They both broke of laughing. "Annie…" Ryan mumbled, "what did you think about them?"

"Well, they sure were enthusiastic!"

"And…" he coached her.

"Loud, they were very loud."

"And…"

"Listen Ryan, I know what you're getting at and I'll level with you. I'll have to admit, it was way more than I expected. I mean honestly, those girls have got mouths on them!" Ryan and Annie both laughed.

"Yeah, they do! There's no way I'm not going to hear them!" Ryan paused. "I need to know if it's something you can handle."

"Ryan," Annie's tone was confident, "you have proven your love to me time and time again. You make me feel secure in our love. I don't feel threatened in any way. I feel safe." Annie smiled at him. "The way you look at me makes me feel like the most cherished girl on the face of the earth."

"That's because you are to me."

Annie nodded slowly. "I know that Ryan. You show me that all the time through your love and your actions toward me. I feel like that if we continue to put God first in our lives and our relationship, if we love each other with all our hearts and always talk as honestly and openly to each other as we are right now, we'll be fine."

Ryan hugged her. "I agree completely but we must also guard our relationship. We must never let anyone or anything get between us. Promise me Annie, "Ryan said urgently, "that if anything is ever bothering you, whether it's big or small, promise me that you'll come to me so we can talk it out."

"I will and you do the same."

Ryan grinned. "No problem on this end. You know I'll come after you! I mean, I've been coming after you for almost a year now. I'm a man who knows what he wants."

Annie laughed. "Yes you are!"

"What I want is you!"

"I'm almost all yours Sweetheart. I love you, Ryan!"

"Right back at you! I love you too, Annie!"

Ryan paused thoughtfully. "So, you think you can really handle the screaming chicks?"

Annie smiled. "Ryan, as long as I know that your heart is close to God and I'm the only girl for you they can scream all they want. I mean, I think some kids just need to have someone to look up to in a really big way. Keep pointing them to God Ryan. He's put you in such a special position to reach a dying world."

"I know Annie. I aim to give God my best."

"In spite of the screaming girls?"

"Definitely in spite of the screaming girls!"

Fourteen

The morning of the wedding, the house was as busy as a crowded airport. The relatives had flown in from all parts of the country and people were scurrying around trying to get ready for the evening wedding. Ryan and Annie sat at the kitchen table watching the mob run around the house. Ryan suddenly laughed. "I think we're the calmest people in this house. Even Banjo seems nervous."

Annie smiled at the dog. "I think he's feeling nervous because he's been invaded by all these strangers. He will feel better when things get back to normal."

By mid afternoon, Ryan left to oversee the wedding site and David went with him. They took their tuxes and planned to change at Tag and Sadie's house. They wanted to leave the main house for all the girls to get ready. The rest of the afternoon consisted of a fingernail painting party and helping each other with hair and make up. Annie was so excited when the time came for her to put on her gown. She loved her dress and was so glad that Ryan had talked her into getting it.

The girls were still getting dressed so Annie made her way down stairs and into the kitchen. The sound of her stomach growling reminded her that she hadn't eaten dinner. She went to the frig and grabbed the contents to make a turkey sandwich. As she began to eat it, Amy came flying around the corner.

"Mom!" she gasped. "What are you doing!"

Annie smiled. "Eating dinner," she answered calmly.

"You're in your dress!" Amy seemed totally panicked.

Annie had to laugh. "That's right. Do you love it, or what."

Amy sighed loudly. "Aren't you afraid that you're going to spill something on it?"

"No," Annie said confidently.

"I would be so nervous!"

Annie laughed. "You are so nervous!" She smiled at her daughter. "Listen, I was hungry and I knew if I didn't eat something my stomach would be growling all through the ceremony."

"I'm so nervous I don't think I can eat at all."

"Why are you nervous? You're not getting married."

"I'm nervous because you're not nervous at all. How on earth can you sit there so calmly?" Amy had lost it.

"Sweetie, I am calm because I have given this a lot of thought. I didn't rush into it. I know Ryan is the man for me."

"I'm glad Mom," Amy dropped down into a chair next to her. "Just ignore me while I have my nervous breakdown."

"You should try to relax. I want you to enjoy tonight."

"OK," Amy sounded like she was trying to convince herself, "I am going to relax."

"Good. Now while you're relaxing, can you go tell the other girls that the limo just pulled in?"

Amy screamed. " The limo is here! Oh no. The limo is here. I'll go tell them." Annie laughed as her daughter ran from the room. She prayed Amy would be able to pull it together enough to enjoy the evening.

The limo ride was fun with all the girls. Amy was beginning to calm down some and actually seemed like she was enjoying the ride. As they pulled into Victorian Park, the driver brought Annie up to the main house. She was to wait there for the ceremony to begin. The girls were to go to the area where the gazebo was.

Annie walked around the old mansion trying to kill time before the ceremony. As she came to a large room off the entranceway, she abruptly stopped. A man was standing there with her back to her. She noticed two things about him right away. He was very tall and he was dressed in a wedding tux. As he slowly turned around, time stood still for a moment. Finally, she found her voice enough to whisper, "Ty."

Tyler quickly crossed the room and took his mother in his arms. He gave her a big hug and then suddenly pulled away." I don't want to wrinkle you. You look so beautiful."

"You can go ahead and wrinkle me all you want. I want another hug!"

As mother and son embraced, tears ran down both of their cheeks. "I have missed you so much," Annie held Tyler tightly. "Tell me, how did you manage to get here?"

Tyler smiled. "Mom, you're not going to believe this, but one of Ryan Jones's biggest fans is the President of the United States."

"Tell me you're kidding," Annie was in shock.

Tyler shook his head. "No. I'm not. Ryan called the President of the United States, and asked him if he could free me from my duties for a few hours."

"I can't believe this!"

"Neither could I, but, he is the President and the commander in chief of the armed forces. So," Tyler shrugged, "I had a private escort from my ship in the Med. to Tennessee. I felt like I was the President!"

"I prayed that God would get you here, I just didn't think it involved the President."

Annie and Tyler sat down on the couch. Annie laughed as she wiped her face with a tissue. "My makeup claims that it's waterproof, but I'm pretty sure that I'm going to cry it all off by the end of the night."

"Mom, you don't need that junk. You're naturally very beautiful."

Annie squeezed Tyler's hand. "You're naturally very sweet. Someday, you're going to make some girl a wonderful husband."

"I'm in no rush Mom."

Annie laughed. "Neither am I, that's why I said someday."

Annie and Tyler could hear the music start up and knew that was their cue to make their way toward the gazebo. Tyler gave his mother his arm, and they slowly walked toward the crowd.

"I'm so glad that you're here to give me away," Annie whispered emotionally.

"Mom, so am I. I am so proud of you."

Annie turned and looked at her son. "I'm so proud of you too."

As they made their way to the back of all the white wooden guest chairs, Annie felt stunned by the beautiful scene in front of her. The park had been transformed into a fairytale world. The gazebo was decorated with greenery and so many white roses and baby breathe that the twinkling white lights had to peek out from behind them. The roses in the park were at their peak. The fragrant flowers, in all different colors, surrounded the gazebo and wedding area adding their own natural beauty. Annie smiled. Enchanting was the only word she could think of. Everything looked so charming and utterly enchanting.

Annie watched Heidi slowly walk down the white runner toward the gazebo. The runner had flowering white dogwood trees on either side of it. Heidi made her way through the white flowery tunnel, performing her flower girl duties very seriously. She carefully, almost methodically dropped the pink rose petals on the runner. Everyone was smiling at her because she was just so cute. When Heidi had finished her job, she took her seat between Bob and Jude.

As the wedding march started, Annie and Tyler began their walk through the white flowering tunnel. When Annie's eyes locked with Ryan's, she didn't notice anyone or anything else but him. He held her complete focus.

Ryan was so excited to see Annie that he leaned down and kissed her quickly on the check. "Now son," Rock said in his deep baritone voice, "you're supposed to follow certain rules here. You're supposed to wait until I pronounce you man and wife before you kiss your bride."

Ryan smiled while the guests laughed kindly. Suddenly all the patience he had over the last few months was gone. This beautiful woman standing next to him was ready to commit to him for better or for worse and he was more than anxious to start forever with Annie.

As Rock began the ceremony, Ryan gently took Annie's hand. She smiled up at him and couldn't help but notice how incredibly handsome he looked in his black tux and top hat. He looked like a very attractive Dickens character come to life. He saw her staring at him and winked. She smiled back. She didn't care if others saw her staring at him. He was her man and in a few minutes they'd be legal.

The love in Ryan's eyes captivated her. He let his heart shine through his eyes and the love she saw there simply took her breath away. She had never felt more cherished in her entire life.

Rock cleared his throat and Annie suddenly snapped out of her trance. She looked at him with questioning eyes and he shook his head and laughed. "I've been waiting for you to join us again, Dear. This is the part where you say your vows." Rock smiled at Annie and she nodded.

She slowly repeated the words that she had memorized. Her vows were short but meaningful. She pledged to Ryan her love and loyalty. She vowed to be a good wife and friend and stand by him in the good times as well as the hard ones. She promised to help him grow closer to the Lord and support him in anyway she could. Her heart belonged to him. She finished her vows in a voice that was so tight she felt she was choking. As she looked up into Ryan's eyes she could see he was fighting to hold back his own emotions.

When it was his turn to say his vows, he let go of Annie's hand and turned and picked up a guitar that he had hidden nearby. He sang a love song to her that he had written just for the wedding. It was a beautiful song that declared his love for her and his promise to be a good husband and father. He promised to cherish her and help keep her heart close to the Lord. By the time he had finished his song, there was not a dry eye in the place.

As Ryan came back over to stand next to Annie, he leaned down and kissed her on the check. Rock laughed. "I can see that you have absolutely no respect for the rules here Mr. Jones."

Ryan laughed. "I'm being as patience as I can Rock. You'd better get to the I do's."

That's the next thing that Rock did. He pronounced them husband and wife, and then said loudly, "Now, you may kiss the bride." The cheers rose up around them and Ryan whisked Annie down the aisle and into the limo. As the door closed behind them, they couldn't stop smiling at each other.

"I love you, Annie."

"I love you, too."

"You know," he winked at her, "I'm very tempted to tell the limo driver to go to the airport instead of the restaurant."

"Are you a little anxious to begin our honeymoon?" Annie laughed.

"I'm extremely anxious to begin our honeymoon. I don't want to share you anymore."

"Well, now I'm Mrs. Ryan Jones, we'll have our whole lives to spend together."

Ryan took her hand and pulled her to himself. He leaned down slowly and kissed her passionately like he'd wanted to do since the first time he met her. A few minutes later, he reluctantly released her. "That is only a preview of things to come Sweetheart."

Annie smiled. "If that's the preview I can't wait until the main show."

Ryan leaned down and kissed her forehead. "I love you, Annie. We're so good together. I know that we're going to have an awesome life together."

Annie smiled back at her prince charming. "I agree. Life has been pretty awesome since we met. I look forward to spending my life with you and growing old with you. I love you, Ryan. I love you with all my heart."

"I love you too. I can't imagine life getting any better than this but I know in my heart that it will. This is just the start Annie. God has brought us together and God has blessed us. This is only the beginning of a very wonderful and special life together."

As the limo driver took off for the Covered Bridge Restaurant, Ryan spent the rest of ride kissing his bride. God had been good to them. He had blessed them both with a second chance at love, life and true happiness. As Ryan looked at Annie for a minute, he couldn't imagine a man more blessed than himself. God had been good and this was only the beginning. Everyday with Annie was going to be an adventure, and he looked forward to each one.

Penny's Cove

Penny's Cove can be found just off of Cedar Island, which is one of the three hundred, small, quaint islands located on Lake Winnipesaukee. Set in the heart of the White Mountains of New Hampshire, this fast-paced novel is filled with mystery, suspense, romance, comedy, and intrigue.

Abandoned by her mother and with a father who is rarely around, Meghan Kane tries to be both mother and father to her mischievous five-year-old sister, while keeping the family marina afloat. As Meghan runs the water taxi between the lakes many islands, her long time boyfriend, Daniel Hatch and his father pilot the Sally G., which is the last operating United States Mailboat in the entire country. Meghan falls into a routine taxiing her passengers between the islands and the mainland and to the popular boater's church service at Alton Bay on Sundays.

As the summer rolls on, a rich and very beautiful debutant from Boston tries to steal Meghan's boyfriend away, while at the same time, Reid Kensington, the very popular and extremely handsome senator's son becomes determined to win her heart.

Amidst endless summer evenings, small picturesque New England villages, boardwalks, beach parties, and late night bonfires Meghan learns firsthand how much people really can change and how empty promises can be if they're not based on God. She's learns that God is truly a father to the fatherless and one she can rely on her entire life.

One

*M*eghan leaned against the white wooden railing and curiously watched the docks below. It was a Friday night and the waterfront at Weir's Beach was alive with activity. Behind her, the boardwalk was full of people. There were walkers, joggers, bikers, eaters, rollerbladers and the kids on skateboards that loved the challenge of swerving in and out of a large crowd.

There were parents pushing babies in baby carriages, some happy and some not as happy. Meghan smiled at a group of little girls that walked by with a mom. They all had pink balloons in one hand and pink cotton candy in the other. They looked very cute and very coordinated.

The smell of cheeseburgers and hot dogs drifted through the air, and as if on cue, Meghan's stomach growled. You could get almost any type of food down at Weir's Beach. Meghan laughed. Whatever was passing in front of her at the moment was the food she found herself craving. It all made her mouth water.

Meghan watched a little boy that looked to be around four years old pass by with his mom and dad. He was holding a double decker chocolate ice cream cone with both of his chubby little hands wrapped around it. He had a very determined look on his face as he carefully attacked his ice cream cone. Meghan smiled as she noticed he was wearing not only a cute blue sailor suit, he was also wearing a good deal of his chocolate ice cream as well.

A scuffle on the north side of the docks drew Meghan's attention. Some tourist teenagers had pushed the mascot for the Taco House into the lake again. Jimmy Stewart, the local Sheriff at Weir Beach, was helping the costumed person out of the lake. Meg felt sorry for the mascot. Dressed as a large taco, the mascot roller-skated around the boardwalk trying to draw customers to the Taco House. At least once a week, a group of mean kids would grab the taco man by the arms and skate him into the lake. Meghan frowned at the sight. That was a job she would never do in a million years. She could think of many other ways to embarrass herself without doing that.

Meghan turned around and lazily looked out at the docks again. The docks were lined with almost every kind of boat imaginable. There were jet ski's in every color, sailboats, both big and small, and of course, the ever-popular powerboats. Meghan laughed at the thought of how her Aunt Birdie called powerboats stink boats. Aunt Birdie was a sailor at heart. She couldn't imagine anything nicer than the quiet solitude of a sailboat as it noiselessly glided through the water.

As Meghan continued to watch the docks, she spotted Mr. Hatch working on his mailboat. He spied her at the same time and waved. Mr. Hatch was like a second father to her. The Hatch family lived on Pine Tree Island, which was only thirty feet from Cedar Island where Meg lived. She spent a lot of time with their family and felt more at home in the Hatch house than she did in her own house.

Meghan loved and respected Mr. Hatch. He was a strong Christian man and still happily married to his high school sweetheart for over twenty years. Mr. Hatch was always so nice to everyone, whether they were a friend or a stranger. His opinion of strangers was simply that they were friends that he hadn't had the pleasure of meeting yet.

Meghan smiled as she watched Capt. Hatch get his mailboat ready for the next day's deliveries. The Sally G. was a floating treasure on Lake Winnipesaukee. The boat was extremely popular with tourists and loved by locals as if it were their own.

As Meghan turned back to the boardwalk, she saw Daniel coming toward her. He smiled and waved at her and a moment later was at her side. "How's the most beautiful girl on the lake doing tonight?"

Meghan beamed. He always made her feel treasured. "Great now that you're here."

Daniel leaned over and kissed Meg softly on the check. "I love you," he whispered in her ear.

"I love you, too." She couldn't stop smiling. Every time she was around Daniel Hatch she couldn't help but smile. He was everything that she had always dreamed of. Daniel was tall, dark haired and extremely handsome. He carried himself with a confidence that was well beyond his years. He was kind and gentle to all and sensitive in ways that she never thought a man could be. The little things in life counted with Daniel and he was so good at reminding her how much he loved her. He was a dream come true for her.

Daniel's face turned in the direction of the docks below. When he saw his dad, a quick smile spread across his face. "Hey Dad," he shouted toward the Sally G., "do you need any help with your baby?"

Mr. Hatch laughed loudly. "No son, I'm just getting Sally ready for tomorrow's deliveries."

"Do you have a heavy load?"

"Yes," Mr. Hatch took his handkerchief out of his back pocket and wiped his brow. "A family from Boston has bought the Bannister mansion and they'll be moving in tomorrow. I have a lot of boxes to deliver in the morning."

"If you want, I'll ride shotgun with you Dad," Daniel's love for his father was clearly evident. "Maybe I can get some of the gang together and we can help you. It should make things go quite a bit faster."

"I'd appreciate it Daniel," Mr. Hatch sounded very grateful. "Thank you."

As Mr. Hatch went back to work, Meghan looped her hand through Daniel's. "Do you ever look at your dad and feel like you're seeing yourself twenty years down the road?"

Daniel smiled and nodded slowly. "All the time."

Daniel squeezed Meg's hand as they stood quietly watching the Mount Washington ferry slowly pull away from the dock. The Mount Washington was the largest ferry on the lake. It had four wide decks and boasted a passenger capacity of over a thousand. Every day they had a variety of entertainment to amuse their passengers and their dinner buffet was prepared by some of the finest chefs in all of New Hampshire.

As Meghan watched the passengers on the decks of the Mount Washington, a smile grew and slowly spread across her face. Some of the passengers were waving good-bye to people on the boardwalk; others had already starting enjoying the buffet, while others were watching her as she watched them. She laughed and Daniel glanced at her curiously. "People watching is so much fun. There's never a dull moment."

Daniel grinned. "It's the best sport of all and I'd have to say, most of the time, very entertaining."

A loud booming voice could be heard over the ferry's P.A. system. Daniel shook his head and laughed. "Capt. Jimmy is beginning his entertaining dialogue of the lake."

Meg smiled. "That man is so funny. Once he gets a mic in his hand, it's like his standup comedian role begins."

Daniel laughed at a joke that Capt. Jimmy was telling his passengers. "I'll tell you, Broadway is missing out on the biggest ham that ever lived."

They watched the ferry for a few more minutes as it slowly made it's way to Rockport Harbor. Meg loved how the little white lights outlined the top of the ship. It made the Mount Washington look romantic and whimsical. More than one local had called the ferry the Love Boat and she could see why. It was a floating opportunity for many.

Daniel gently squeezed Meghan's hand. "I've got something for you."

Meghan loved the way Daniel's brown eyes twinkled when he was excited. "What?" she asked curiously. Daniel was a master at giving good surprises.

Daniel's face grew thoughtful. "It's something that I've wanted to give you for a long time."

Meghan stared at her boyfriend. She was more than interested to what he might be up to.

Daniel smiled lovingly. "A very, very long time." He paused as he dug into his blue cargo shorts. He pulled out a small plastic box and gently placed it in Meghan's hands. "It's only a token Meg. It's a promise of things to come."

Meghan's heart began to race. When a guy says that to you, marriage, white dresses and diamond rings run though your mind. Meg opened the little box and gasped. A bubblegum machine, diamond engagement ring sat in the middle of a clump of cotton ball. Meghan's heart melted as she watched Daniel take the bubblegum machine ring and slide it onto her engagement finger.

"Meghan," his voice had grown husky with emotion, "I'm going to get you a real engagement ring as soon as I've saved up enough money." Daniel's voice cracked and Meg felt the emotion of it strike her right in the heart. "I love you Meghan. I always have and I always will." He turned her head slightly so their eyes met. "Will you marry me?"

The brilliant smile that covered Meghan's face answered the question before she could. In a voice filled with wonder, awe and excitement, Meg answered Daniel confidently. "Yes, Daniel, I will marry you. I love you."

Meghan couldn't stop smiling. She had always loved Daniel Hatch. She honestly couldn't remember a time when she hadn't love him. They had grown up on Lake Winnipesaukee all their lives. They had played together since they were babies, yet as they grew up, a love that was special and deep grew between them. He was her childhood sweetheart, her Knight in Shining Armour, her trusted confidant and friend and now she was wearing his ring. Nothing could have made her happier.

Meghan looked down at the ring on her hand and smiled again. Even though Daniel had only spent a quarter on it, in her eyes it was priceless. It represented a life that was to come that they would share together. It represented love, hope and a promise of a happy life together. Someday a real diamond would replace this one but this bubblegum ring would mean no less in her eyes.

"Meg," Daniel whispered, "look under the cotton ball."

As she slowly lifted the cotton ball, her mouth dropped open in shock. There, hidden under the cotton was a beautiful sapphire ring. The small stone had two diamonds on either side of it. It was gorgeous.

Meghan looked at Daniel with questioning eyes. He grinned at her. "After careful consideration, I didn't think the bubblegum ring would hold up very well. I liked the idea of giving it to you but it's not very practical to wear every day. I figure that sapphire ring can be your engagement ring until I can get you a real diamond."

"It's absolutely stunning." Meghan felt like she was in a trance. Daniel slipped the bubblegum ring off her finger and slid the sapphire one on. "Save the bubblegum ring as a token and wear the sapphire one to let the world know that you are mine."

"Gladly," Meghan looked up into Daniel's big brown eyes. She felt so happy that she thought her heart would explode with joy. Life had been hard for her and her sister Lindy, but now things were turning around. From this point on, she wouldn't look back at the past. She would keep her eyes focused straight ahead on the future. That's where the promise lay for her.

Daniel leaned down and softly kissed Meg on the lips. "I love you," he whispered as he pulled back an inch from her lips. "I have always loved you."

"I love you too," Meghan smiled. Today she was going from Cinderella to a true princess.

Daniel stepped back and held both of her hands in his. "I know that some people are going to say that we're too young."

"Some will," Meghan nodded thoughtfully.

"Not many people can say that they've known each other for sixteen years," Daniel grinned.

"Not many people can say that they've played with their future husband in a playpen either. " Meg laughed. "We really do have some serious history going on between us. I don't know anyone, except for your parents and mine, that I've known as long as I've known you."

Daniel smiled. "Same here Honey. I'd like to get married right after we graduate from high school if that sounds OK to you."

"That sounds great."

"Then we can go off to college together," Daniel wrapped Meghan in his arms.

"That sounds good too." She turned her head and smiled up at him. "I can see you've given this a lot of thought."

Daniel nodded. "I've been thinking about marrying you all my life. I'd say that's a lot of thought."

"Will you wait for me Meg until we graduate?" The hesitancy in Daniel's voice broke Meghan's heart.

"Daniel," she hugged him hard, "I have waited for you all my life too. What's two more years?" Her eyes were tearing up. "I will wait for you forever."

Daniel wiped her tears away with his shirttail. "Hopefully we won't have to wait that long."

Meghan smiled. "I hope not, but I will Daniel. I love you so much."

"I love you too," he whispered right before he leaned down and kissed her again. Meghan was right for him. He hugged her harder. She was good for him and they had always been so perfect together. It was as though God himself had designed them just for each other.

He looked forward to becoming her husband and starting a family together. For now, Daniel thought as he touched the sapphire ring on her finger, it would have to do. Being engaged was the first step but being married was what he really wanted. Daniel sighed. He prayed that the next two years would pass quickly. He knew he really wouldn't be content until Meghan was at his side for good. He needed her like he'd never needed anyone. He sighed again. Two years was going to be too long. It was going to seem like forever and in this case, forever couldn't come soon enough.

About the Author

Sharon Snow Sirois, a former teacher,
has been writing stories all her life. She
and her husband have been active in youth
ministry for over twenty years. Sharon is
an avid reader, who enjoys hiking, sailing,
biking and skiing. She is a home schooling
mom who lives in Connecticut with her
husband and four children.

Sharon loves to hear from her
readers. You can write her through
Lighthouse Publishing or email
her at: sharonsnowsirois
@hotmail.com